THE WATER
CLOCK

By Jim Kelly

THE DRYDEN MYSTERIES
The Water Clock
The Fire Baby
The Moon Tunnel

THE NIGHTHAWK SERIES
The Great Darkness
The Mathematical Bridge
The Night Raids

THE WATER CLOCK

JIM KELLY

Allison & Busby Limited
11 Wardour Mews
London W1F 8AN
allisonandbusby.com

First published in Great Britain in 2002.
This paperback edition published by Allison & Busby in 2020.

A CIP catalogue record for this book is available from
the British Library.

10 9 8 7 6 5 4 3 2 1

ISBN 978-0-7490-2520-5

Typeset in 10.5/15.5 pt Adobe Garamond Pro by
Allison & Busby Ltd

The paper used for this Allison & Busby publication
has been produced from trees that have been legally sourced
from well-managed and credibly certified forests.

Printed and bound by
CPI Group (UK) Ltd, Croydon, CR0 4YY

For Midge

THURSDAY, 8TH NOVEMBER

THE GREAT WEST FEN

Out on the Middle Level midnight sees the rising flood nudge open the doors of the Baptist chapel at Black Bank. Earlier the villagers had gathered for a final service loaded down like Balkan refugees with suitcases and bundles. Now the water spreads across the Victorian red-brick floor; a creeping congregation, lifting the pews which shuffle forward to press against the altar rail. Finally the wooden lectern lifts and tips its painted golden eagle into the chocolate-coloured flood. But no one hears the sound, all are gone. Outside, below the flood banks, fenceposts sucked from the sodden peat pop to the surface. On what is left of the high ground hares scream a chorus from an operatic nightmare.

The flood spreads under a clear November moon. Cattle, necks breaking for air, swim wall-eyed with the twisting current. At Pollard's Eau, just after dusk, the Old West River bursts its bank, spilling out over the fields of kale and cabbage. A dozen miles away the lookouts in the lantern tower of Sutton church take the noise for that of a train on the line to King's Lynn. They wait, fatally, for the fields to reflect the stars, before raising the alarm.

Burnt Fen Farm, now a ruin, stands on its own shrinking island.

Philip Dryden climbs the stairs of the farmhouse in which he was born.

His knees crack, the damp air encouraging the rheumatism which waits in the joints of his six-foot-three-inch frame. He stops on the landing and the moonlight, falling through the rafters, catches a face as expressionless as a stone head on a cathedral wall.

He leans on the twisted banisters and feels again the anxieties of his childhood — welcome by comparison with the present and approaching fear.

Will the killer come?

Outside the ice creaks on the Old West River. Unheard, small voices of perfect terror rise with the approach of death. Rats dash in synchronised flight to beat the flood, crowding into the steep pyramids of winter beet.

Shivering, he walks through the hallway and pushes open the slatted door to the attic stairs. He climbs again to the old schoolroom where he was the only pupil. The view from the dormer window frames a snapshot of memory: his father, sat in a pool of midsummer sunlight in a blue-striped deckchair, dozing under a wide-brimmed cherry picker's hat.

Outside the wind brings the slow crash of a tree subsiding into the flood. A dying cow bellows and briefly, with a gust of heavenly sound, church bells ring the alarm too late from Littleport. The lightning cuts a gash across the night and Dryden sees the serried rows of waves marching south.

Waiting for a killer on Burnt Fen. A single, double, killer, coming.

On the horizon occasional car lights thread to Quanea. Locals, quitting at the nicely judged last moment, speed to the high ground. One stops, the headlights swing round, and the car idles beside the

Eighteen Foot Drain. A false alarm: it executes a three-point turn, a dance of light from yellow to red, leaving Dryden's heartbeat rattling. He shivers now in judders which make it difficult to hold the torch.

Another car on the fen. So quickly is it there his eyes struggle to focus on the headlights as they snake nearer. He's come from the south, along the drove. He's almost here and Dryden's underestimated him. Threading through the fields along the narrow banks of the lodes.

Half a mile away the car stops. The headlights die.

They sit and wait. A trickling minute passes. Then five. Sitting, watching, water rising. He's answered a message from a dead man. Dryden examines the roar of the flood for other, lethal, noises.

The moon finds a cloud, the wind drops, and in the sudden suffocating silence a car door closes without a slam.

He's coming.

THURSDAY, 1ST NOVEMBER

SEVEN DAYS EARLIER

CHAPTER ONE

Humphrey H. Holt's licensed minicab crept across the fen like the model motorcar on a giant Monopoly board. The Ford Capri was an icon – from the fluffy toy dice hanging from the rear-view mirror to the beaded seat covers. The back window was stacked with dog-eared children's books hoarded by his daughter – who had fitted the red plastic nose to the radiator and the Jolly Roger to the aerial. Emblazoned with a triple H motif the cab was, not surprisingly, rarely in great demand for weddings. It had once made up the numbers in a funeral cortège – and the family had had the presence of mind amidst their grief to ask for their money back.

Philip Dryden shifted in the passenger seat as they cleared the railway crossings at Queen Adelaide, and turning up the collar of his giant black greatcoat he eyed the cab's meter. He coughed, drawing in the damp which was already creeping out of the fields. The meter read £2.95. It always read £2.95. He could see the frayed wires hanging loose below the dashboard. The cab hit a bump and the exhaust struck the tarmac with a clang like a cow bell.

Humph wriggled in his seat, setting off concentric rings of wave-like motion in his seventeen-stone torso which he had snugly slipped into his nylon Ipswich Town tracksuit top. Somewhere, deep inside, a large length of gut cavorted.

Another bump on the drove road put the car briefly into flight before it returned to earth with a bone-shaking thud. The suspension, a matrix of rusted steel, was not so much shot as dead and buried.

The jolt dislodged the passenger side vanity mirror which dropped neatly in front of Dryden's face. He stared at himself in irritation: his imagination was romantic and he found his own face a dramatic disappointment, which was odd, as most people, and almost all women, found it striking if not handsome. But self-knowledge was not one of his virtues. The bone structure was medieval, the face apparently the result of several blows of a Norman mason's chisel into a single limestone block. Jet black hair followed the architectural design – cropped and severe. It was the kind of face that should have been illuminating an Anglo-Saxon chronicle.

He flipped up the vanity mirror and smudged a porthole in the condensation of the window. 4.10 p.m. A lead expanse of chill cloud over the fen, occasionally lit by the red and green of half-hearted fireworks. The temperature had not risen above freezing all day and now, as the light bled away, a mist crept

16

out of the roadside ditches to claw at the cab's passing tyres.

Dryden checked his watch. 'We could do with being there,' he said. Like most reporters he'd learnt the hard way that patience is a vice.

Humph adopted an urgent posture which produced no discernible increase in speed. The cab swept on while beside them a flock of Canada geese, just airborne, began its long slow ascent into the sky.

Two miles ahead a blue emergency light blinked – a lighthouse in the dusk. A mile away to the east the fairy lights of a pub twinkled in the gloom.

'Tesco trolleys,' said Dryden, searching his coat pockets for a pen. Instead he produced a miniature pork pie, the remnants of a quarter-pound of button mushrooms, and an untouched half-pound of wine gums.

Humph adjusted the rear-view mirror by way of answer. He'd known Dryden for two years now, since the accident which had put Dryden's wife, Laura, in a coma. Humph had ferried him to the hospital through those first critical weeks. In that time he'd learnt to let Dryden finish his own sentences. If you can have a conversation entirely based on rhetoric then they did.

Dryden kicked his feet out, irritated that the cab afforded no more leg room than the average car. Had Humph answered? He was unsure.

'I bet you. Three sodding Tesco trolleys and a hubcap. If we're lucky. Brace yourself: another Pulitzer Prize.' Dryden stretched scepticism to breaking point: it was often, wrongly, seen as cynicism.

They came to the sudden T-junction. They were common in the Fens, abrupt full-stops in the usually uninterrupted

17

arrow-flight of the drove roads. Death traps. Overconfident drivers, lulled by seven miles of tarmac runway, suddenly found themselves confronted by a bank, and then a ditch with ten feet of iced water in the bottom.

A signpost stood at an angle beside the road: FIVE MILES FROM ANYWHERE CORNER. Dryden laughed, mainly because it wasn't a joke.

Across their path lay the bank of the River Lark, a tributary of the Great Ouse – the Fens' central artery. They parked up, short of a yellow and black scene-of-crime tape.

As Dryden reached the top of the bank an industrial arc lamp thudded into life, picking out a circular spotlight on the ice. *Cue Torvill and Dean*, he thought.

In the dusk the bright circle of light hurt his eyes. The Canada geese, having caught them up, flew startled through the arc lamp's beam like bombers picked out in the searchlights of the Blitz. They attempted a landing on ice downriver – a disaster of flailing webbed feet shrouded in gloom.

Dryden started listing hardware in his notebook – a sure sign he knew he might be short of facts to pad out a story. Eight vehicles were drawn up along the foot of Lark Bank. Two local police patrol cars – blue stripes down the side of Ford Fiestas, the county police force's diving unit in a smart purple-striped Cavalier with trailer, the fire brigade's special rescue vehicle, a Three Rivers Water Authority Ford van, and an unmarked blue Rover which might as well have had CID in neon letters flashing from its number plate.

Out on the river four frogmen were trying to break through the ice to attach cables to something just below the surface. One called for oxyacetylene torches and soon the diamond-blue flames hissed, generating vertical mushroom clouds of steam in the frozen air.

What Dryden needed was a story line: and for that he needed a talking head. What he didn't have was time. *The Crow*'s last deadline was 5 p.m.

He scanned the small crowd. He ruled out the senior fireman – politely known as 'media unfriendly' – and ditto the water authority PR who was even now smoothing down a shiny silver suit under a full-length cashmere coat.

With relief he recognised a plain-clothed detective on the far bank. Detective Sergeant Andy Stubbs was married to one of the nurses who cared for his wife. They'd met occasionally at the hospital, both keeping a professional distance. Dryden decided businesslike was best: 'Detective Sergeant.' It was nearly a question – but not quite. An invitation to chat.

Detective Sergeant Stubbs turned it down. 'Dryden.' He zipped up an emergency services luminous orange jacket. The body language shouted suspicion.

Dryden looked out over the floodlit river with an air of enthusiasm more suited to the terraces at Old Trafford. He grinned, rubbing his hands together with excitement, then he made his pitch. 'What's all this about then, Mr Stubbs?' A mixture of deference and jollity which Dryden judged the perfect combination. The jollity was more than a front. He suffered from the opposite of clinical depression – a kind of irrational exuberance.

'County has put a stop on all information, Dryden. We're not quite sure what we've got. We've been out here three hours. Give me ten minutes and if nothing has come up I'll give you a statement.'

'I need to file in twenty minutes to make copy.'

DS Stubbs nodded happily. He didn't give a damn.

In the distance Dryden could see Humph's cab. The internal light was on and dimly he could see the taxi driver gesticulating wildly. Humph was at conversational level in four European languages which he had learnt from tapes. This year it was Catalan. In December, to avoid Christmas, he would take two weeks holiday in Barcelona – alone and blissfully talkative. Typically he sought fluency in any language other than his own.

Stubbs appeared to have the same problem.

Dryden tried again. 'Car then – under the ice.' He beamed in the silence that followed as if he'd got an answer.

Out on the frosted river the frogmen were attaching four metal cables to the car roof at its strongest points, having melted the surface ice with hand-held blowtorches fed by gas lines running back to the fire brigade's accident unit. The steel cables ran to the county police force's portable winch, which in turn was connected by cable to the fire engine's generator. An industrial pump was churning out hot water in a steaming gush from the bank, gradually producing a pond of slush which bubbled around the divers. Beside the single arc lamp uniformed police officers were setting up scene-of-crime lights along the bank. One of the firemen was filming the scene with a hand-held video camera. There was enough hardware for the climax of a Hollywood disaster movie – on ice.

Dryden had seen it all before. The emergency services could never pass up an opportunity to wheel out their toys and put in some real-time training. He half expected the force helicopter to *thwup-thwup-thwup* into earshot.

'Quite a show, Mr Stubbs.'

Stubbs looked right through him. The effect was oddly unthreatening. Dryden felt better and grinned back.

For a detective sergeant of the Mid-Cambridgeshire Constabulary Andy Stubbs managed to radiate an almost complete absence of authority. His face was so undistinguished it could have been included in a thousand identity parades, and his eyes were an equally forgettable grey. His hair was short and fair, echoing the talcum-powdered dryness of his skin. He reeked of Old Spice.

Dryden fingered his collar. Stubbs's colourless coolness always made him uncomfortable. He put on his desperate face: one down from suicidal and one across from murderous. He stepped closer. 'Any ideas? I'm a bit pushed for time.'

Stubbs decided to talk, not because he could see any advantage in it, but because he liked Dryden, or more accurately he envied him: envied him his lack of order and responsibilities, his freedom, and his untied existence. And he pitied him. Pitied him for the very reason for that freedom: a beautiful wife confined to a hospital bed for the rest of her life.

'There's something under the ice,' he said.

Dryden screamed inwardly. He could see that for himself.

'And that's off the record – it's all off – OK?'

Dryden held out both hands to indicate that his notebook was back inside the greatcoat – not that that had ever stopped him remembering a good quote. 'We never spoke, Mr Stubbs.'

'The river froze last night around 2 a.m. – the frogmen say the sheet of ice was unbroken. So the car went in before then. The nearest habitation is the Five Miles from Anywhere, the pub over there. Must be a mile. They don't get much trade in winter. They've heard nothing – saw a few fires around last night – but that's par for the course around Guy Fawkes.' As if on cue a distant percussion echoed round the fen. They turned to see a cascade of orange and red fireworks burst over the distant silhouette of Ely Cathedral, standing two hundred feet above the black peat Fens.

'Who found it?'

'Kids. Skating. You can see something clearly from above. But today's the first day they've been out on the river – so it could have been there for weeks.' Stubbs looked reluctant to go on. 'I've got no real idea what we've got, Dryden, and that's off the record too. I can't afford some damn fool quote in the paper.'

Not again.

Six weeks earlier Stubbs had responded to an emergency call relayed from county headquarters. An anonymous member of the public said a car had crashed in a field known as Pocket Park on the edge of town. It was a local landmark and the site of Ely's annual fair. By the time Stubbs got there it was dark and there was no sign of the car in the field. So he called it a hoax and went home to tea.

The following day they found the driver dead at the wheel in the next field. The coroner ruled that the victim, an eighty-four-year-old pensioner, had died instantly from a heart attack, having swerved off the main road and carried on into a ditch.

It was the local TV that crucified Stubbs. A two-man team from Cambridge caught him on his front step the next night. The house was in worst Barrett Estate Tudor. His wife, Gaynor, made the mistake of coming out to greet him with the two kids – a show of solidarity which made good TV. The news crew flooded the front garden with an arc lamp and blinded the kids, who started crying. It was just about the worst time to be asked the one question he couldn't really answer.

'Any message for the family of the dead man, Detective Sergeant?'

Fatally, Stubbs tried irony: 'We all make mistakes.'

It was a great headline and excruciating TV. Stubbs was up for a police tribunal – failing to follow proper procedure. It didn't help being the son of a former deputy chief constable. So no more quotes. And no more cock-ups – which explained what appeared to be massive overreaction to a dumped car.

Dryden was running out of time. 'No problem – all off the record. Just a short statement saying nothing is fine, but give us a clue. I've got a story to file – at the moment it looks like "mystery surrounds". Bit thin. Any idea if the driver is still on board?'

Stubbs started to answer and then they heard it: the *thwup-thwup-thwup* of the county helicopter following the Lark upriver from Mildenhall.

'Well, we are honoured.' Dryden made a mental note to get some stills off the fire brigade's video for *The Crow*'s sister paper, *The Express*.

Stubbs popped some chewing gum and tugged at the overtight tie and starched white nylon collar of his shirt. 'It's a car. It must have been doing sixty to get that far out from the bank. Either the driver's in it or he got out just in time – and if he got out just in time he knew he was ditching it. So why ditch it that far from the bank? There are some fairly fresh tyre marks running to the edge, but no signs of a skid on the road. And as far as we can tell no other tyre marks at all in the last twenty-four hours.'

The detective walked off to indicate the end of the conversation. The helicopter arrived on the scene and hovered about sixty feet above the frogmen, adding its searchlight to the blaze of electricity. Dryden checked his watch. He had another ten minutes in which to file – tops. The downdraught from the helicopter had taken a few more degrees off the temperature so he walked to the high flood bank, and then eastwards beside a bleak field of winter beet.

He looked out over the black water and shivered at a memory from his childhood. Another frozen river and a skating child. The sound of cracking ice and the sudden plummet into the shocking water. The colour had been extraordinary. The painfully clear blue of a winter's sky seen through the crushed white lens of the ice. He'd sunk, drifting downriver, away from the jagged circle where he had crashed through the ice. Looking up into the receding world, he had been too young to know he was drowning. He'd felt like sleeping after the first panic of the fall. Sleeping where the light was dimmer and wouldn't hurt his eyes. Below. He had been ten, and drowning, looking up into a world he didn't want to leave.

Boxing Day. He'd been given skates but told to stick to the frozen pond behind the barn. But that was dull. The channel which began by the barn led away from Burnt Fen on its tiny island and out into the secret maze of drains and ditches frozen silent in that bitter winter. He'd skated faster, faster, and finally out, with a great whoop, into the wide expanse of the river.

He still loved that place – not ten miles from where he now stood. It had been his world. He could see for ever and see no one. He hadn't been a lonely child. He had a voice inside him to keep him company. But the voice failed him that Boxing Day morning. It didn't see the thin ice where the swans had slept.

But the voice had not deserted him. As he sank, it whispered a single word. 'Skates.' They'd been his best present. He'd sat by the Christmas tree to open the blue and silver parcel. 'Skates,' said his voice again. And he'd understood. So he pulled the laces and watched them sink into the gloom below.

He'd risen until his head bumped the ice which froze to his hair, anchoring him to the spot. He wanted to cry then, for the rest of Christmas he was going to miss. His voice had gone. Or too far away to hear.

That was the one moment he would always remember. The unhappiest moment of a happy childhood. The empty desolation of being on the wrong side of that sheet of ice, in the cold sterile water, while the fire burnt at the farm and the smell of Christmas food seeped out of the kitchen. And above him always the criss-crossed pattern of his own skates.

Humph hooted from the cab. Dryden ambled over, drained of energy by the familiar chilling memory. *The Crow* had called on the mobile and they wanted copy. Humph delivered all messages in a flat monotone – indicating indifference. 'I told 'em the police were about to issue a statement and you were holding on for that . . . another ten minutes. They'll ring back . . .'

Dryden slammed the cab door and leant on the roof with his notebook. As so often when faced with a white sheet of paper and a deadline Dryden thought about something else. He saw Humph on the steps of the high court, the decree nisi in one hand, and his daughter by the other. It was the last time he'd seen him smile.

Humph waved the mobile at him through the side window. Dryden kicked the side of the cab and began to compose a paragraph for the Stop Press. In the best traditions of British journalism it said nothing with great style.

He was steeling himself for the ordeal of filing it to Jean, *The Crow*'s half-deaf copytaker, when the fire brigade's winch started to whine. As the cables took the strain he heard the ice crack. By the time he got to the bank a spider's web of silver lines had appeared across the ice. The helicopter dropped thirty feet and the downblast swept the loose ice to the banks. The car jerked up a foot, the steel frame creaking and howling under the strain. The metallic blue roof appeared, then the rear windscreen, and then the boot. By the time it reached the bank, water was pouring from two broken side windows. It came to rest on the bank top and, as the cables held it fast, the frogmen searched the inside by torchlight.

It took thirty seconds for their body language to tell him everything he needed to know. He could see relaxation in every practised movement. No sign of a driver or passengers.

Dumped car – big deal. But he got the details. A Nissan Spectre. Latest registration. No bumps, scrapes or window stickers. Road tax paid. Glove compartments empty. They put the torches on the boot and bonnet. Dryden was getting into the cab when one of the firemen gave a shout. He sprinted back, telling Humph to hold the copytaker on line.

They had the arc lamp trained on the open boot. For a second Dryden could not understand what he saw: it looked like the back of a butcher's van. Inside was what was left of a large slab of ice glistening with melted water. Inside that was a body in an unrecognisable form. It had not been cut to fit, but compressed and twisted into the space.

A great Guy Fawkes rocket burst overhead, the stark white light making the image burn into his retina.

There was one body. Male? The face stared at them – one

particular eyeball so close to the surface of the ice it reflected the blue electricity of the arc lamp back into the night. The thick, greying, corn-blonde hair was matted with dried blood.

At first Dryden thought the head had been severed from its body. It lay twisted and back over its own shoulder. Then he saw the knuckle of bloodied vertebrae protruding from the neck and the thick flap of flesh that still joined shoulder to head. The sudden exposure to the heat of the lamps was melting the ice quickly, the fingers of one hand beginning to protrude along with a naked, blue-veined foot. Around the flesh streaks of black blood made the white skin look like ice cream drizzled with chocolate.

One of the frogmen was sick in the long grass. Stubbs was unmoved. In control. He called the police photographer over to capture the position of the body before the ice melted. Then he used the squad-car radio to get the pathologist, coroner's officer, and forensic team. Murder enquiry procedure.

Dryden told the copytaker the story was coming: he did that twice to make sure she'd heard the first time. Three hundred and fifty words by five-thirty. He wrote the intro and gave the rest off the top of his head. It wasn't great – but it was in time.

Police launched a murder hunt yesterday after the butchered body of a man was found locked in the boot of a car winched out of the frozen River Lark, near Ely.

The police recovered the car – a new blue Nissan Spectre – from fifteen feet of water two miles south of the village of Prickwillow after children skating on the river spotted it below the ice.

Det. Sgt Andrew Stubbs of Ely Police, said: 'Clearly we

are treating this incident as suspicious. We have begun a murder enquiry and would appeal to anyone who can help with information to come forward.'

The police were unable to provide any clue to the identity of the dead man or the ownership of the car. Forensic experts from Cambridge were due to arrive at the scene late last night. The body was being prepared for removal to the city mortuary at Waterbeach.

One eyewitness to the recovery of the car, Ely taxi driver Mr Humphrey H. Holt, said: 'When they got the car out it was a block of ice. Then they got to work on it with the blowtorches. All hell broke loose when they opened the boot. It must have been a horrible sight – they were obviously distressed.'

Detectives will concentrate on trying to identify the dead man. It is understood that his head was nearly severed. House-to-house enquiries were underway last night to see if anyone had heard or seen anything suspicious.

Detectives will be hampered by the isolated nature of the scene of the crime. The nearest building is a public house – the Five Miles from Anywhere – over a mile to the east. Traffic at the T-junction is extremely rare. Field work in the area has been halted during the current bad weather.

Dryden got the copytaker to read the story back and then checked with the news desk that he was in time. He was.

The firework display was reaching its climax over the cathedral and the sky was now a riot of lurid colour. The forensic team had got the corpse out of the Nissan and placed it on a body bag. Two medics in protective white suits were struggling to get the stiff limbs inside the plastic shroud. Dryden moved closer while

Stubbs was busy on the mobile. The corpse's feet were still visible, tucked grotesquely into the small of the back. Around one ankle was a short length of heavy rope attached to what looked like a cast-iron pulley block. And one arm hung loose. The hand was tanned and strong and on the wedding finger was a single gold band. *Somewhere*, thought Dryden, *the long wait has begun.*

CHAPTER TWO

By the time Dryden got back to the office, via a chip shop with Humph, the newsroom looked like a cabin on the *Marie Celeste*. The advent of the computer had brought with it a lot of talk about the paperless office: but it was just talk. And *The Crow* – established 1882 – was hardly at the leading edge of new technology. Waste paper covered almost the entire floor and plastic coffee cups lay in small heaps by the PCs. An ashtray fashioned from an old hubcap contained the contents of a small volcano. Spikes – supposedly banned with the introduction of the PCs – still bristled on every desktop to collect used copy and notes, and the occasional passing eyeball. The newsroom consisted of three reporters' work stations, a larger mahogany news editor's desk in the bay window, a subs' table with two dumpy make-up computers, and a copytaker's table complete with acoustic hood salvaged from a skip in 1965 when the old post office was demolished. Splash, the office cat, was curled up on the single fax machine for extra warmth. Behind a glass partition was the editor's office. The glass had been obscured by various absolutely essential pieces of paper carrying information ranging from the tide times at Brancaster to the constitution of the Three Rivers Water Authority. This paper camouflage had been erected by reporters over the years and now entirely baffled any attempt by the editor to see his staff.

The office was on the first floor of *The Crow*'s premises in the centre of Ely, above the front counter and telesales. It looked out on Market Street where, tonight, frozen rain slanted across the amber blaze of the street lights. The top deck of the Littleport bus had just drawn up at the stop directly outside and, barely visible behind the streaming condensation, was what appeared to be the entire cast of St Trinian's.

Dryden's story, not surprisingly, had made the lead: HUNT FOR FEN KILLER in sixty-eight point across two decks shouted from the proofs left lying on the subs' table. The top-single beside it was hardly in the same league: FIREWORK WARNING OVER KIDS' PRANK.

He was rereading the copy when Kathy Wilde, his fellow senior reporter, thudded up the stairs, kicked open the newsroom door, and deposited the office's allocation of fifty freshly printed copies onto the floor with a wallop that lifted the floorboards on which Dryden was standing.

Kathy, a red-haired Ulster woman, distracted attention from lurking depression and a tendency to put on fat by a nearly continuous exercise in extrovert behaviour. She knew someone would be in the office from the lights. It was one of her less dramatic entrances.

'Would yer effing believe it.' The Ulster accent was sharp enough to make the windows rattle. 'Page eight! Stark-bollock naked in the front of his bloody Mondeo with a blow-up doll and these tossers stick it in the briefs on page eight!'

'Pity he didn't keep it in his briefs,' said Dryden.

He liked it when Kathy laughed. She let herself go – one of Dryden's litmus tests of character. She advanced towards him.

Kathy had developed a kind of catwalk designed to draw attention to her hourglass figure. It was an ample hourglass through which a lot of sand had passed, but an hourglass none the less. The effect was mildly hypnotic and Dryden froze like a rabbit in the headlights of an oncoming car.

Kathy invaded his personal space – in Dryden's case an area slightly smaller than Norfolk. When she moved she sounded like a mobile in the wind – the earrings, necklace, and bracelets tinkling together.

She removed a piece of imaginary lint from Dryden's shoulder. 'You tell me – go on. I'll take it from you. Tell me I don't know a decent story when I see one.' She thrust a mangled copy of the paper – hardly hot off the presses but still warm – into Dryden's hands.

Kathy had come to England to do feature-writing shifts on the Fleet Street Sunday papers. She'd cut her teeth as a reporter on the stricken doorsteps of the Troubles. *The Crow* was a day job that paid the bills and gave her a base within striking distance of London for her lipstick-red MG sports car. She had a low view of *The Crow*'s professional competence and had not taken kindly to the occasional lecture from the paper's poorly talented senior staff. For Dryden she made an exception: his Fleet Street track record put him on a pedestal. It also made him doubly desirable. She liked the emotional distance, the unselfconscious good looks, the scruffy oversized clothes on the six-foot-plus frame, and the shock of jet black hair. But she loved the CV most of all.

She realised, suddenly, just how close she was standing and backed off in confusion. Subsiding into the newsroom's one battered armchair she burst into angry tears. It was a regular but effective performance. Her face, impish and animated, slumped and crumpled. A considerable amount of make-up began to coalesce giving her a tragic theatrical appeal to which Dryden was just a little susceptible.

He snapped out of it. 'So they wouldn't know a decent story if it bit them on the arse. What's new?'

Kathy stemmed the floods to a series of appealing snuffles.

Dryden admired the front page splash. He'd been a reporter ten years and had often written the front page lead on the *News* – circulation one million. But he got just as big a kick out of *The Crow* – circulation 17,000 and falling.

Kathy's snuffles threatened to upgrade to sobs. Action, he decided, was the best way to head-off emotion. 'Look, I've got a night job – civic opening at the Maltings. Why don't you come with me? We can have a drink and discuss Henry's news judgement at the same time.'

Henry was *The Crow*'s ancient editor and the constant object of critical attack. In one memorable harangue Kathy had told the assembled newsroom staff of *The Crow* – in Henry's absence – that the editor was to modern journalism what 'shit pie is to haute cuisine'. Dryden had found this hugely amusing while the rest had made a mental note to look up 'haute cuisine' when they got home.

Kathy was transformed. She stood and swung her suitcase-sized handbag over a shoulder, narrowly missing Dryden's head. 'You're on. Let's go. I could do with a drink and I'm buying.' One of the many things Dryden liked about Kathy was that she would.

The Maltings, part of the old Ely Brewery, had been converted into a cinema and restaurant complex on the riverside. The district council had put up most of the money with help from the Millennium Fund. As a result Ely's civic dignitaries were out to squeeze every last drop of publicity they could from the project. Tonight marked the showing of the first film: *Waterland* – based on Graham Swift's portrayal of life in the Fens.

As they walked down Forehill towards the river Dryden and Kathy found themselves in picture postcard country: the willows, dusted with ice, hung over a skating rink of river. Smoke drifted up into the snowclouds from the renovated waterside cottages which had attracted incomers into an area once infamous as a damp slum. On the opposite bank had stood the medieval suburb of Babylon, but now the marina sulked in the darkness, punctuated by the ghostly white shapes of floating gin-palaces up on blocks for the winter. Beyond them stretched the water meadows, gently suffocating below a freezing mist.

At the water's edge a crowd had gathered around a narrowboat moored by the Cutter Inn. The excruciating sound of splintering, tortured wood echoed in the silence. The boat sat at a dizzy angle, her plant pots smashed on the ice and her gay green and yellow painted boards twisted and cracked. A dog barked at the creaking wood.

The crowd, warmed by the prospect of witnessing a minor tragedy, had formed a small amphitheatre around the *Sally Anne* – the name just showed above the ice – as the owners ferried valuables out through her side windows and hatch.

Dryden fished a notebook out of the folds of the greatcoat – always a good way of getting attention. A young man in an old sailor's blue cap gave him a suspicious look.

'Can I help?'

In Dryden's experience this was a euphemism for 'fuck off'. The man was about twenty-five, tall, fit and sporting an outdoor tan.

'Philip Dryden, *The Crow*.'

Kathy shimmied up and struck a pose. 'Kathy Wilde – also with *The Crow*.'

'You must be desperate – sending two of you . . .'

'We were just passing actually. Sorry to bother you, especially now. Can you spare us a second?'

It was nicely judged. Dryden's body language, like Kathy's, was relaxed and vaguely bored. Years of experience had taught them both that excited aggression – the normal stock-in-trade of the Fleet Street reporter – was inappropriate in almost all situations outside TV drama.

'Paul Camm, Camm's Boatyard. This is one of ours.'

Dryden nodded, biro poised. Kathy walked along the towpath checking the other boats. She too produced a notebook and started interviewing one of the river authority's watermen who had turned up to catch the last hours of the *Sally Anne*.

Camm was in a hurry to tell his story. 'She's stove in. It's minus 2C. Probably cracked her boards early this morning and slipped under when the air warmed up during the day. Now she's locked in again. She could well go under completely tomorrow.'

'Don't you heat them during the winter?'

Camm scowled.

Tactless, thought Dryden. *Concentrate*.

Camm broke eye contact and looked out over the water meadows: 'Yeah – usually anyway. But we've got thirty boats. We're short of people – this one got left out. The heater must have run out of oil.' Camm looked distracted. Worried, yes. But about more than the narrowboat.

'Heaters do work though?' Dryden pictured his own boat out at Barham's Dock. He'd refilled the heaters with paraffin that morning.

'Oh yeah. Yeah.' Camm's eyes searched the far bank, the middle distance of reeds and trees white in the frost. 'No problem. Or just leave the pump on and keep the water moving around the outflow – as long as there's somewhere for the ice to expand to. But this one we cocked up.'

Dryden nodded to a pile of kitchenware, cushions, books, and ornaments. 'Whose stuff?'

'Just standard fittings – we hire them out as part of the package. TV, all mod-cons, corkscrew. That's what most of them really want – a chance to relax and get pissed for a week.'

'Must cost a few bob these?'

It was a nice try but Camm was no fool.

'Enough.'

'How much do you hire them for?' Reasonable question – and if he didn't answer Dryden could find out.

'Four hundred a week in summer – it sleeps eight.'

'Bit of a warning to others then?' That, Dryden decided, was what the story needed – a forward-looking angle.

'Yeah. If we can lose a boat anyone can – especially in this weather. It's going to get worse as well.'

Dryden scribbled the quote – relying on his erratic spidery shorthand.

Inside the Maltings the ceremonies had begun. The place was an industrial palace in newly pointed brick. All the usual suspects were up on a makeshift stage, most of them with some variety of bent-spoons strung round their necks. A crowd of about a hundred, enlivened by a free sherry, was prepared to listen politely to a speech by the Lord Mayor, Councillor Roy Barnett. Kathy started taking a note and gave Dryden her wallet.

At the bar he ordered a pint of bitter and a Campari and soda – he could not resist that sickly red colour. Inside the wallet was a picture of Kathy's father, Eugene. Dryden had heard the story several times, always in a bar. A Catholic lawyer in Londonderry, he'd specialised in taking cases against the IRA – harassment, punishment shootings, extortion. He'd stood and been elected to the new Ulster Assembly, until a midnight knock at the door had left him with a gunshot to the head. He was the most potent of all role models for his daughter – a dead one.

The mayor was speaking from what appeared to be handwritten notes in green ink: two bad signs in one. He looked no better than usual – a Bobby Charlton haircut spread over skin the colour and texture of grey lard. Kathy was taking a crude note which she would tidy up into proper sentences later for a piece. She knew that if most politicians were quoted accurately they'd sue.

Beside the mayor sat his wife, Liz, a Labour councillor herself and one-time leader of the party on the district council. The mayor's office was largely ceremonial. The party leadership had involved the wielding of some real political power – even if it had been on a tiny provincial stage.

Roy Barnett's speech was rambling, incoherent, and extremely badly delivered. A model of its kind, it also ran for twenty-three minutes. Kathy had time to visit the bar regularly and both she and Dryden were much happier by the time the mayor sat down – the gasp of delight this produced being a mark of relief not admiration.

Kathy recognised a couple of pliable councillors and slipped off to see if they were in an indiscreet mood. Liz Barnett caught Dryden's eye across the second round of sherries and motioned him towards the bar. By the time she got there Dryden had bought her a large malt whisky and for himself a deliberately understated brandy and Babycham.

She noted the malt with a slight nod of appreciation and Dryden's drink with horror. 'The press,' she said, as a toast.

Liz Barnett was one of those women who inspire two questions. How, followed promptly by why: how did the appalling Roy get her to the altar in the first place and why had she stayed with him for more than thirty years? She had been a beauty once and was still striking. Auburn hair turning grey, with no attempt to cheat nature. Strong features and a naturally tanned skin supported by industrial quantities of make-up expertly applied. Her secret was colour: she wore shawls, dresses, headscarves, and various layers of material in bright gypsy designs. She was fifty-four and looked good: husband Roy was sixty and struggling to keep a beer gut inside a nylon shirt.

The mayoress's political assets were impressive. She could give an impression of genuine, rapt interest while being shown round a basket-weaving class for the fifth time in a year. She had proved adept at slipping into the clothes of New Labour while preserving a sharp edge of social antagonism towards the middle classes. Socialism had never been a great force in the Fens – radical Liberalism being the natural successor to religious nonconformism and rural deprivation. But Liz Barnett had channelled some of those forces into support for Labour during the Thatcher decade. If she hadn't been a woman she'd have made it to Westminster. But being a woman had taught her one thing, the corrosive evil of prejudice. Dryden looked at her feet. She still wore an ankle bracelet, a gypsyesque touch that had caused a scandal at Roy's investiture as mayor at the start of the year.

Liz Barnett was also ferociously streetwise and had realised early the power wielded by the press. Her friendship for Dryden had been – at first – entirely manipulative. There was now a grain of genuine respect as well.

'Your wife?' she asked, nodding to the barman to repeat the malt whisky and Dryden's concoction.

Dryden could never answer this particular question without feeling that he was lying in some way, keeping back some part of the truth.

'The same. No better, no worse. What can I say?'

She was enough of a professional not to apologise for the question. She stepped a foot closer. Dryden appeared to be having one of those days. It was a tribute to the mayoress that she could produce such effects at such a tender age. Her husband was holding forth on the other side of the room to a captive audience that looked as though it had been injected with concrete. His face was mottled crimson with a dash of what could only be called cardiac blue.

She leant in close as the noise in the room rose with the consumption of free sherry.

'You will have seen the planning and resources committee's agenda on the request for extra funds for the cathedral restoration?'

It was a rhetorical question. Liz Barnett was one of his best contacts.

She pressed on. 'Frankly they've got a bit of a cheek. It's virtually a demand for a £30,000 contribution because they've discovered, at the very last moment, that they need to put up scaffolding around one of the transepts to reach the high gutters.'

She broke off to kiss a passing councillor who got her name wrong and then staggered away. 'Anyway, apparently they needed to clear gutters ahead of a thaw. If the water collects and freezes, then cracks the stonework – it's gargoyles crashing to the ground, plagues of frogs, that sort of thing.'

'What's the problem?' Dryden could feel the effects of the alcohol as it stole over his modest intellect. He burped and ordered a fresh round of drinks.

'The point is, why wasn't this eventuality foreseen – cold weather in winter not being a totally unexpected development.' She tossed her hair. 'Apparently there's some argy-bargy between the diocesan authorities and the contractors. You'll need to put the questions. But it's a bit of a shambles if you ask me.'

Dryden looked hopeful.

'Although if you did, I would, naturally, be unable to comment at this time.'

Kathy appeared at Dryden's elbow and ordered another round of drinks. The mayoress declined and drifted off to rescue a tray of alcohol from her husband's embrace.

Dryden felt the room sway and was acutely aware of Kathy's lips which had begun to whisper in his ear. He struggled briefly with an amorphous feeling of guilt. But the room was on the move and it seemed sensible to hold on to something. Their bodies touched in several places – in fact an increasing number of places.

Suddenly a woman screamed in that theatrical fashion usually reserved for amateur-night productions of *The Mousetrap*. Dryden thought two things very quickly. First that he was late visiting Laura. Second that he had somehow caused the scream.

But Roy Barnett had caused the scream by the simple expedient of collapsing to the floor – courageously holding on to his pint glass. He was now in the arms of two rather startled WRVS women who had been listening to his anecdotes for the last half hour. It looked like a modern-day re-enactment of the Death of Nelson. Liz Barnett was calmly calling an ambulance on her mobile. She hadn't spilt her drink – and she was ordering another.

Dryden called Humph's mobile and woke him up in a lay-by. The ambulance beat the cab to the Maltings by thirty seconds.

'Follow that ambulance,' said Dryden, enjoying himself. Humph happily handed Dryden a miniature bottle of

Campari from the glove-compartment bar and slammed his foot down on the accelerator, but they had to imagine the screech of tyres.

Kathy watched them streak off into the night. She would recall little about the evening the next morning but the memory of the kiss lingered like a hangover.

CHAPTER THREE

The Tower Hospital had begun life as a workhouse in 1788: decorative stonework failed to offset the mean windows and the poor gothic humour of the single belltower. Standing on the edge of town it shared the high ground with a great railway-brick water tower of monumental ugliness. The hill and the rough common around it were known as The Ropes — a reference to the fact that it was once the site of the common gallows.

Here, in 1812, a group of seven luckless land labourers were hanged before a hungry crowd in broad summer sunshine. The so-called Littleport Rioters had made the mistake of drinking a large quantity of beer on starving stomachs and then embarking on two days of spectacular lawlessness. They were left for a month on the gibbet, like slaughtered crows on a line.

The workhouse closed without sorrow half a century later. With awful predictability it limped into the next century as an asylum: residency of the Tower being a local euphemism for anything from mild eccentricity to stark lunacy. By the 1950s the interior was a scandal: cracked tiled walls, Victorian plumbing, and unshaded light bulbs. It finally closed after a fire gutted the building and brought down the roof of the great hall, the scene of thousands of joyless communal meals.

What was left was bought by the Steeple Trust, private health care specialists, who fitted it out in the kind of unclinical luxury that would make any patient reach for their wallet. The Trust produced a glossy brochure boasting a heated swimming pool, saunas, and gym. It held a maximum of fifty 'guests'. But the £2 million spent on the rebuilding completely failed to obscure the building's innate malevolence. It stood against the night like the Victorian horror-house it had once been.

Roy Barnett had been detained overnight after being discharged from the local hospital's accident and emergency department. His condition was described as comfortable. This was hardly surprising as he had had at least twice as much to drink as Dryden, who didn't know what day it was.

There was a suggestion, however, that a mild heart attack had joined forces with the alcohol to produce the collapse. Dryden would check his condition in the morning. Next time he had a chance he would also ask the mayor, chairman of the local Labour Party's public services pressure group, exactly why the NHS wasn't good enough for him.

Liz Barnett didn't bother to visit. Roy slept soundly and unloved.

Laura Dryden was in 'Flat 8' on the ground floor of the Tower – a suite comprising a bedroom, bathroom, WC, and visitor's room. It cost the insurance company £360 a week, a fact Dryden hardly appreciated given his complete disdain for the management of risk. Laura had taken out the accident insurance policy without his knowledge and lodged it with their solicitor, alongside, as it turned out, a batch of policies covering Dryden and her parents, all paid for by the proceeds from the TV soap opera *Clyde Circus* through which she had become a minor celebrity.

The bedroom, nearly two years after the accident, was almost free of medical equipment. A small computer screen showed Laura's pulse and other vital data against a soothing corporate blue background. A clutch of multi-coloured plastic pipes at her wrist brought in liquid food. Others, discreetly hidden, ferried out the waste. The room struggled to look non-utilitarian. But the institutional cleanliness, and the precise neatness, made it appear like an exhibit in a museum of modern life – 'Contemporary Bedroom'. Personal effects were arranged on the table and a single shelf in that self-conscious way typical of a house opened to the public. It could have been a room inside a glass paperweight.

There were two bedside tables. One held fruit and some fresh bread rolls, broken, with a glass of Italian sparkling white wine. The other, hairbrushes, make-up, and a small picture of Laura's parents marked 'At home – Torino, 1958'. There was a picture of Laura with Dryden – 'Honeymoon, 1990, Rome'. They looked criminally confident.

At first the national tabloids had 'monstered' the story – sending their best reporters and snatch photographers out to the Fens to provide a string of '*Clyde Circus* star fights for life' exclusives. Dryden had felt ambivalent about the group of dishevelled characters who set up a temporary camp outside the Tower's main gates; he vaguely knew some of them, but had drunk with them all. In bad weather they ran a rota with one snapper on duty to catch celebrity visitors while the rest fortified themselves in the Rifleman, a pub half a mile out of town.

Dryden met them there by agreement and read them brief bulletins on Laura's progress, letting out snippets of newsworthy trivia: the letter of support from the rival cast of *Coronation Street*, the personal visit from the leading lady of *Clyde Circus* who was reported to be Laura's arch-rival, and the personal get-well message from the director-general of the BBC. They loved it and thanked him, organising whip-rounds to buy Laura flowers. But he knew it wasn't enough.

The inevitable request for a picture, made a month after the accident, caused a wave of nausea and a hot spit of self-loathing for his trade. But he knew the pressures: news editors were tired of Laura's fight for life and bored with the reality of a colourless and featureless coma. The story was changing from hope to tragedy and the lifeless picture exclusive was the next inexorable step. If he refused he knew the consequences: the super-telephoto lenses, the bribes to hospital staff, the invasion of his own privacy, the unpeeling of their lives. And, despite Laura's deepening coma, he felt a bond with the hacks out in the cold. He had been there too, on Fleet Street, desperate for the story.

When the picture of Laura finally appeared he was stupidly thankful that they had all chosen the most lifelike and appealing of the set he had provided. Laura's parents, on the first of several flying visits from retirement in Umbria, asked for a copy: a request which strangely disturbed him – perhaps with its hint of family surrender – so that he sank his face into Laura's pillow and cried for the first and only time at what the accident had done to him.

The newspapers dropped the story relatively quickly after that. Laura had been written out of *Clyde Circus* with ease; her character, GP's-nurse-turned-drug-addict Jane Corby, flew without notice to Australia in answer to a telegram from her long-lost father Bill. With each episode, postcards, read to the locals at the Palm Tree, told of suburban happiness with Bill's family and lurid tales of romance on Bondi Beach. It was increasingly clear that Jane would not be returning home and that if she did few would remember what she had looked like when she left.

Medical interest in the case was more enduring. The newly diagnosed condition of 'locked-in syndrome', or LIS, was attracting large private sector and government research funding. LIS had a brief but spectacular history. First diagnosed in a Cape Town road traffic victim in 1985 it had quickly become verified by a string of similar cases from around the world. A conference at Berkeley in 1992 had set down the basic criteria for clinical diagnosis: the trauma which triggered the condition had to be both physical and mental – a combination of severe physical shock and intense stress. The Cape Town road traffic victim had been trapped in the back of a burning minibus, unable to break the windows or brave the flames which had engulfed the engine. The clinical symptoms were simple: the patient became comatose physically while all basic bodily functions operated as normal. The crucial difference between LIS and other comas was a high level of brain activity, a symptom only traceable with modern equipment. The victims remained aware of their surroundings, in some degree, throughout the 'coma'. The result was what Second World War submariners would have called 'silent running' – vital systems only, vigilance, but otherwise no signs of life.

The number of cases was still small enough to secure Laura a kind of minor medical celebrity. Doctors came, professed themselves fascinated, made their examinations, took their readings, and left. Their professional objectivity led them to visit the illness rather than the patient, and they offered increasingly perfunctory sympathies for the victim. Dryden had negotiated anonymity through the British Medical Association and Laura appeared only as Case X – a device which protected her privacy but relegated her to the status of a forensic exhibit, pickled in a theoretical jar. The doctors who bothered to talk to Dryden rarely met his eye: in the thirty-four cases of LIS so far officially diagnosed only four had returned to normal life. All had said they recalled varying forms of consciousness while in the coma, ranging from almost total recall to a surreal remembrance of passing dreams.

Dryden had his doubts. He suspected he'd lost Laura for ever on the night of the accident. The nurses at the Tower preserved a professional optimism. They threw open the windows on fine days, used Laura's room to chat and work in, and encouraged him to surround her with stimulating reminders of the life her mind continued to reject.

There was little doubt exactly what Laura's mind was seeking to evade: the memory of the crash in Harrimere Drain. Three hours trapped in a car beneath the black water of the ditch. Three hours in which she could have had no choice but to blame him, as she struggled to understand why he wasn't there, slowly retreating into a coma which denied the unacceptable reality that she had been abandoned to die. He had driven the car but escaped without her: as a bald statement of guilt it was as seemingly inescapable as the black water through which he had swum towards the moonlight.

He wanted her back so that he could tell her what really happened. What he didn't want was a recovery which was incomplete. She was the perfect patient as she was: he wanted her back as she had been. What he feared most was a lifetime spent caring for someone who hated him, or worse despised him secretly. He had to be able to tell Laura exactly what happened that night at Harrimere Drain – and know that she believed him.

She had to know that it wasn't his fear of water that stopped him going back.

Scared of water, or just scared? Cowardice born in the single image of the criss-cross pattern of his skates in ice seen above his drowning ten-year-old head.

Meanwhile the insurance company went on paying the bills – an unavoidable act of grace after Dryden had dropped the good name of the Mid-Anglian Mutual into every interview he had given in the months following Laura's accident. One day they would resort to the small print on the policy and withdraw the funding, or at least take it to the courts. But he was prepared to move on to their savings, such as they were, and Laura's parents had offered as well, willing to see their dreams of retirement modified, then abandoned. But the alternative was unspeakable – or at least unspoken. A steel bedstead in some tucked away anteroom in a hospital which would resent her consumption of scarce resources. Or worse, doctors willing to end it without pain.

Dryden began his ritual visit.

He threw the black greatcoat over a chair and unpacked the fresh food he had brought. Laura's parents had owned a small Italian cafe in north London. He had used it as home when he was on the *News*. From the street it had looked like a sandwich bar but down a long dim corridor was a small dining room, lit by coloured Victorian skylights, with red-checked tablecloths on a dozen tables. Laura had introduced herself by spilling a plate of fresh tortellini into his lap. Clearing it up had been oddly erotic.

Laura was short, compact, and olive brown. Her eyes were liquid brown and huge, her mouth was full – largely with gleaming teeth. Her hair was that particular coppery brown reserved for the Mediterranean. Laura projected a sense of humour, and a slight cast to one eye added a sexy nonconformism. She had the personality to fill a room and overwhelmed Dryden in the time it took to reorder the tortellini. In many ways she was his opposite: sensual, emotional, and a natural actor. She sprang from a family which had never failed to support her, which had never withheld its love, and she placed complete trust in those she loved as a result. Within a month Dryden had slipped effortlessly into this group assuming, unawares, a terrible responsibility.

Her father, a miniature Italian bandit perpetually dressed in a white cook's apron, specialised in home-made pasta, fresh figs, and fruity sparkling wine for a small, but plump, group of expatriates. Laura never weighed more than seven stone, harbouring a morbid fear of ending up like the tribe of aunts which ate at the cafe on Sundays: black widows who brushed both sides of the corridor as they struggled out after a light meal that had taken two hours to eat. Her four younger brothers were slim and fit and Laura's teenage life as a surrogate mother, while her own worked in the cafe, had left her little room for indulgence. She concentrated, instead, on the smell and texture of food. She would sit and wait for others to start a meal, taking in the flavours by scent. She breathed food and broke it, like good bread, to enjoy the physical sensations of eating. She filled their flat with fragrances of food, crushing coffee beans and pounding peppercorns, getting Dryden to make a larder below the stairs with a mesh window to let the aromas of cheeses, vegetables and herbs permeate their home.

So each day he brought fresh food. He poured two glasses of wine, always the light Frascati she loved, a little ceremony of hope. He brought music too and set the timer on the CD player to bring the sound on for a few hours each day – at dusk, and in mid-morning when he knew that if Laura was listening she would want the company of Motown and Verdi.

He always made himself look once at Laura's face. A deathmask: quite unlike the real thing, but more compelling than a favourite snapshot. He always thought she looked frosted: dusted perhaps with a light covering of caster sugar, a perfect face set on the surface of a wedding cake.

Then he turned the lights down and sat looking out into the gardens. Tonight the frost was already white on the trees. The effects of the alcohol were fading fast. It was late but the sounds of the hospital continued: a trolley squeaked past in the corridor, somewhere teacups clinked, and a nurse's sensible shoes tapped past on the lino outside the door. In the room above Roy Barnett was sleeping off his beer while his heart tip-tapped to an irregular beat.

Dryden's routine started with reading out the cards, the letters, or sometimes just a newspaper. The doctors said from the start that he should talk to Laura. At first he had taken her hand and constructed animated one-way conversations. He'd almost believed them himself in those first weeks, desperately misunderstanding every facial tick as a subtle appeal to understanding. But with time his speeches had become soliloquies, delivered with no real conviction that they were ever heard.

But he never lied. He told her often that he had not deserted her that night. That he had been powerless to help. But he feared she couldn't hear, and if she couldn't hear then she must still believe he had put his life before hers. That was the thought which brought him back each night to talk to her. The first sentence was always awkward: like the opening line of a bad play delivered to a half-empty theatre. Stagy, inappropriate, and inevitably feeble. Before delivering it he allowed himself a single cigarette – the only one of the day. Greek, acrid, and cinder hot. He projected the smoke out now into the still air of the room for Laura to smell.

'And I thought it was going to be a Tesco trolley – shows how wrong I can be.'

He glanced at the bed. The coppery hair was lifeless and artificial. Laura's breathing whistled slightly like a cat's.

'A great story – at last. They'd even be interested in this one on the *News*. The body of a man found dumped in the boot of a car and then run into the river. Neck broken – snapped – his head nearly severed. The river freezes and wraps him in an ice cube. There's only one set of tyre marks leading to the spot. The ice stops the river traffic so it could have been there for weeks – anyway there's virtually none in winter – but kids spotted it skating.'

Dryden stubbed the cigarette, disliking the habit as he did at the end of every smoke.

'Now DS Stubbs thinks, according to the local radio news, that this is a London job. Nasty, vicious crimes being a typical capital offence.'

He enjoyed the weak witticism and missed Laura for not spotting it.

'The Regional Crime Squad has been contacted but the script is written: south London thugs decapitate their victim and drive into the Fens to dump the body. By the time some weekend Captain Pugwash had banged his cruiser into it the body would have been fishmeal. Gangland is hardly weatherwise – so they can be forgiven for overlooking the possibility of the ice. And it's a good spot – lonely even by Fen standards. You get winter croppers in the fields but they never stray far from the shelter of the picking machines. The pub, the Five Miles from Anywhere – you remember it, we sat by the river in the summer – it hardly opens in the winter.

'But a gangland killing? If you've got the presence of mind to drive the victim's body here in the first place, why dump it in a river in a car that can be traced – the police have the registration number, even the tax disc. OK, it's almost certainly stolen but it still represents an additional risk. It gives the police somewhere to start. And these are supposed to be professionals?

'And then they've deliberately stranded themselves in the middle of the fen. It's night, presumably, and by this point well below freezing. The police now say that there are no unaccounted-for tyre tracks within half a mile of the dumped car on any of the drove roads. So he, she, or they, have to walk to a second vehicle, or several miles to the nearest main road. The police are starting house-to-house in the morning. To walk to the nearest rail station would have taken three hours.'

Out in the dark garden the moon rose through the branches of a monkey-puzzle tree.

Somewhere in the Tower the gentle sob of someone in pain punctured the thick luxurious silence.

'So my guess is that if they were outsiders they panicked for some reason – were forced to dump the car – and then set off across the fen on foot. In which case there must be a chance they're still out there – and if they've been unable to find shelter they must be in bad shape. If they have found shelter then somebody else could be in bad shape, especially with the coppers blundering around doing house-to-house.'

Dryden stood and pressed his nose against the ice-cold window. In the walled garden the monkey-puzzle tree cast bizarre Byzantine patterns of shadow – tangled limbs of deeper shadow in which it was easy to imagine the shape of a figure standing watch.

'So I think it's much more likely they're local. In which case their victim is likely to be local too.'

He heard the cathedral bell toll midnight. Under the monkey-puzzle tree he thought he saw the shadows move. A tiny pin-point of red, which he had mistaken for the reflection of his own cigarette, fell to the ground. Out onto the frosted grass strolled a security guard, an Alsatian loping behind.

He took Laura's hand, lifting it like an exhibit from the unruffled linen sheet. He fought back the guilt that always rose when he left – the result of his own self-pity. And he fought off a cynical laugh – a sign, he knew, that he no longer really felt this lifeless form was his wife.

If this was a charade, who was it for?

'I'd better get back to the boat,' he said too loud. 'The ice is breaking up and I'd better get the pumps going. Your parents have written – a long letter. I'll read it tomorrow. And there's some pictures, I'll bring those too.'

He placed the dead weight back on the sheet. At the door he forced himself to complete the ritual parting.

'Goodnight, Laura.'

He closed the door and in the silence listened. Sometimes he wished so hard to hear her call his name that he conjured up her voice. It was an illusion so strong there was a danger that one day he would miss the real thing.

Sometimes, just before dawn, he would lie in the dark trying to see behind the headlights, and the glare of the two fog lamps, straining beyond the dazzle to see a face behind the wheel. But there never had been time. A second? Two? No sooner had the car pulled out than it was slewed across his path. The two seconds that changed his life.

It wasn't his fault. Nobody ever said it was. But he had been day-dreaming, he'd admitted that much. They said it didn't matter. The tyre marks told the story.

They'd been to dinner at New Farm. 1999. Winter. A Friday evening in late November. Dryden and his mother had left Burnt Fen in '79, two years after his father's sudden death. A local farmer let the land while the old house crumbled. They moved to London and his mother taught full-time in a comprehensive in the featureless suburb where they lived. The dream was over then.

His parents had met at Cambridge. His father, a physical scientist, wanted to run an organic farm. His mother, a teacher, married him and the life he wanted to lead. They bought Burnt Fen in 1965 at auction. His mother provided the cheap labour they needed to pay the bills. Dryden, born within a year, was taught at home after a brief bureaucratic battle with the local education authority.

But his father's death broke the slender thread of reason which had kept them on the land. The ten years in London were stable, streetwise and not unhappy. His mother retired in '98 and New Farm was ready by then. It stood within sight of Burnt Fen, across Sandy's Cut. Close but unreachable. That's how his mother wanted the past.

After dinner Dryden and Laura had talked about moving back. There was room. But for him it was still too early. Perhaps if children came.

They'd waited too long before setting out, wanting to postpone the dismal journey back to London through the grey suburbs with their shambling Friday drunks. Laura was asleep in the back of the two-door Vauxhall. Hour and a half to London. Forecast: fog patches, ice later. Concentrate.

But the mind wanders on the railway-straight roads of the Fens. And then the headlights. They'd swung onto the Soham Road from a side track. The police had retraced the journey. A local, they said, cutting across country at speed. Zig-zagging on the drove roads. It was reckless, swinging out across both carriageways, meeting him head-on. He'd swerved right and felt the car bump over the low verge and then, for what can only have been hundredths of a second, it flew in a shallow flight between grass and water. He had always thought of water as being soft and yielding, even if it inspired in him an absolute fear. Since childhood and his fall through the ice he'd held its touch in his memory – clinging and soft, deadly but yielding. But the car met it with a juddering thump, its speed suddenly halted, and he felt the pain across his shoulders as the seat belt cut in, breaking first the collarbone and then a rib.

Until that impact he could recollect no noise: then it came in a distorted rush only to be muffled, swallowed by the enfolding water. He heard Laura scream, just once, as she strained against her seat belt. Through his body he heard another rib break. The engine raced and then with a backfire died. The dashboard lights flickered out. Shock, physical and mental, froze the world around him.

How long did they float? Laura, he was sure, had passed out in those few seconds. Then the car lurched to the left and slid down. He knew he panicked then. He remembered kicking his feet and finding water round his shoes. A thread of sanity tried to hold, telling him to search for the door handle, search for the window handle, pull back the seat for Laura. But it was no good. The terror rose and his consciousness retreated, blacking out.

Then he was back. Brought back. By what? A distant sound perhaps, a faint echo of rescue. He gulped for air but found water. The dull race of the river came to him, just heard behind the lurching beat of his heart. Gravity told him he hung from the seat belt facing down towards the engine. His thrashing hands found the seat-belt buckle and he flicked it open, setting himself into a slow fall. He gulped water in painkilling mouthfuls – stilling the scream of agony across his chest.

He sensed the sound again – a percussion through the water. Then someone broke into his dying moment. He felt the hands searching blindly in the dark. At first they repelled him, seeking him out, clutching, unseen. But he must escape, so he lunged towards them and they instantly contracted, catching his arms and pulling him with startling force across the front seat towards the semi-light beyond.

Did he think of Laura then? He tried to imagine he had. This was the single second he relived the most. The point when he willed himself to believe that he had tried to stay, or at least promised to return.

As the hands lifted him towards the open door his face broke free into an air pocket and he gulped, in a frenzy, filling his lungs. Then he was breathing water again, but rising, up towards the silver surface of the drain. He was unconscious by the time he reached it.

He came to on the forecourt of a hospital. He was in a wheelchair, just beyond the bright circle of light cast by a security lamp over the main doors, and slipping in and out of consciousness. But he had no idea if it was hours or seconds between each painful bout of reality. He thought he saw someone once, hurrying away from the light. Had he dreamt it? He was unable to shout or speak and the figure was gone in a second, like the hint of a sail at sea.

A canopy above the entrance was marked PRINCESS OF WALES HOSPITAL. Inside, he could see the low lighting of a reception desk where a nurse sat, her head dipped below the counter, rising only intermittently to answer the phone.

He passed out for what seemed like a very long time. When he came to it was with a jolt and a fresh surge of guilt and anxiety. For the first time he remembered the accident, the moment of impact was beyond recall, but he knew that he had escaped and that Laura was still there, now, below the black water of Harrimere Drain. He knew the water was filling the car but he also remembered the gulp of sweet air he had taken as he escaped.

He dropped a foot to the tarmac and felt the pain run down his nerves, a cold bolt of electric agony. He used the weight of his arms on the wheels to edge closer to the doors — four feet away the sensors picked him up, the glass swished back, the nurse looked to, and he passed out.

But as consciousness swam away that last time he saw one image from the night. He was lying in the back of a car, full-length across the back seat. The car was speeding, he felt the lurches, but no pain. Occasionally, and more frequently as the journey continued, they would pass under a street light. The back of the car was large, even spacious, and he recalled the smell of leather, real leather, not plastic imitation or leatherette. There was nothing on the back seat by his head except a blanket which had been furled up under his neck. He remembered the smell of it. A mixture of oil and dog. Beside his head on the floor behind the passenger seat lay a large parcel. It was one foot by two feet and wrapped in bright blue paper dotted with silver stars, and a single golden full moon.

FRIDAY, 2ND NOVEMBER

CHAPTER FOUR

Dryden had slept badly on *PK 122*, his floating home since Laura's accident. He'd concocted a nightmare of which he could remember only a single image: butchered meat hanging from the branches of the monkey-puzzle tree in the gardens of the Tower. The unremembered climax had brought forth a short audible yell just after dawn: he had heard the echo, and then the frightened chattering of the ducks on the ice. It was a rare nightmare, free of the suffocating presence of water – an elemental fear as much a part of his life as his fascination with water, a dynamic irony which he knew was very likely to kill him.

PK 122, a superannuated 1930s naval inshore patrol boat, was moored at Barham's Dock, an old channel off the River Great Ouse about a mile south of the quayside at Ely. The dock was now no more than an overgrown ditch with just enough water at its mouth to moor the boat out of the mainstream. Underneath the long grass and bulrushes was an old timber quay, once used to load barges with vegetables and salad crops direct from the peat fields for the railhead at Ely and the London markets.

In a lonely landscape it was the loneliest of spots. Below the bank the boat was, effectively, lost to the outside world. Dryden's mobile phone was the only link – except for the occasional passing pleasure boat on the main river, or dedicated hikers trying the towpath route seventeen miles south to Cambridge.

The crash that had put Laura into a coma had undone so many things they had planned together that he was determined to live a temporary life, with as little material luggage as possible. Most of their savings remained untouched, but three months after the crash he'd withdrawn £15,000 of the money he'd got for their flat to buy *PK 122* and have her refurbished in the town boatyard.

He'd taken six weeks' leave from the *News*, although they'd made it plain their good nature would stretch no further. *The Crow* had offered him a job after a few casual shifts he'd taken to fill up the time. He soon realised that the freedom of working for a weekly would allow him to visit Laura each day at the Tower, where she had been transferred immediately after the crash. The alternative had been to move her to a London clinic while taking his chances on the *News* with a newsdesk unlikely to listen sympathetically to requests for regular days off.

His mother died that first winter, having never fully recovered from the shock of the accident at Harrimere Drain. Then he rented out the new house and channelled the cash into an account for Laura. The *News* offered him terms to go quickly and he took them. Perhaps, somewhere, there was a hint of relief. Ten years as a reporter had sapped his enthusiasm even if his inquisitiveness remained undimmed. *The Crow* gave him a full-time job as senior reporter. He felt idiotically satisfied when he saw his first by-line.

PK 122 had spent most of her working life at Weymouth patrolling the naval harbour. She was steel, aluminium grey, and fitted out to weather a typhoon. The powerful single Merlin engine was new and mighty. On her polished wooden instrument panel a small silver plaque said simply: DUNKIRK. 1940. It was a romantic touch he could not resist. From the mahogany-panelled cockpit a hatchway gave into a naval wardroom from which a corridor ran to the prow, giving access to the galley, two toilets and a double shower he'd had put in to replace a tackle room. The cabin had six berths. Dryden had paid for her to be sealed against the damp and fitted with Calor gas heating. The contents of their London flat had been placed in long-term storage but he salvaged their books and filled the wardroom's fitted shelves: a reaffirmation that they had, at least, a shared past. An oil-fired generator provided lights and powered the galley. On deck *PK 122* boasted the latest in wind-powered generators, a nod to Dryden's sometimes shaky environmental credentials. It cut in over the boat's usual power supply when the wind speeds were high enough – which this far out on the fen was for most of the winter, and an uncomfortable chunk of the summer as well.

Their car, a write-off anyway, had been sold for scrap after the crash in Harrimere Drain. Since the night of the accident he had never driven and still rode in cars with at least one window slightly open in all weathers, and never in the back seat, even in a four-door. Running *PK 122* was cheap. He used his wages from *The Crow* to outsource his transport needs to Humph.

Each morning the cabbie parked up about a hundred yards from the dock on the drove road which led to Barham Farm, where Dryden bought milk and eggs every week and paid his monthly £8 mooring fee. Humph, a delicate cook, rustled up fried egg sandwiches at home and brought them along. Dryden's contribution was two cups of bitumen-strong coffee.

The nightmare had upset Dryden's routine. He sloshed what was left of his third mug of coffee out over the ice and jumped back on board to get his overcoat and two fresh refills. He bristled as he heard Humph honk from the cab.

Dryden disliked anger and felt it was a defeat for self-control. But Humph's duties as an alarm clock were taken just a little too seriously – especially for someone who spent most of his time at work asleep.

But Dryden couldn't argue with the service: as a cut-price chauffeur Humph was difficult to beat. The bills were presented weekly and bore all the hallmarks of fiction. Too low by a factor of ten, Humph refused to amend them repeating, mantra-like, that 'he'd been going that way anyway'. Dryden had secured £40 a week from *The Crow* as standard expenses when he'd signed up and he made sure all of it got to Humph in one way or another – either as fares, shared meals, books, tapes, cigarettes, or, his other real vice, the occasional miniature bottle of spirits. The Capri's glove compartment looked like an off licence in toyland.

'Freezing,' said Dryden, unnecessarily, getting into the car and handing over the coffee in return for a fried egg sandwich.

Dryden straightened his legs out in the cab and knocked his head on the roof prompting another surge of early morning irritation.

'You could walk down and call me up, you know – the horn isn't compulsory. Fresh air doesn't kill.'

Humph retaliated by saying 'good morning' in Catalan and pressed the pause button on the cab's tape deck. A silky voice repeated the phrase with almost identical pronunciation. Humph asked – again in Catalan – how Dryden had slept. He pressed the pause button again and the silky voice repeated the phrase.

'Very impressive. Get a lot of Catalan speakers on the school run?'

Humph glugged coffee. The cabbie's head, like his feet and hands, was completely out of scale with his duvet-sized torso. His face was child-like, his eyes a cornflower blue. For someone who never actually went outside he showed an enormous interest in the weather. 'Minus 0.5C and steady,' he said.

The cab, expelling carbon monoxide in a black drift from the exhaust pipe, clattered along the drove road and out onto the A10. The hangover from his drinking binge the night before had locked Dryden's brain in neutral. He opened the glove compartment and retrieved his diary. Its contents were largely irrelevant, especially this morning, as the Lark murder was likely to dominate his schedule until the next deadline on Monday. Four days. He suppressed the frustration and tried not to think about what he'd be doing if he was still on the *News*. With just two senior reporters *The Crow* demanded the talents of a jack of all trades, and certainly didn't offer the luxury of covering one story a week, however sensational.

He hated Fridays anyway. Too much time to think. Too many grim diary jobs that he thought he'd left behind on his first weekly paper a decade earlier. Flower shows, WI meetings and, worst of all, the golden weddings. And the complaints – the day after press day was plagued by serial whingers who'd spotted tiny mistakes, and occasional whoppers. Dryden's particular favourite since joining *The Crow* had been the week they'd included the death notice of Albert Morris in the 'Used Cars' column.

He snapped the diary shut. 'Golden wedding,' he said, 'Jubilee estate. Mr and Mrs William Starr. Must remember to ask them how long they've been married.'

Humph grunted: sore subject. They sat in silence. Humph's divorce had been acrimonious but short. His wife had run off with a plumber from a nearby village who weighed seven stone dripping wet. Part of the allure of cab driving since the separation had been the opportunity he might get to knock the bastard down.

'Fifty years . . .' said Dryden, oblivious of his friend's sensitivities and, for that matter, his own. He didn't know which was worse – the thought that he would never celebrate his own golden wedding, or the thought that he would.

Nine a.m. News on Radio Littleport. The Mid-Anglian Water Board had issued a short-term warning of heavy snow. Dryden felt happier. News was a great distraction if you didn't want to think about your own life. And another item: vandals had attacked St John's Church, Little Ouse. Dryden resisted a memory. His mother was buried in the churchyard there. The stone had been retrieved from the ruin of Burnt Fen Farm.

Mr and Mrs William Starr, the golden wedding couple, lived in a dull house with dull paint on the front door. *Dull*, thought Dryden, and felt a fresh dollop of treacle trickling over his brain. They seemed surprised when Dryden accepted a sherry at 9.30 in the morning, and even more so when he asked for a refill. He made his escape under cover of the arrival of *The Crow*'s amiable photographer 'Mitch' Mackintosh, a miniature Scotsman with no apparent boredom threshold and an addiction to mindless gossip and fake Tam O'Shanters.

Dryden walked back to the office through a light snow shower having dispatched Humph to a lay-by for a nap. There was light in the sky but even now, in late morning, the day was in a long gloomy decline. The town centre was both brightly lit and dismal: that peculiarly depressing combination which smacks of the approach of Merry Christmas. Outside Woolworth's a dog on a rope barked constantly at the too-early fairy lights and a small, wailing child was urinating in the gutter.

Dryden sought refuge in the newsroom. On the mat lay a plain brown envelope marked for the attention of Septimus Henry Kew, Editor, and stamped in red stencil lettering: STRICTLY CONFIDENTIAL. Dryden was rattling the package to his ear and just about deciding it was indeed a video cassette when Henry came up noiselessly behind him. He had a gift for this, an almost supernatural ability to appear at the wrong moment.

Dryden jumped guiltily at the editor's dry cough.

Henry was tall and desiccated like a human praying mantis. His sex life appeared to be confined to the plain brown envelopes and lifetime membership of the Boy Scout movement. Today, thankfully, he was not in full uniform but the lapels of his tweed jacket bristled with insignia. The staff of *The Crow* called him 'Woggle' – but only behind his thin, straight back.

'Just checking,' said Dryden, handing over the envelope. 'You can't be too careful.'

Henry indicated by eyebrow semaphore that Dryden could indeed be too careful. But the editor said nothing, a favourite tactic, and an effective one.

Dryden scanned the newsdesk diary, a dog-eared tome which hung from a lavatory chain attached to the news editor's desk. It was a vital aide memoire even in the age of email. According to the news editor's juvenile block-letter scrawl Kathy was out for the whole day with the WRVS doing a feature for *The Express*, the Tuesday freesheet, on looking after the rural elderly. Gary Pymore, the office junior, was in the local magistrates' court for the appearance of Richard Churchill Hythe, Ely's serial peeping tom.

Dryden dropped coins into the office coffee machine and leant his head against the cool steel fascia. Through the syrup he could just recall Liz Barnett, the mayoress, telling him something useful at the civic reception at the Maltings the night before. Something to do with the council and the cathedral repairs. He also made a note to ring the Tower and check on her husband's condition.

He flipped through his contact book for the home number of Councillor Ben Thomas, the Labour Party's current council leader. He hit an answerphone and swore loudly before the beep. Henry coughed, producing a sound like a death rattle, and retreated behind the glass panel partition of his office.

Dryden left his message in a silky voice and then slammed the phone down, timing a heartfelt expletive to miss the tape. Dryden dealt with the complexities of journalistic morality with simple clarity. Elected officials were fair game, and elected self-important ones were simply asking for it. 'Bastard,' he said again, just for the sound of it. Henry coughed from behind the partition.

He tried to run a hand through his thick, jet black hair, where it duly got stuck. What next?

Gary Pymore, fresh from magistrates' court, clattered up the stairs. Hearing the junior reporter coming was not difficult, Gary had suffered from meningitis as a child and lost a good part of his ability to balance. This had been treated by fitting his shoes with 'blakeys' – small metal plates once designed to preserve shoe leather. The treatment involved smacking his shoes against the ground as he walked and using the sound as a kind of sonic stabiliser. As a result he was, in motion, a human metronome. A metronome with acne.

'Yours,' he said, plonking a takeaway cappuccino down by Dryden's elbow. To be exact it was a Fen cappuccino, and as such unrecognisable as coffee to an Italian.

Gary threw himself into his own chair and put both feet up on the desk. Criminal overconfidence was his tragic flaw, compounded by the illusion that it was the spots. 'Where's Woggle?' he whispered.

Dryden nodded to the partition.

Gary winked – a grown-up trick he had never quiet mastered as he was unable to limit it to one eye. 'What a fucking corker this is,' he said, waving his notebook.

Henry was ominously silent.

'So anyway,' continued Gary, 'he's up this ladder with his trousers down again right . . .'

Dryden was immediately confused, a common problem with Gary's copy: 'Where were his trousers then – at the bottom or the top?'

'Round his ankles course. Broad daylight . . . And, according to the prosecuting sergeant he was in a state of . . .' and here Gary checked his shorthand: 'a state of extreme excitement.'

An odd gurgling sound came from Henry's office.

Dryden's phone rang.

'Ben Thomas. Hi – how can I help, Philip?'

If you snapped Ben Thomas in half you'd find New Labour written right through him, thought Dryden, *and very little else.* On the phone Thomas had the ability to pitch his voice at a tone which suggested he was standing up and in a hurry. This indicated both that he was giving you valuable time and that it was running out. He also annoyed Dryden intensely by using his first name.

'I'll be brief,' promised Dryden. 'I understand the district council is expected to meet an unexpectedly large bill for work on the cathedral restoration this year – due to a late decision to extend work to clear and repair guttering ahead of the cold weather. There appears to be some unease that the financial controls at the cathedral are lax and that council-tax payers are having to foot the bill.'

'Who's uneasy?'

'Some of your fellow councillors. Leading figures.'

'Who exactly?'

'At the moment they are only prepared to comment privately. But I'll run a story – so if you want to comment this is your chance, or chat off the record.'

Dryden had spent nine years on Fleet Street, three of them at Westminster for the *News*. He had quickly learnt that the best way to get a comment from a reluctant politician was to say a story was running anyway. They couldn't stand the idea of missing out – especially to another politician.

'OK. Can we agree a quote at the end?' Councillor Thomas took silence for consent, a provincial mistake which would one day cost him dear. 'The annual restoration work which we bankroll is supposed to include routine maintenance to gutters and stonework. It appears that a very late decision was taken to extend this year's programme to the transept . . .'

'South-west transept?'

'. . . Yup. As I said. We're told that the work is required – public safety being at risk if water collected in the guttering and froze. The question we have to ask is why wasn't the danger spotted earlier? Last year the restoration work was concentrated on the buttresses and stonework on the south-west transept – last year we could have extended that work for very little extra cost. This year new scaffolding has had to be erected, a hugely costly undertaking.'

'How . . . ?'

But Thomas was ahead of him: 'Thirty thousand quid makes a difference, Dryden' – Dryden smiled at the missed opportunity to use his first name – 'in a total council budget of just under six million. I've demanded a meeting with the Master of the Fabric and the Dean – after that we'll move on to the contractors. Basically they have to get the message that this cannot happen again. I intend to get the money clipped off the annual bill spread over five years.'

There was a pause in which Councillor Thomas, Chairman of the Ely branch of the 'Stop Children Smoking' campaign, could be heard drawing deeply on a cigarette.

'What's so dangerous about water gathering in the gutters?'

'Freezing water cracks stone. Thaw results in falling stone. Need a diagram?'

'What's causing the water to gather?'

There was a deep sigh from the far end of the line.

'Leaves. Apparently they're choking the mouths of the gargoyles. All right?'

'Fine. And on the record?'

'Errrrm. The council has responded promptly to an emergency request from the cathedral to extend work on the roof in order to protect the public from the possibility of falling stone caused by frost action. We look forward to discussing with the authorities future funding arrangements – blah, blah, blah . . . Make the rest up – OK?'

Dryden heard the receiver crash down.

'Charming. Have a nice life. But make it a short one.'

Dryden's phone rang again immediately. It was DS Stubbs. Dryden could almost smell the Old Spice.

'Dryden? Just a heads up, thanks for the story by the way, it was fine and – hold on, I've just got another call . . .' After a long pause in which Dryden was forced to listen to a lot more of the 'Hall of the Mountain King' than he really liked, Stubbs was back on the line. 'I didn't want you turning up for the noon presser – there's nothing new on the case. The chief constable has taken a personal interest. He doesn't like the suggestion that the Fens are a nice quiet backwater where bodies can be dumped with impunity. That's all we are saying really: top priority, arrests expected soon, you know the drill.'

'And the truth?' Dryden found Stubbs's solicitousness disturbing. He sensed a bargain in the making.

'Progress. We're pleased.'

Dryden saw his chance: one of the few plus points of working for a weekly rag like *The Crow* was that you didn't have to push hard all the time. 'Fine. Look – I don't suppose you could spare me ten minutes some time? I'd like to do a piece on how you're organising the enquiry; checking the missing people list, tracing the car, house-to-house, that kind of thing. Perhaps we could meet – over a drink?' *What a tart*, thought Dryden. It is quite amazing the bilge people will believe if you flatter their self-esteem. He could virtually hear Stubbs purring on the other end of the line: there was nothing the detective sergeant would like more than to be held up as an example of methodical police work, especially with a tribunal hearing coming up on his spectacular balls-up over Pocket Park.

'I can meet you at the Tower tonight. Gaynor's on late shift – I'll drop her off at ten,' said Stubbs.

'Fine – how about the canteen? They do a nice cup of cold tea.' He sensed that if he hadn't asked for the meeting Stubbs would have. He felt his skin crawl.

He felt the need for action, or at least distraction. According to the newsdesk diary Gary was down for magistrates' court that afternoon. He crossed his name out and replaced it with his own – chief reporter's prerogative. An afternoon of other people's misfortunes would do nicely. He put Gary down for wedding forms, farming news and emergency calls. The newsroom was stuffy and overheated and the rest of the staff would be in soon for a late, publication day, start. He left a message for Humph to pick him up after the court rose at 5 p.m., bought a bunch of lilies on the way to the courts, and rang the vicar of St John's, Little Ouse.

CHAPTER FIVE

The landscape slipped by Humph's cab: a monochrome sea as flat as an ancient mariner's nightmare. In one field of black earth a wild horse stood, its head and neck just clear of the blanket of ground mist. A disembodied mythical animal floating over an invisible land. Telegraph poles stood at crazy angles in the deep black peat – just scratching the low white sky above.

Humph ate a sandwich with one hand while guiding the cab out to Little Ouse with the other: a procedure not so much reminiscent of steering as tacking. He ate with delicate and exaggerated care. He was a finicky eater. As he always said, the problem was his hormones. Dryden imagined they were big hormones with Ipswich Town sweatshirts.

They found themselves running beside the frozen River

Lark. At the spot where the car had been ditched they pulled up by the yellow and black scene-of-crime tape where a solitary PC stood guard. He looked too young to be out on his own let alone in a police uniform.

Dryden wound the window right down. 'Any developments, Inspector?'

Humph smirked. They had few shared pastimes but baiting police constables was one of them.

The copper ignored him.

'I understand the culprits may be armed and still in the area?' This was news to the constabulary. The PC produced a two-way radio and walked off to check out in private how it worked.

Humph drove away before Dryden could do any more harm. They sped past the Five Miles from Anywhere – closed on winter evenings, its beer garden was full of picnic tables dripping in the mist.

A mile downstream was the site of an old cut used by the potato barges in the 1880s, similar to the one in which *PK 122* was moored but much larger. The dock was being redeveloped as a marina. Building work had begun in the late summer and as they drove past Dryden could see lights burning in one of the Swedish-style chalets built to stand on wooden piles above the moorings. The river beyond was blocked by a pontoon above which a single-track bridge was being constructed to provide car access to the marina from the north.

Dryden told Humph to park up. A wrought-iron arch over the entrance spelt out the words: Feltwell Marina.

As Dryden stood listening for signs of life a voice made him jump: 'Can I help?' A body followed in the gathering gloom. The caretaker had seen him coming.

'Saw the lights,' said Dryden by way of explanation. Building work ahead of the big freeze had left the marina's yard with half a dozen deep trenches criss-crossing the site.

The caretaker nodded. He was big and broad and dressed like a lumberjack. He had a ridiculous fur hat with ear-flaps tied up under his chin. Dryden would have laughed, but then he was big and broad and dressed like a lumberjack.

Dryden was always disappointed at his inability to intimidate. At six foot three, in the cavernous black overcoat, he felt he might just occasionally demand some respect. But the lumberjack didn't look very impressed.

'I just wondered,' said Dryden, weakly. 'Any news about the car they got out of the river?'

'Car?'

There was a long silence in which the sound of cogs could be heard turning. Was that a thought crossing his mind?

'Fuck off,' said the caretaker and whistled. An Alsatian dog bounded into the light trailing a line of dribble any rabies victim would have been proud of. Dryden's guts dissolved and the surge of panic was so strong he couldn't move his legs. With what looked like exaggerated calm he flipped open a laminated wallet containing a press card, which failed to impress the dog. Then again it was a decade old, and someone else's.

'Philip Dryden. *The Crow.*'

'Fuck off,' said the caretaker. It didn't count as repetition because it was at least an octave lower and a lot louder.

Dryden fucked off. The last thing he saw was a half-finished sign propped up against the marina's prospective site office. FELTWELL ANCHOR MARINA OPENS: APRIL 1. Work on the bridge would not take as long, but the river would be blocked for several months at least. But for the kids, and the ice, the Lark victim would have stayed undiscovered into the spring.

'Local knowledge,' said Dryden to nobody, fishing in the pockets and producing a packet of mushrooms which he munched as they swept on through the gloom.

The village of Little Ouse lay at the end of a three-mile drove – a long, dispiriting ride across the peatlands on a track constructed of slabs of concrete laid inexpertly heel-to-toe. It had been a soft drove until the war, when the concrete had been laid by the Ministry of Production to speed the supply of vegetables to London. The corrugated surface played a soundtrack back to drivers – a kind of dismal rumbling background beat.

Two rows of brick tied cottages formed what was once the heart of the village. They stood in the lee of the high riverbank. A tortured cast-iron bridge crossed the Lark. A home-made wooden sign hung from its railing in the gloom of a winter's dusk: 'At Your Own Risk'. The church of St John, rebuilt by the Victorians, was demure and neat in contrast to the monumental vicarage, a neo-Gothic classic in damp red-brick, which stood beside it in the same stand of tall pines. Much of the odious decoration was hidden beneath a facade of ivy. Like most poor Victorian buildings it was dominated by a minor feature, the front porch – a stone portico supported by carved caryatids of two clerics with bishops' crooks.

They pulled up and Humph killed the engine. He was asleep before the sound died.

The light was gone from the day and the dusk was violet except for the white ice on the trees. The vicarage loomed over them, some of the windows lighted. Two men came out and made their way to a woodstore beside the church, returning laden with logs for a fire. Beneath the portico they stopped to chat to a figure lost in the gloom. Then they were gone, but the figure lingered. The wind whispered through the pines. A full minute passed before the Reverend John Tavanter stepped out into what was left of the day.

He wore a heavy black overcoat but nothing on his head, which was globe-like and radiated intelligence. Dryden guessed he was in his mid-sixties, a rounded, almost sensual figure with the dreamy childish features of a poet. A teetotal Dylan Thomas. He exuded a comfortable confidence, although his hands fluttered in a minor betrayal of something less assured.

He saw Dryden, spread his hands in a blessing, and looked to the sky. 'Snow soon,' he said, in a pulpit voice.

Dryden slammed the cab door and enjoyed the triple echo. They walked towards the church. They'd met before over the previous two years in a depressing round of parishioners' deaths, farm accidents, and petty vandalism in the parish – and finally at his own mother's funeral. St John's at Little Ouse was the least vibrant of Tavanter's six churches, the solitary Sunday service drawing a congregation of twenty, limping in from outlying farms.

Some, most perhaps, knew the story of the desolation of St John's. In small communities sexual scandal has a half-life as long and corrosive as radium. Tavanter had come to St John's, his first parish, from Oxford in the spring of 1965. The obstacles in his modernising path were formidable – the nagging poverty of his congregation and their almost pagan need for a style of religion he could not condone, let alone deliver. He had arrived with ideas of social mobility then popular in his theological college. He found a congregation which wanted a medieval preacher to take up residence in the manse with a suitable wife. They suspected his motives and eventually, worse still, his morals. For years they despised him while he fought to love them without hatred.

He blamed himself for hiding the truth. So, on Advent Sunday 1975, a bright day full of unforgettable yellow sunlight which managed to flatten a landscape already steamrollered by nature, he announced from the pulpit that he was gay. It was a life-defining moment and one he replayed with pride on the video tape that was his memory. In a single practised sentence he gained the authority he deserved, and lost a congregation. At the end of the sermon the hymn had been Bunyan's 'To Be a Pilgrim'. He had sung it alone.

They drove him out: not in the hail of earth and invective that would have been his punishment a century before, but by indifference and malice. He preached to an empty church for six months. On saints' days they would gather within sight of St John's across the peat fields to pray. He watched them, his vestments blowing uselessly in the wind, while they raised their voices in hymn. He left within a year after a pauper's funeral which he had briefly prayed might be his own.

It was God or chance that arranged the next episode in John Tavanter's life. By then he did not care if it was someone else's God. He joined a team ministry in Stepney, in London's East End, where he helped the poor who asked no questions. In 1983 he used his savings to buy a plot of land on the canal bank beside St Barnabas's Church so that a youth club could be added to the Victorian church hall. It cost him £26,000: the land was of little value to anyone else.

Within a month the diocese had decided to close St Barnabas's and merge two congregations at a new church half a mile away. Developers wanted the land for executive housing – the gentrification of the inner city was then beginning to gather pace. The only obstacle was Tavanter's half acre. He sold for £750,000.

When it came it was a delicious moment. The solicitors handed over the cheque in their wood-panelled offices in Bow High Street. Cold rain ran in rivulets down the fake mullioned windowpanes.

£750,000.

The figure hung in the air despite the weight of its astonishing implications. He returned to Cambridge and founded a centre for the care of terminally ill patients with AIDS. He called it, in one of many acts of retribution, the St John's Centre. In return for transferring ownership of the hospice and its financing foundation to the local diocese he was appointed team vicar for a group of six Fen parishes, based at the vicarage of St John's. He used the rambling building as a centre for the carers of AIDS patients, in need of somewhere to escape the pressures of the deathbed.

It was a victory and John Tavanter spent most of the rest of his life trying not to glory in it. Those parishioners who remembered him treated him like a ghost.

Dryden and Tavanter liked each other in that kind of instant superficial way which can be the first step in a long friendship. Tavanter saw in the reporter a fellow outsider, someone who watched life as a spectator, a game devised for ordinary, normal people. Dryden recognised in Tavanter the wry attitude of someone estranged from society, and not entirely unhappy with the arrangement. When his mother died he chose Little Ouse for the burial. Tavanter had been matter-of-fact, helpful and humane.

They walked to St John's in silence. In the porch a single electric light bulb shone on a squalid scene: cigarette butts, a few bottles of cider, two condoms and a syringe, in a nest of old clothing and newspaper.

'Kids,' said Tavanter, nudging the nest with his foot. 'The syringe is for show. But one day it won't be.' He flicked an imaginary strand of hair from his forehead, a constant mannerism which reminded nobody of the thick blonde hair of which he had once been sinfully proud.

'Place must have changed,' said Dryden, expertly leading his witness on.

Tavanter was aware of the reporter's skills but trusted him: in the past they had talked privately about stories and the result had been sympathetic and intelligent.

'Some. About two centuries in forty years. When I first came to St John's they didn't have teenagers. They certainly didn't look like teenagers – they had the same windblown faces and hand-me-down clothes as their parents. But they dreamt then about the same mundane things: owning a TV, running a car, sex and marriage. I don't think I married a woman at St John's who didn't turn out to be pregnant at the altar.'

'Now . . . ?'

He shrugged and gave Dryden a first, direct look. His eyes were beautiful, even Dryden could see that, a turtle-dove grey with enough depth for a drowning. Tavanter unlocked his church. St John's was Edwardian, built on an earlier medieval site. The church interior was as neat and cold as a crypt.

They passed into the vestry and out into the churchyard. This had survived the Edwardian construction and the rebuilding of 1947. The yew tree and a spectacular vine were much older than the church and several of the headstones reached back into the sixteenth century. His mother's headstone stood by an old rubble wall. He deftly replaced the lilies with the fresh bunch he had brought, and, as always, took a pebble he'd collected by the river from his pocket and set it on the stone. He didn't pause to remember but followed Tavanter through a gap in the hedge into a small enclosure full of cheap, standard headstones. Some graves were unmarked and others carried simple wooden crosses. The grass was unkempt and there were no flowers. With the dusk a gentle fall of snow had begun and was peppering the ground. An owl hooted ridiculously like a sound effect from a TV thriller.

They laughed, relieving the tension. 'Paupers' graveyard,' explained Tavanter, taking a deep breath of ice-cold air. 'Rather a lot of them, I'm afraid. As you can see someone has taken exception to them.'

Most of the stones had been badly damaged – presumably with something heavy wielded by someone determined. Few had survived intact, most were split in two, the fragments scattered in the frosty grass.

'Why the publicity?' The radio report would have come from police calls. It was rare for them to advertise vandalism.

'Not my choice. Police think I should have told them about what was going on in the porch. They think publicity will scare them off. I told 'em that was why the kids did it. To get noticed.'

'This is the first . . .'

'Oh yes. Nothing like this before.'

Dryden bent down and matched some of the broken stone shards to their disfigured headstones. Jack Gotobed 1823–1860. Martha Jane Elliot 1891–1976. Peter Noah Jones 1901–1964. Marjorie Phyllis Carter 1900–1972.

He felt the corrupt damp rising from the ground. He shuffled his feet. 'Any relatives still around?'

'Hardly. Rural depopulation. The last burial here was in the 1980s. Still consecrated ground, of course. Anyway, you don't ask questions about relatives out here. Old joke but it's true. When they ran a school here in the 1930s there were four family names on the register and twenty-eight children. They have family trees – they just don't have any branches on them.'

They laughed together, the sound crackling in the frosty air.

'Cost? Repair?'

'Don't think we'll bother.' Tavanter folded his hands inside his overcoat in a fluid movement which spoke of a lifetime in vestments. 'Tidy up perhaps. I might get the tops of the stones rounded off. I'll make a point of popping in over the next few weeks, leaving the lights on, generating some activity. But it won't fool anyone. We might get a security light – but in the end it'll make no difference.'

'Any fears for the rest of the church?'

Tavanter sighed. 'I can't tell you what to write, Dryden, but why give 'em ideas? It's totally vulnerable of course. There's six churches in the circuit I cover – to provide security for all would wipe out our income. And they're only churches – stone and mortar – we try to concentrate our resources on the people. They could take the windows out I suppose, although they're meshed. If they got in there's arson, but they won't push their luck that far.'

'Kids then, you reckon?'

Tavanter gave him an old-fashioned look. 'It's not the only theory, as I am sure you've guessed. The police consider the sanctuary here at St John's a hotbed of perverts. Buggery and vandalism – what's the difference, eh?'

'Where there's kids there's parents.'

Tavanter nodded, enjoying himself. 'On the whole they come under the heading of what I think our American cousins call white trash. Poor white trash.'

Dryden raised his eyebrows in mock shock.

'We're all allowed our prejudices,' said Tavanter, buttoning his overcoat to his neck.

They stood awhile in what had become the night. The only light came from the thick frost now underfoot. They turned together and retraced their black footsteps etched out on the grass.

Dryden stopped before the gap in the hedge that led back into the main graveyard and put a finger to his lips. He pointed down to a track of footsteps which had come out of the trees, shadowing their own to the paupers' graveyard, but stopping short by the hedge. In the frost a cigarette butt smouldered. They heard a door open somewhere across the fields, letting the sound of a TV drift on the air. A dog barked and stopped when a door slammed.

'Kids,' said Tavanter, like a mantra.

CHAPTER SIX

Laura, the immobile victim of locked-in syndrome for nearly two years, had moved. When Dryden arrived they took him into a consulting room and gave him a cup of tea in a pea-green cup. The consultant neurologist, Mr Horatio Bloom, had a face like a horse, and an incessant insincere smile.

'Your wife,' he said, beaming with self-satisfaction.

'My wife,' said Dryden, sipping from the pea-green teacup.

Bloom stiffened. They disliked each other. Bloom was not used to insubordination. Dryden was struggling with some complex emotions – not all of them uplifting.

'Since, er' – here Bloom referred to his notes – 'since Laura's accident your wife has not moved at all, complete paralysis. Obviously the internal organs have been operating but all muscle movement, including that associated with deep sleep, has been absent. Today she moved. I think we should be encouraged, Mr Dryden.'

Dryden sipped. He wanted her back, of course. But he wanted her back as she had been. What he did not want was a painful and tortuous recovery which left him caring for a mumbling shell with a disintegrating personality: a human being by name only, demanding attention but giving nothing in return.

'And nobody could have moved her?' Dryden asked.

Bloom readjusted his steel-rimmed glasses. 'Mr Dryden. The nurses and staff here at the Tower are acutely aware of the importance of your wife's posture. She is moved regularly to avoid bed sores and circulation problems but these alterations are logged with the charge nurse on duty.'

Dryden didn't really know why he asked the next question. 'Is that charge nurse ever Gaynor Stubbs?'

Bloom's eyes flickered over the notes before him: he coughed and avoided a direct answer. 'Your wife was checked by the physiotherapist at 5 p.m. today. She did undertake some work with her arms and neck, which she recorded when she returned to the nurses' station. When she checked again at 5.45 p.m. your wife's body was very nearly out of the bed, she had turned over on her right side and one arm was hanging outside the bed.'

'No one else could have got into the room?'

Bloom clasped his hands tightly as though restraining temper. 'All visitors must sign the book and there are security cameras, as you know, in the main corridors.'

Dryden thought of the open window: and beyond, the spreading darkness of the monkey-puzzle tree.

'Can I see her?'

Bloom led the way. A nurse was reading beside Laura's bed.

Bloom tapped a pen against the VDU screen: 'The level of brain activity is slightly higher – perhaps five per cent more than normal at this time of the day compared to the average over the last two years.'

Dryden sat and took up Laura's hand. If she'd turned to the right, as the physiotherapist's evidence implied, she would have been reaching for the pictures on the bedside table. He felt a stab of hope.

'What next?' But he knew the answer, loathed its Kiplingesque preachiness.

'We wait and watch, Mr Dryden. Time . . .'

'. . . is the great healer,' finished Dryden.

'We shall, with your permission, install some monitoring equipment so that we can pick up any movements and record them. Then we can work on the limbs that seem to be most active.' Bloom took Dryden's indifference to this request as the signal to leave.

Dryden leant in close to Laura's face: as close as he'd been in two years – but not quite touching. His lips were almost on hers: he spoke to them. 'I wonder,' he said, aloud.

He walked to the window and tried to lift the sash. It moved smoothly letting a sudden cold blast into the stuffy room. Out in the dusk the monkey-puzzle tree glittered with frost.

Dryden poured two fresh glasses of wine. He replaced the bread and some of the fruit, turned the lights off and sat looking out into the gardens. Beyond the high wall he imagined Humph waiting in the cab.

'Humph sends his love.' His voice was too soft and the sentiment came out half-hearted and limp. He turned to the bed in apology and repeated himself. 'You'll meet him one day – you'll like him. There's a lot to like.'

There was a knock at the door and DS Stubbs's head appeared. He still looked crisp and neat at the end of a fifteen-hour day.

'Sorry. I have to scoot. Could we meet now?'

Despite Laura's immobility it was unthinkable that they would use the room for a private chat – an inexcusable admission that she was more an object than a silent witness.

They slipped down the corridor to the hospital's heated pool. There was no one swimming in the cool Radox-green water. A cluster of plastic chairs was arranged on the poolside beside an automatic drinks machine. Dryden paid for coffees. The pool glowed with underwater lighting. They sat for a moment in the dappled light, the only sound the faint hum of the electric pumps, which creased the surface with miniature waves of vibration.

Body language was a study Dryden enjoyed. At the moment Stubbs's was all wrong. He leant forward in his chair, hands together, attentive. He wanted something, and it made Dryden wary.

He also seemed unable to begin the conversation. Dryden decided to get what he could as quickly as he could. 'So. Our man in the car – details?'

'Prelim. autopsy results show time of death to be around twenty-four hours before the body was hauled out of the Lark, an entry bullet wound at the back of the skull and an exit through the mouth. That's where all the blood came from. None of this came out at the press conference by the way – you didn't miss a thing.'

'Bullet wound?'

'Yup. The traumatic injuries to the neck came after death. There are some threads of heavy rope – similar to that used to attach the iron pulley to one of the ankles. Doc thinks the body was hanged after death, causing the rupture of the neck muscles and the snapped spine at the base of the skull.'

'But otherwise he was perfectly healthy?'

Their laughter rebounded off the white tiled walls. It was easy to be cynical about the dead. Stubbs showed tiredness for the first time. He closed his eyes and rested his head back over the chair. Above him the sickly reflections of the pool weaved themselves across the ceiling like a slow-motion disco.

'Yup. A picture of health if he wasn't on a mortuary slab. In his fifties. Naturally tanned skin, well-developed muscles and tendons, lean torso. Liver clean as a whistle, no sign of cigarettes. Exceptional lung capacity in fact. His skin suggests an outdoor job. Good quality blue overalls, woollen socks. One oddity.'

Dryden tried not to look interested. He already had enough for a decent story and the words 'off the record' didn't mean he couldn't use the information. He'd just leave Stubbs's name out of the paper.

'Despite the clean liver a high level of alcohol in the blood.'

'So the killer got him blitzed first – anything else in the blood?'

Stubbs gave the reporter a look which just might have been admiration. 'Sedative. Pretty massive dose apparently.'

'Tricky slipping a Mickey Finn to a complete stranger – suggests he knew him well?'

'Suggests,' agreed Stubbs, adjusting the strangulated tie.

'The ropes?'

Stubbs was reddening slightly at the cross-examination. Not so much at the implied insubordination as its expertise.

'Best lead we've got. Cut roughly after death with a knife. The pathologist reckons he must have dropped at least thirty feet to produce the neck injuries. In which case there's a long cast-off lying around somewhere. Two short lengths were cut to fasten the pulley to his foot.'

Dryden cast around for a line: ship's ropes, haulage ropes, bell ropes, tug-of-war?

'Odd chemical traces on the ropes: chlorine and machine oil mainly. Lab at Cherry Hinton is doing a full set of tests now.'

Dryden breathed in the vapours of the swimming pool: ozone, no hint of chlorine.

Stubbs tried to read Dryden's face and failed. The medieval features were blank.

'What about the hands on the victim – prints?'

'Checking. Anyway, the killer appears to have made at least one mistake. On October 31st, the day before the victim was found, the blue Nissan Spectre was involved in a road traffic accident on the Littleport by-pass. Just after 10 p.m. There was a shunt at the roundabout and he got whacked in the boot by the driver behind.'

'Hell. Do you think he had the body in the back?'

Stubbs ignored the question. He unwrapped some spearmint gum and began to chew audibly.

Dryden cracked his fingers one by one. If they were going to play irritating noises he'd win.

'Driver behind reported it because our man in the Nissan Spectre wouldn't give his name – instead he offered the bloke £50 cash to get lost and save his no-claims bonus. He thought the damage would cost more than that to repair. Chummy drives off but our man gets the registration number.'

'And a description of the driver?'

'You'd have thought so, wouldn't you?' Stubbs stretched his legs. He looked tired and worried: the prospect of the approaching police tribunal seemed to be giving him sleepless nights. Dryden felt better. 'The witness is a teacher from one of the secondary schools in town. Intelligent bloke, mid-thirties, all his faculties. But about as observant as this plastic cup.'

'Anything?'

'The suspect wore a hat – US cap-style. No glasses. That's it. He didn't get out of his car.'

'Not much of a photofit there then.'

'Quite. Which is where I'd like your help.'

Dryden didn't believe in fate but he felt that he'd been waiting for this moment for two years. Stubbs wanted a favour – and favours deserved repayment. He saw a fading manila envelope in a locked filing cabinet marked 'Dryden – Laura Maria: RTA. Confidential'. Inside, perhaps, was an explanation and a clue. An explanation of why the police had so far refused to let him see the file and a clue to the identity of the man who had pulled him from Harrimere Drain and driven him to the hospital. Now, at last, he saw a way of getting to read it.

Stubbs coughed unhappily into the echoing silence of the pool. 'We're getting the witness into the station on Monday to try and put together a poster.'

'How many pictures of heads with caps on have they got?'

Stubbs's face creased in what might have been anger. 'Look. I've been honest . . .'

Dryden made eye contact.

'. . . as I can be . . . We now think our man is local. He may well be working with others – also local. If they read in the paper that the police are confident they can put out a photofit of the killer then they may panic.'

Dryden always looked at people's hands when they said the word 'panic'. Stubbs were dry and still.

'They may do a runner. Break cover. Try to build an alibi.

We – I – would like you to run the story in *The Express* on Tuesday. It'll get picked up everywhere else and we'll arrange for a separate briefing for the *Standard* in London – just in case our boys are outsiders. You can write what you like . . .'

'But you'd like me to refrain from the truth – that the photofit, if it was ever published, would simply remind half the male population of East Anglia under fifty of the other half . . .'

'Indeed. In fact we'd be happy if the article gave the impression that we were confident the photofit – which we will say we plan to publish on Wednesday – will bear an uncanny resemblance to the man we are seeking urgently in connection with the Lark murder.'

Dryden could guess the rest. When the photofit did not appear the police would simply announce that they were close to an arrest and did not want to alert the killer by revealing his identity. He crushed his plastic coffee cup and attempted to lob it into a bin – it caught the edge and bounced back into the antiseptic pool. They watched it bob on the miniature waves.

But that, thought Dryden, was only half the plot. 'And your disciplinary tribunal is when?'

Stubbs blushed, the blood breaking through the barrier of talc. He looked suddenly younger and uncertain. For the first time Dryden considered the possibility that they were the same age.

'Tuesday.'

'Bit desperate, isn't it?' Dryden could see them now. Stubbs waiting nervously outside while they read the front page of *The Express* and its promise of a breakthrough in the hunt for the Lark killer.

Stubbs watched the cup bob in the pool.

'What are their options?' Dryden was beginning to enjoy himself.

He fished in his jacket pocket and retrieved a half-eaten sausage roll.

Stubbs's complexion reflected the watery green of the pool. 'Demotion. Slapped wrist. Who knows?'

'But if they spend Tuesday reading how the Lark murder enquiry – under the inspired leadership of Detective Sergeant Andy Stubbs – has got one up on those flash bastards from the Regional Crime Squad they might be more inclined to put the Pocket Park incident down to inexperience?'

They smiled together. Dryden's normally immobile features were lit by a rare flash of real excitement. Stubbs made several small movements designed to signal that the meeting was over. Dryden contrived to miss them all.

'And all this would amount to a favour?'

Stubbs looked wary. 'Of sorts. Clearly you'd be ahead on the story.'

'Although the story would be hogwash of course, even if it was exclusive hogwash.'

Dryden looked at the detective sergeant's hands. He was nervously tracing the crease on his trousers. He decided to let Stubbs sweat a bit before offering a straight swap – the story in the paper for the file on Laura's crash.

'I'll think about it,' he said. 'Let's keep in touch.'

Dryden pushed his chair back, letting the plastic screech as it tore across the tiles.

CHAPTER SEVEN

Dryden found Humph's cab waiting for him just outside the Tower's gates. He was asleep but he had a paper note tucked into the chest pocket of his Ipswich Town tracksuit. The cab driver's memory was poor and important messages were always consigned to paper and prominently displayed.

Dryden slipped the note free without waking his friend.

Gary phoned. Cathedral crawling with coppers. He'll see you there. Wake me.

There was no need. A nerve-crackling squeal of tyres signalled DS Stubbs's rapid exit towards town. He'd clearly just got the same message. Humph was on his tail before he'd cleared the gates of the Tower. They followed the unmarked police car effortlessly through the deserted streets and parked up on Palace Green, an open triangle of grass in front of Ely Cathedral's Norman west front. Overhead the county force's helicopter swung as if on gyres, its solitary searchlight playing across the vast lead roof. Dryden had seen more police hardware in twenty-four hours than at any time in the last two years.

The clock tolled midnight and the sky, which had been weeping snow for the last hour, looked ready to unload a blizzard. The great grey-white lid of the sky was low enough to pick up the aluminium-white lights that illuminated the central Octagon Tower of the great church.

At ground level a solitary ambulance stood quietly, its light flashing a useless warning. There was none of the anxious rush associated with an accident, nor the almost tangible excitement that goes with the scene of a crime. A group of about a dozen uniformed PCs were standing around smoking and chatting in the hush habitual outside church.

Gary Pymore, junior reporter, stood shivering by the police incident van despite the ever-present full-length leather coat. He'd acquired a polystyrene cup of coffee and a sticky bun from the police mobile canteen. He fingered his ear stud as Dryden approached.

'Hi. Thought I better let you know what was up. I can handle it of course.'

'I'll tag along,' said Dryden, taking what was left of the bun out of Gary's hand. Gary replaced the bun with a cigarette and Dryden watched with joy as the teenager's eyes clouded with the effort of stifling a cough.

A small, tubby man stepped out of an ageing black Jaguar that had been parked up by the cathedral's west doors. He had an overfed face, a neatly trimmed white beard, and the kind of pitted bald head that can put you off your food. His builder's overalls were spotless and his plastic hard hat had the logo NENE & SONS on the front. He had the scrubbed neatness of a VIP visitor. He wore a heavy scarf at his throat and his eyes were brown and muddy, like the water in a building-site ditch.

Stubbs had acquired a clipboard and command of the scene. He bustled up officiously: 'Josh Nene?'

Nene touched his hat and sniffed loudly. He looked to be fighting a mild temperature and a grumpy disposition.

Dryden left Gary by the mobile canteen and hung around just within earshot as Nene and Stubbs looked up at the scaffolding they could see against the night sky.

'OK, sir. Can you lead the way up?'

By way of answer the builder unlocked a small wooden hatchway cut into the great oak doors of the cathedral.

Stubbs called Dryden over. 'You can tag along. But this is a favour. One that I expect to see repaid on Tuesday morning.'

Dryden put his thumbs up. A wordless bargain he would be more than happy to break.

He stepped through the hatchway last and inhaled the scent of candles while suppressing the memory of a north London Catholic childhood. The vast nave was too dark to see but it was impossible not to sense the cavern of still space above them. They stood on the Norman tiled maze of the floor while they were issued with hard hats and fluorescent jackets.

Somewhere a door slammed and footsteps slapped on stone. With time Dryden's eyes began to discern the dim symmetry of the vast church, the arches of the nave like the ribcage of a great whale that had swallowed them whole. Directly above he could see the warm gold glint of a Christ-figure decorating the high Victorian painted roof.

Nene slipped with surprising agility through a small door in the massive south wall of the cathedral and they followed, Dryden feebly attempting to convince himself that he was unafraid of heights, and enclosed spaces, although he forgot both at one point when Nene's torch failed and he remembered he was even afraid of the dark.

The party of three came to a stone landing lit by a single unshaded light bulb with a wire cover. Two corridors met here at right angles, while ahead of them was a small door. The staircase turned onwards and upwards towards the viewing platform of the West Tower, 215 feet above the ground. Set in the wall were the massive steel ties of the emergency restoration in the 1960s, which had saved the great tower from collapse as its weight distorted the Norman foundations. The small door stood open, letting in silver-grey light. A policeman stood guard, hastily crushing a cigarette underfoot. Dryden recognised Sergeant Tom Pate, a man whose incompetence was legendary. His appearance in court giving evidence for the prosecution was almost always enough to secure an acquittal. Sergeant Pate looked with horror at the reporter. Stubbs looked with horror at the cigarette stub.

Nene led the way through the rusted iron doorway into the white light beyond. They were standing at the point where the narrow stone gutter of the nave met that of the south-west transept at a right angle. More than a hundred feet below them was the old cloister garden, set out in geometrical neatness like a model village. A golden retriever ran in tiny circles on the grass lawn illuminated by the yellow light streaming out from the French windows of the Bishop's House.

Above them the sloping roof climbed to its apex, almost lost against the lead-coloured sky, and behind them the massive bulk of the West Tower rose up towards the low clouds, its outer walls studded with the heads of decorative imps and demons put there nearly eight hundred years earlier to ward off evil. A couple looked like Dryden's relatives.

There was no handrail, just a low stone wall at knee height. Dryden, a dedicated physical coward of extraordinary range, felt the back of his knees wobble. He attempted a cough and produced instead a squeal of remarkable pitch and strangulated stress which everyone kindly pretended not to notice.

As they paused to catch their breath the snow began to fall at last – a sigh of relief from an overburdened sky. The large wet flakes seemed to make the heavens brighter as they fell in damp clusters. The fall accelerated visibly, quickly obscuring everything except the walkway on which they stood.

Nene, who was probably in his mid-fifties but looked older, wheezed with the effort of the climb and leant back against the stone until his breathing returned to normal. In the frost his lips had an unhealthy blue lustre.

Dryden took in the rooftop world. The darkness had gone in the flood of white but nothing was visible. Almost nothing. Through the blizzard a bright halogen-blue lamp stood out, about fifty feet along the transept gutter. Dimly a group of silhouettes was gathered round the light. It looked like a Christmas card of the nativity.

This was clearly their destination. With sickening inevitability Dryden considered the journey that lay ahead. He took the first step unasked, knowing that any delay could result in embarrassing hysterics. Fleetingly he considered how much of his life was focused on doing things he feared just to prove to himself he wasn't a coward. The gutter was floored with a once treacherous layer of ice. One of Nene's men had taken a pick to it, scouring the ice deeply to provide a safer footing. The stonework glittered around them with the first signs of a hoar frost and the snow was swaddling the ranks of gargoyles. Griffins, imps, dragons and cockatrices stared out into the white night.

As they approached the group it broke from its stiff tableau to reveal a crouching gargoyle where the crib of the nativity should have been. To Dryden the stone figure appeared to be some kind of horserider seated on a mythical animal – part dragon, part lion. Nene stepped round it and stood back on the far side, putting a foot casually up on the stone parapet for support.

All moments of recognition are emotionally charged. Most bring delight but in the few seconds it took Dryden to realise exactly what he was looking at the short black hair on his neck bristled and he felt the lurching impact of disgust. Logically his brain assembled the evidence of his eyes: the dry wisp of hair still clinging to the rider's bowed head, the exposed yellow-china bones of one hand attached to the gargoyle's neck with lichen, the verdigris-covered remains of an overcoat. But it was the skull he would remember. The yellowed dome was marked by the tiny canals which had once carried blood to the brain – an intelligent pattern now interlaced with the silver mucous trails of slugs, one of which, orange and fat, was heading for the dark safety of the unseen eye sockets.

'Jesus,' said Dryden.

One of the three men in the group that they had joined crossed himself. An owl flew through the lamplight and disappeared instantly into the snowfall.

Most of the body had collapsed into the gutter. There was no flesh left on the exposed hand, arm, or the skull – most of which was tucked unseen into the wing folds of the stone gargoyle's back. The attitude of the body suggested that he, or she, had tried to stand, using the gargoyle as support, but had only managed to raise one arm to the task before death had intervened. Lichen, like glue, had fixed the scene.

'Jesus,' said Dryden again, automatically searching his overcoat pockets for the cigarettes he had given up ten years before – except for the packet he kept in Laura's room for the ritual evening smoke. Nene recognised the gesture and produced a packet, leaning gingerly across the body to offer one. They lit up in silence and flicked the ash and match over the gutter's edge.

Stubbs, even more colourless now in the white world of snow, produced a crisp white notebook: 'Mr Nene?'

Nene coughed weakly as though preparing for a speech. 'Not much to tell.' His voice was reedy and high-pitched. 'I came up about five o'clock to check the roof ahead of tomorrow's work. You can't see the gutter from anywhere, except the Octagon Tower to the east – this stretch is obscured anyway by one of the pinnacles which rise from the walls of the nave. And we're too close to the base of the West Tower for this to be visible from the viewing platform. We were going to raise some scaffolding to clear the outer guttering in case water was trapped in the freeze. I found, er this, as you see it – and raised the alarm with Mr Hodgson.'

The cathedral policeman nodded. It was he who had crossed himself. Dryden knew Hodgson. *Sanctimonious bastard*, he thought and gave him a sympathetic smile.

'Any suggestions?' asked Stubbs.

Nene's eyes were rheumy and ill. 'My guess would be that he jumped from the tower – hit the roof and slid down to the guttering. Looks like he didn't die straightaway – but managed to crawl into a half-sitting position behind the griffin.'

'Date?'

'We did work at this end of the cathedral twelve months ago – but much lower down. The last time anyone actually came up here to walk the gutters was probably in the mid-sixties, when the West Tower started to shift and we had to pin everything with steel rods.'

Dryden drew deeply on the illicit cigarette. 'Aerial photographs?'

Stubbs winced. An obvious question he would never have thought of asking. It was a small consolation that Stubbs knew how bad a detective he was.

'My guess is you wouldn't have seen it unless you were looking for it,' said Nene.

Dryden threw the remains of the cigarette over the wall and watched it drop like a miniature distress flare into the blizzard. He fought back the urge to ask for another. He tried a question instead. 'Was the work on this roof part of the special extension of the restoration programme?'

The builder nodded. 'Last part. We were going to run scaffolding up tomorrow – although I doubt we could have in this weather.'

'Couldn't you have done the work from here?'

Nene shook his head. 'Health and safety regs. You need a working platform of a certain width – it's OK to come up and survey it by foot but if you have to work on the stone you need more room. Much more room. And some of the gargoyles are choked at the mouth end – that's several feet over the edge.'

Nene looked down but Dryden took his word for it.

'So how long do you think our friend has been up here?' repeated Stubbs, pointedly turning back to Nene.

Dryden leant forward and edged towards the bone hand which had become joined to the gargoyle's frosted neck. 'It certainly didn't happen yesterday. Lichen is a slow grower – there must be several summers' worth here. Ten? Twenty? Thirty? More?'

'Is that possible?' asked Stubbs.

Nene lit a fresh cigarette before answering. 'Yes. Yes, it is. It could be much longer. There's not much left, even given the place is running with rats, and the gulls will have pecked it.'

There was an uncomfortable shuffling of feet. Those that could studied what was visible of the corpse.

Two ambulance men appeared from the small doorway in the West Tower carrying a collapsible stretcher and a silver body bag.

This I don't need to watch, thought Dryden. Then he spotted something on the frosty stone ledge by the corpse. 'You might want to look at that.' He put his finger within an inch of what looked like a lichen-covered coin. Stubbs gravely produced a clear plastic exhibit bag into which he dropped the coin with a pair of callipers.

Stubbs studied it by the light of the arc lamp. 'Half-crown. 1961.'

Dryden moved back into the light. Stubbs was holding two other exhibit bags – both containing what looked like the remains of documents.

'Pockets?'

Stubbs nodded. 'Standard procedure. This was from the back pocket of the trousers, or what's left of them. They were inside this.' He produced another plastic evidence bag inside which was a fisherman's oilskin pouch. 'Waterproof. Otherwise nothing would have lasted.'

He held the bag to the light. 'One's a driving licence. The name's gone but the number's still legible. We can trace it through vehicle registration at Swansea. The other's what looks like a betting slip.'

Stubbs flipped the plastic bag over and turned the torch on the faded white paper. A misspent youth told Dryden all he needed to know. The betting slip was pre-computers. An on-course bookie's mark had faded beyond recognition. But the torn halves told a happier story: the winnings had been collected.

Dryden kept nodding while he memorised what he could read: *£5 to win – Bridie's Heart. 50–1.* The rest was partly destroyed but read: *£5 . . . Ayers Ro . . . 50–1.*

Dryden shivered. 'Well – at least we know something for sure. He – or she – liked taking risks.'

Bright sunshine fell that day on Stow Bardolph Fen fifteen miles north of Ely. The single-carriageway A10 crosses it from south to north en route for the coast at Lynn and the popular windswept beaches at Hunstanton, Brancaster and Cromer. That summer the first hovercraft service had opened from Ramsgate to Calais but, despite the growing attractions of 'abroad', thousands still braved the North Sea for a traditional British holiday.

The Crossways filling station stood, and still stands, although much altered, at the junction with two byroads – one out to the farms at Cold Christmas, the other to the sluices at Denver. Then it was a state-of-the-art roadhouse: an outpost of sensational modernity. Teenagers came on scooters to view the automatic drinks dispenser and buy cigarettes and pop. Today it is a Happy Eater.

That afternoon Amy Ward was alone in the shop minding the till. It was no ordinary afternoon. In London, at Wembley Stadium, a crowd of 100,000 was about to watch the World Cup Final. Saturday, July 30th, 1966. England would play West Germany in a game nobody who saw it would ever forget. Amy would never forget that day either, but for very different reasons.

She was slim, dark and plain – but dressed to catch the eye. She wore a pink sweater pulled tight over her breasts while a miniskirt, clipped at the waist by a broad leather belt, clung to her thighs. Resourceful, unimaginative, and self-contained the twenty-four-year-old Amy was reading the Radio Times. *The front had a colour picture of Bobby Moore, England's tall, blonde, and imperious captain. Amy lingered wistfully over the image.*

George was at home in their newly built (George always said 'jerrybuilt') bungalow directly behind the shop. The two buildings were joined by a short corrugated-iron covered walkway. George was watching the build-up to the game on TV, along with millions of others around the world. He'd given Eric Dean, the Crossways' resident mechanic, the afternoon off. It was a sore point with Amy. She wasn't a football fan – and she wasn't interested in listening to the game on the radio – but she'd have liked to have seen it. The Queen was there. George's brother had phoned that morning from New Zealand. He was watching too. Everyone was watching except Amy. She'd strung bunting over the forecourt of the garage and a Union Jack flew from the flagpole. But George hadn't even asked if she'd like to watch. It wasn't as though they'd be busy. She hadn't seen a car go past since two o'clock that afternoon. The roads were deserted. Next day the papers would all say the same thing. It was the day the nation came to a standstill. The day England won the World Cup.

So it was just George and Eric who sat on the Wards' new sofa and shared a packet of Embassy Filter Tips. Between them on the new purple and blue shag-pile carpet ('This is luxury you can afford – buy Cyril Lord') stood a crate of bottled Worthington White Shield. Just before the game began Amy smiled, despite herself,

110

when she heard George, always patriotic, joining in the chorus of 'Jerusalem'. It was her last smile.

Bored, she began to clean the counter top methodically, until it gleamed and perfectly reflected the sunlight. She heard the roar as the game began and felt the tension of the opening ten minutes. Even Eric, already the worse for half a dozen bottles of Worthington, was strangely subdued. Outside nothing moved. It was a perfect summer's day but in most homes the curtains were drawn to enhance the flicking black and white pictures from London.

West Germany's first goal was greeted with silence. George swore and she heard a bottle smash in the grate. She glanced at her watch. 3.13 p.m.

She would say later in her statement to police that she didn't know what had caught her attention. She found three men standing with their backs to the plate-glass window of the shop. Interviewed at Lynn Royal Infirmary she would tell detectives that she was sure they must have walked to the Crossways. She had a fine ear for a car pulling up on the forecourt and she was certain none had. She was right. The scene-of-crime team found tyre marks on the grass verge 500 yards to the south.

There had been some traffic that morning. What George called 'bucket-and-spade specials'. Overexcited children in the back seat, bleary-eyed parents in the front. But there were no children that afternoon. Just the three men with their backs to the plate-glass window.

Amy Ward was puzzled rather than alarmed She had never seen random violence, at least not until the new TV had shown the Mods and Rockers fighting on the promenade the summer before at Clacton and Brighton. She lit a cigarette and put the Radio Times *away under the counter.*

She told the police the next few minutes were incoherent in her memory. Without word or apparent signal the three men moved at once: the man she would later describe as having blue-black hair, young and slim and dressed in the new-style US jeans, strode away to stand by the two petrol pumps. He carried a rag and a wrench but she never saw his face which was partly obscured by a US-style peaked cap.

The man she would later describe as the leader moved quickly to the shop door and, stepping through, pulled a knitted black balaclava over his head and a sawn-off shotgun from a large ironmonger's holdall. The other followed less confidently, fumbling with a balaclava. Amy's bloodstream flooded with adrenalin. She stood, knocking her stool to the ground, and took a breath to call George. But the first man moved with surprising speed to bring the shotgun up to her chest. His voice, muffed through the jagged slit of the wool, said: 'No. Not a sound.'

The other man hesitated in the doorway.

The leader clicked his fingers and said:

'Till.'

The week, with plenty of traffic running up to the coast, had been a good one and there was nearly £600 in notes – including two £20 bills which George had swapped for change with one of the delivery men.

There were also three wage packets: one for the mechanic, and two for the drivers who ran the Wards' small road-haulage business. The wages in cash totalled a further £48. The second man counted the money while the leader watched Mrs Ward – so close his breath played on her skin. He traced a finger down her sweater, from neck to belt.

She remembered saying: 'Please don't.' She told the police she was sure he meant to rape her.

He breathed into her mouth: 'Silver?'

She fumbled at a key held by a clasp to her belt and nodded to a reinforced wooden door to her left: 'Storeroom,' she said, or possibly: 'In there.' Her statements differed on this small point. He brushed past her, produced two large burlap sacks, unlocked the door, and disappeared inside, switching on the light.

George Ward's collection of silver football trophies, some his own, but many just in safe keeping, was kept in neat rows on green baize. George had been an outstanding local sportsman until a knee injury had shredded his cartilage four years earlier. He compensated now by helping run local leagues and had always offered his storeroom as a safe place for sporting silverware. The entire collection was uninsured but its value would later be assessed at around £800–£1000. The cups were put into the sack and passed to the second man who added the cash and wage packets from the till. The leader stood at the strongroom door and said, 'Come and give me a hand clearing up, darling.'

They all heard the sound of talking at the same time. Out on the forecourt the one with the American-style cap was putting petrol into a caravanette and chatting with the driver. He was taking the customer's money and searching in his pockets for change.

Amy flipped up the counter flap and took three steps towards the plate-glass window. She said later she hoped to make some sort of signal to catch the attention of the driver. She heard the shotgun being cocked and turned to find the leader standing behind her. He had the gun in the crook of his arm and she remembered that his eyes, which were very dark, reflected the sunshine pouring in through the window.

She heard the caravanette pulling off and said: 'You can't get away with this. I know you.' She may have said something more, but her memory could never retrieve it.

113

The several statements she made to police never explained these words. She denied that she did know him, and was unable to say why she had said what she said, other than to guess that it was an attempt to buy time.

Then they heard the cheers. The tension of the first twenty minutes suddenly released. England had equalised. George was whooping. Another bottle smashed in the grate, then another. They sounded close, next door, not thirty yards away.

That was the moment that changed her life. The gang leader fired the gun at a range of between six and eight feet slightly to the left side of her skull. The blast tore away her right cheekbone and jaw and shattered into bonedust her left collarbone. She would taste the lead and cordite in her mouth for months. Metal shot and bone fragments were retrieved from the brick wall six feet behind her. She lost her right eye and the sight in both. Shreds of tobacco from the cigarette, which she had held in her mouth throughout the robbery, were embedded in her wounds and were a constant source of infection. At the time she recalled no pain but distinctly remembered a voice she had not yet heard saying: 'Christ. Christ. You've killed her.'

Later she recalled, briefly, her husband whispering to her that the ambulance was coming. Then no more. She would not regain consciousness for nearly three weeks. The rest of her life was punctuated by severe bouts of depression and the recurring image of the jagged slit of a mouth in a black, woollen balaclava. The teeth she recalled were small, white, and perfect, like those of a child.

SATURDAY, 3RD NOVEMBER

CHAPTER EIGHT

At weekends Dryden abandoned time but embraced food. *PK 122*'s handsome ship's clock had stopped at 9.19 a.m. – in 1948. He removed his wristwatch on Friday night, a tiny ceremony which gave him immense pleasure. During the week he grazed on a conveyor belt of pork pies, crisps, sweets, and anything else he could get in his pockets. At the weekend he ate Big Time: and first call was the Box Cafe, affectionately known to a small but undiscerning clientele as Salmonella Sid's. He walked to town along the riverbank in the hyper-clear air which follows a snowstorm. About six inches had fallen in the night and it was still held by frost to the pitched cathedral roof on the horizon. He stopped on the bank and studied the south-west transept through pocket binoculars. The scene-of-crime lamp was still in place – as was a single policeman, huddled in the high doorway through which he had climbed last night. He hoped it was the incompetent Sergeant Pate.

Salmonella Sid's was a steam box. A wall of hot air and grease hit you when you came through the door. Dryden ordered the Full English and settled down with a discarded copy of the *Mirror*. The body on the roof of the cathedral had made a paragraph on page ten: HEAVENS ABOVE! Nice touch. He made a note to bill them – like most of Fleet Street they were lousy payers. He'd check the rest of the tabloids when he got to the office. He'd filed 350 words for the *Telegraph*, *Times*, and *Independent* as well; they'd ordered and would eventually have to pay up whether they ran the copy or not. The *Guardian* had just taken a paragraph and he guessed they might send a staffer out to do a colour piece. The *News*, his old employers, had taken 350 words. He doodled on the *Mirror* with a biro. If the tabloids used it as well as the serious papers he'd make about £700.

Not bad for an hour's work even if it had been at one in the morning.

Loaded down with enough cholesterol to block the Channel Tunnel he headed for the office. The front counter was open taking ads but the rest of the building was empty. Henry had a flat above the offices on the third floor but enjoyed a private entrance from the backyard to his flat. At weekends the only indication of his existence was the occasional creaking board and the strains of Radio Three. Jean, the bellowing deaf telephonist, had Saturdays off. A long line of temps dealt patiently with enquiries from readers who all seemed to like shouting.

Dryden checked his answerphone.

'Dryden?' He recognised the languid tones immediately. He imagined the Reverend John Tavanter at the payphone mounted in the hallway of the retreat at St John's. 'Bad news I'm afraid. The vandals returned last night after we'd left. Persistent, aren't they? They attacked the stones again and crushed the pieces nearly to rubble. Dreadful mess. No one heard anything of course. I thought you might want to know . . . I'm at home Sunday evening if you need to ask any further questions. You mentioned a picture. If the photographer rings me at the centre in Cambridge I can meet him there any time Sunday afternoon. Cambridge 666345. Goodbye, Dryden.'

However hard Dryden tried he could never imagine Tavanter saying: 'God bless'.

A second message: 'Andy Stubbs here. Swansea have come up with the name of our man on the roof.'

Dryden cursed loudly; he'd hoped it would take them longer. This way the dailies got a crack at the story before his next deadline. It was another favour from Stubbs – and a useless one.

'It's Thomas Shepherd, no middle name. Shepherd spelt S-H-E-P-H-E-R-D. Official address given as Belsar's Hill – that's a gypsy site out on the Great West Fen. We've checked the files and at the time of his disappearance in the summer of 1966 he was a suspect in a robbery and attempted murder investigation. The robbery took place at . . .'

Stubbs's notebook crackled.

'The Crossways garage on the A10 on July 30th – you may have a file on that if *The Crow* was published. Our file is pretty pathetic. His finger . . .' Dryden's tape cut out.

Third message: 'Sorry. As I was saying – his fingerprints were found at the scene. He went to ground immediately after the

119

robbery. His family claimed he was in Ireland. He was never seen again by a reliable witness. He was nineteen. On the run, clear evidence which would have put him inside for fifteen years at least, and half the force looking for him – looks like a reasonable scenario for suicide to me. There were two other members of the gang, never identified. The enquiry was closed down in 1968 but had made very little progress once Shepherd had disappeared. Hope that helps.'

There was one more message. It was Stubbs again.

'Hi – sorry, you asked about cause of death. That far back it's impossible to make even an educated guess. Coroner likely to go for death by misadventure and leave it at that. He's already released the body for burial. The pathologist says both thighs were broken and one leg – the right I think – had broken in so many places it was virtually powder. The right arm was also badly broken. Looks like he fell on that side. Left arm and leg are intact. One oddity. All the fingers on the right hand are broken just above the middle knuckle.

'Anyway, he must have hit the roof with a hell of a crash, probably near the apex, and then slid into the gutter. Our blokes say that with injuries like that he couldn't have lasted more than a few minutes – especially on a cold night. I didn't tell you any of that. Everything is non-attributable. Bye.'

Stubbs was clearly trying hard to win Dryden's help in publishing the photofit story. There must be a good chance they were going to demote him. Embarrassing at the best of times, but even more so for the son of a former deputy chief constable.

The Crow had been published every Friday since the beginning of 1946. Before that it had come out on Thursday – market day. In 1982 Henry had launched *The Express*, a downmarket tabloid for Tuesday. It was designed to protect *The Crow*'s Friday circulation by deterring free newspapers.

Paper copies of *The Crow* were too unwieldy to store, but the library had them on microfiche. Dryden inhaled a cup of coffee from the machine and wrapped himself in the greatcoat. The library was a brutal sixties block nicely situated right outside the cathedral. The cold snap had kept the borrowers at home. Dryden headed straight for the records room in the basement.

He found the first report on the robbery in early August – the Friday following the raid. There was an update each week and plenty of coverage throughout the summer's so-called silly season when news was scarce. The location of the Crossways filling station on the main route north to the coast helped keep the story topical throughout the school break. The condition of Mrs Ward also kept the story going. She was on the critical list for four weeks and did not finally return home until Christmas.

According to the cuttings, the Crossways was a very different place from the one she had left in an ambulance on 30th July. Her husband had sold out to Shell and the cafe had closed. An interview with the couple in February 1968 said they had decided to keep the bungalow and run the garage on a franchise. The mechanic, the other witness in the robbery, left to work in King's Lynn.

Dryden read and reread the reports. The evidence against Thomas Shepherd was conclusive: his fingerprints at the scene and the description given by the motorist who stopped for petrol were good enough. But his decision to flee the police hunt was just as eloquent of guilt.

Had Shepherd been on the run for years before his death on the cathedral roof? Or did he jump within hours of seeing the injuries to Amy Ward at the Crossways and hearing the radio news that the police were on his track?

One thing made Dryden uneasy – it was a fact rather than a question. The identity of the police officer who had first led the hunt for the A10 robbers before Scotland Yard had been called in to take over the investigation in early 1967: Detective Inspector Bryan Stubbs, then at the start of a career that would take him to the giddy heights of Deputy Chief Constable. A fine career in detection that he must have then hoped would be carried on by his son, Andrew.

Dryden got back to the office via the High Street butchers where he bought a hot steak and kidney pie and three sausage rolls. No point in dying of hunger.

He looked Stubbs Senior up in the directory. It was a Newmarket number. Dryden was surprised it wasn't ex-directory – most ex-coppers were. A rare display of public accountability? Or arrogance?

Stubbs Senior answered on the tenth ring. After a brief introduction Dryden said what he wanted. He reckoned he had less than a one in fifty chance of getting anything out of him – and even that was certain to be background only.

'It's about a case you investigated in 1966. The papers called it the World Cup Robbery . . .'

Dryden left silence as a question.

'Yes. Yes, of course, I remember it well.'

'There's been a development.'

If the former deputy chief constable made a reply it was lost in the chimes of what sounded like a shopful of clocks.

Dryden checked his wristwatch: 11 a.m. precisely.

Stubbs Senior didn't bother to explain. 'Don't tell me that gypsy kid has finally turned up?'

Dryden wondered how close the Stubbs family was. Had they talked that morning?

'You could say that. Could we meet, briefly? It would only take a few moments.'

There followed a pause worthy of a deputy chief constable. 'Dryden, you said? Philip Dryden?'

Dryden decided this needed no answer.

'I live at Manor Farm – on the Newmarket to Lidgate road. Any time after four would be fine.' He repeated the address and put the phone down.

Dryden tackled the weekend calls. There was a rota for the chore but he picked up the job most Saturdays. In return Henry looked kindly on his expense claims. One incident worthy of the name: the fire brigade reported an overnight blaze at the circus wintergrounds on Grunty Fen, a stretch of bleak bogland beyond the reclamation skills of even modern drainage engineering. It was an area known locally as The Pools. The police said they were investigating arson. By the newsroom clock he just had time to visit the scene and make his appointment with Stubbs Senior.

Mitch, the gibbering Scotsman, minded his High Street photographic shop on a Saturday and didn't take pictures for *The Crow* or *The Express* unless in an emergency. Dryden grabbed the office camera, an antique that looked like a prop from a Charlie Chaplin film, and headed for the taxi rank.

Humph was first in line. The cabbie had dealt with the

impact of divorce on his private life by simply expanding work to fit the empty hours now available. An hour off meant sixty minutes' kip in a lay-by.

'Newmarket by way of The Pools. Top speed,' said Dryden not bothering with hello.

Humph thrummed his delicate fingers against the steering wheel in anticipation of the drive.

They clanked through town past the occasional dedicated shopper flecked with snow. On the market square a few traders had put up stalls for the Saturday craft market but most were watching proceedings from inside the Coffee Pot cafe. The Salvation Army band played stoically at the foot of the war memorial to a crowd that consisted of two dogs and an unaccompanied, and empty, pushchair.

They swept down Forehill and out onto the fen. It took them ten minutes to get out to The Pools. At this time of year the fields of snow were punctured with ponds of ice. Three months a year, out of season, it was the wintergrounds for a travelling circus. It was Kathy's beat and she got a steady stream of stories, mostly about the animals. Chipperfield's it wasn't; nothing more exotic than a llama amongst the livestock, and the usual old-fashioned rides like dodgems and a small rusting Ferris wheel. The scene was bleak to the point of beauty, like a TV ad for the Irish Tourist Board.

They pulled in beside a circle of caravans, each smoking gently from a stove pipe on the roof. A fire crackled orange-red in the freezing air inside a large open brazier fed by a gaggle of children. The Ferris wheel stood out against the fading light of the sky, dripping a fresh winter crop of lurid orange rust.

Dryden took in the scene: *Dogs*, he thought.

A Dobermann pinscher strained at one leash and an Alsatian at another. He sat for a few seconds to check the radius of their movement and then got out of the car, pausing to check no unleashed dogs were lurking. Humph made an entirely unnecessary settling-in movement which indicated he was going nowhere.

The flimsy metal door of one of the caravans jerked open and a large man, wrapped in several sweaters, jumped down and came over with a well-measured combination of hostility and nonchalance. He put the open fire between them and said nothing while holding at his side the largest wrench Dryden had ever seen.

A decade of experience had taught Dryden that in such situations ploys are unlikely to work. 'Hi, *The Crow*, Ely. We heard about the fire. Could I have a few words?'

It was hard to see the man clearly through the rising heat which distorted the air between them. He might have been handsome once. He was at some age over fifty but an outdoor life made any estimate beyond that less than a guess. The hair was tyre-black and full. The face was hard and muscular and made up of flat clean facets, like the bodywork of a truck. The eyes were small, green, and intelligent. One arm of the overalls was empty and folded neatly back to the chest: his disability went unhidden, more – he wore it as a badge of experience. He kept the fire between them but eyed Dryden's camera out of interest rather than concern.

'If you're taking pictures, mister, I'd like to see some . . .' The accent was a tussle between Ely and the Bronx – and New York had won.

Dryden pointedly eyed the straining Dobermann.

'Insurance,' said the man. Dryden was unsure if he was

referring to the dogs or the need for pictures of the fire damage.

The gypsy snapped suddenly at the dogs. 'Shut it, boys.' They shut it and, whimpering, skittered under the caravan.

'Joe Smith,' he said, picking up an iron bar and prodding the wood in the brazier.

Fine by me, thought Dryden, who'd made up less believable names.

Smith held his one hand out over the fire and kindly shooed the kids away.

Dryden stepped into the circle of heat. 'So what happened?'

Smith slipped a piece of chewing gum into his mouth. 'Could've killed us. There's a dozen kids on the site. No warning – nothing. Just set light to the stables.'

Dryden tried an expression of world-weary cynicism – a subtlety lost in the weaving heated air between them. 'Police didn't seem to think . . .'

'They think we did it to get the insurance. Gonna print that, fella?'

'Dryden. The name's Dryden. So . . . who . . . ?'

'Never saw 'em. They stuffed straw from the stables under the caravan as well – didn't light it. Just a gesture. Nice people.'

'But the dogs . . .'

'Inside. Cold. They're pets. They lit the fires and drove off – we heard them reversing on the drove road, looked like a van, a Ford perhaps. We were too busy fighting the fire to follow.'

'All of you too busy?'

This observation was apparently a mistake. Smith came round the fire. Dryden estimated that a blow with the wrench would be fatal – or even a promise to deliver one. The potential weapon had now assumed the proportions of a small fork-lift truck.

'You'll want to see the animals.' He walked off towards the stables and Dryden followed. Inside the straw was burnt and wet. Sprawled innocently in the debris were the charred bodies of two ponies. The smell was pure Salmonella Sid's – overcooked greasy meat with a hint of burnt toast.

'Oh shit,' said Dryden and put his breakfast in the sawdust. When he finished retching and stood up Smith was standing ready with a metal canteen of water.

'You found them like this?'

'Nope. If we hadn't got to them the whole block would have gone up – we've got nearly fifty animals. These two had gone down with the fumes. The half-doors had been bolted and a petrol bomb tossed in. Some of the fairground stuff is stored in there – we dragged that out but a lot of it's trashed.' Smith looked around and shook his head. 'Don't ask me why.'

Dryden couldn't resist. 'Why?'

Smith tried a grin. 'If you want a list of our enemies we'd betta sit down.'

Perhaps the police were right – perhaps they were making it all up for the insurance money.

'You the owner?'

'Nope. We just look after it from the fall onwards. Feed the livestock, oil the machines, run 'em now and again to keep it all moving. Do a bit of painting as well. Circus people come back in February from Ireland, pick her up and off on tour.'

'So you're not the insurance policy holder?'

'Nah. But we're all in cahoots. Gypsies are like that – ask anyone.'

'You tour?'

'Some of us go, work the stalls and the rest. Others stay here – keep an eye on things. Earn an honest dollar.' He looked

Dryden straight in the eyes. He said it again. 'Honest dollar.'

Dryden started taking his pictures. Smith got two of the kids to pose with some of the charred circus rides – an old merry-go-round and some dodgem cars. Nice pic – very nice pic. A woman who might be the kids' mother hovered by the caravans tending the fire. If you'd asked the average bigot what a gypsy woman looked like she was the opposite: neatly dressed in designer jeans and trendy sports windcheater. She had short blonde hair and bright cat's eyes like Joe Smith – and shared his accent without the undercurrent of the Fens.

She inveigled the children into posing for the pictures and smartly slapped one who asked Dryden for a fifty-pence piece for his trouble.

Dryden took a set of pictures for the insurance company showing the extent of the damage. Smith insisted on a shot of the burnt-out stables. Dryden was relieved to get back out again into the fresh, cutting air.

His mobile chirruped. It was Andy Stubbs. 'Hi. You OK to talk right now?'

Smith had returned to the fire and was chatting with the children. 'Yeah. Fire away.'

'Chummy in the car boot – we've found the record that goes with his prints.'

Dryden waited. 'There's a link with the body on the roof. The prints were found at the Crossways garage – next to Tommy Shepherd's on the shop counter. No ID of course, they never found the rest of the gang. But a link.'

Dryden's imagination wheeled. The body on the cathedral roof was that of the prime suspect for the Crossways robbery. The victim in the boot of the car fished out of the Lark had been there too – but never identified. And the Lark victim died forty-eight hours before his one-time partner in crime Tommy Shepherd was discovered on the cathedral roof.

'Look, I've got an incoming call – better go. You still OK on the photofit story?'

'I don't remember saying I was.'

Stubbs's desperate need for help was becoming cloying. Dryden guessed that he was getting increasingly worried that the tribunal would chuck him out of the force. The station must be full of rumours and most of them would be fuelled by the natural desire of his colleagues to see the golden-boy son of a former deputy chief constable publicly humiliated. Stubbs needed the story to run. And he needed it to run Tuesday morning, so Dryden was his only hope. The local evening wouldn't touch the story, they'd just want to wait for the photofit itself. And the nationals had already moved on. Dead body found in the Fens. A story on day one. Not much on day two. But Dryden needed to string Stubbs along. He wanted that file. But he could afford to wait, he was holding all the cards. He faked some static on the line and switched the mobile off.

He rejoined Smith at the fire. The gypsy looked happier, so Dryden tried his luck: 'Ever have anything to do with the camp at Belsar's Hill, Mr Smith?'

He gave Dryden an old-fashioned look. 'Some. They buy and sell horses a bit. Why?'

'I had some news for a family that used to live out there – name of Shepherd?'

'Common name – same as Smith.' He let a smile touch his eyes. 'I can take a message unless you want to go in person.'

'It's about someone called Tommy Shepherd – a kid really,

teenager. He went missing in the sixties. There might not be anybody left who cares – but his body has been found. Perhaps you might ask if one of the family could give me a ring – on the mobile.'

He scrawled the number on a page of his notebook – Henry's budget didn't run to business cards. 'I'll drop the pictures by – but you'll ask at Belsar's Hill?'

Smith looked to the woman. 'What do you want me to tell 'em? Where was he found?'

'It's a long story. They found him on the roof of the cathedral – in one of the gutters. He'd been there thirty years – perhaps longer. Suicide the police say – jumped from the West Tower.'

Smith nodded. Went on nodding. Poking the fire.

'I'll have more by Monday,' said Dryden. 'The autopsy. That kind of thing. They can ring if they want. I can put them in touch with the police who are investigating. If they want.'

Smith nodded by way of goodbye. As Humph's cab pulled away Dryden watched him in the rear-view mirror. The New York gypsy with the giant wrench watched him back.

CHAPTER NINE

Newmarket has the most northerly siesta in Europe. Stable boys, grooms, and jockeys snooze after lunch having risen at dawn to get the thoroughbreds out on the gallops. Without the crowds who flock in on race days the town slumbers deeply in the late afternoon. Dryden and Humph rolled in just after 1 p.m. Snow covered the gallops on the heath near the town and a string of glistening thoroughbreds, steaming under winter blankets, clip-clopped across the dreary High Street doing a passable impression of coconuts being knocked together.

Humph stayed in the car park of the Winning Post, a pub with a very low bar, while Dryden ferried him a pint of orange juice and a salad sandwich. Dryden administered two pints of best bitter and nearly managed to finish a grisly meat pie, remembering, too late, the aroma of Joe Smith's stable.

He found the National Horse Racing Museum just off the High Street, by the headquarters of the Jockey Club. Galleries on the history of the 'Sport of Kings' and the lineage of its great horses had been lovingly filled with priceless memorabilia and were completely deserted. Dryden was instantly depressed, recalling dull Saturday childhood afternoons in front of the TV and the unmistakable voice of Peter O'Sullevan. He repeated to himself the observation that if betting was illegal horse racing wouldn't exist. A squealing group of schoolchildren crowded into one room where an oversized ex-jockey had coaxed them into trying a mechanical riding machine.

He found the archives in a small basement room which unaccountably smelt of horse manure. He eyed the curator with suspicion. Johnnie Reardon was Irish, compact, and skittish. He informed Dryden within thirty seconds that he had won the Oaks in 1980 on Pilot's Error. A black and white newspaper picture of horse and jockey in the winner's enclosure hung on the wall. The print was unprotected by glass and Reardon's countless attempts to point himself out had worn his image into a white ghost-like form. Dryden gave him the benefit of the doubt.

He told Reardon exactly what he wanted and why he was there.

'That'll explain it then.'

'Explain what?'

'The police. They called. They're sending round a bobby this afternoon. I'm to be on hand. Bloody cheek. I might get plastered in the Bay Horse and miss 'em, eh?' Reardon belched slightly indicating with little doubt that it would not be his first visit to the Bay Horse that day.

Dryden could recall precisely the details on the betting slip. The question was, when was the race run and did Tommy Shepherd win? The police clearly didn't think the details vitally important – a 'bobby' sounded pretty routine. But Dryden wanted to know whether the nineteen-year-old thief died a winner or a loser.

They took a gamble, appropriately, on Tommy's death being soon after his disappearance in the summer of 1966. They also took a gamble on his last bets being waged on a race at Newmarket. Reardon fished out some leather-bound record books. The cartridge paper creaked with age. Dryden checked his watch – it took Reardon six minutes to find the first entry. Bridie's Heart had run in October 1966. It was unplaced despite being the clear favourite.

'Now that's odd, isn't it?' said Reardon.

Dryden nodded, not knowing why.

The ex-jockey checked a reference book. 'Now here she is. That's why. She'd won that year already. July 30th – *Daily Mail Stakes*. Fifty to one outsider – that's more like it, eh?'

July 30th – the day of the Crossways robbery. Had Shepherd set up the bet as part of an alibi – an alibi that wouldn't stand up in the face of a set of fingerprints found at the scene of the crime? Did he ever get to spend his winnings?

Reardon tracked down the card for that day's racing. Ayers Rock – also at 50–1 – had won the three o'clock. At the precise moment Amy Ward had crumpled to the floor, Ayers Rock had ambled over the finishing line, a clear winner by two lengths.

'How much did yer man put on 'em?'

'A fiver each to win.'

133

Reardon whistled. 'Five hundred and ten pounds – including the stake back. Not bad. Not bad at all.'

'A fortune,' said Dryden, noting the speed of the jockey's mental arithmetic. The picture of Tommy as a luckless suicide looked less substantial by the minute.

'That's a win,' he said, winking.

It is, thought Dryden. *But you're still not getting a tip.* Then he thought again. Perhaps an afternoon in the Bay Horse might give him a half-day lead on the police investigation. He gave him a fiver and told him not to drink too much.

Dryden walked briskly back to the car counting en route the number of remarkably small men he passed on the street. It was like a day out in Lilliput.

Humph was juggling with a pair of large fluffy dice – the kind usually reserved for the front window of the Ford Capri. Luck was a subject of fascination to the cab driver – or in his case, the lack of it. The cab was fitted out with an array of rabbit's feet, and a horseshoe had been fastened above the rear-view mirror. It obscured just enough of the rear view to invite an accident.

Dryden banged the dashboard. 'Lidgate. Chop chop.'

They set out through the plush villages in the hills above the town, villages in marked contrast to the damp-soaked drabness of the Fen towns. Clear of the peat of the Fens medieval buildings had survived the centuries. Whitewashed stones bordered trim village greens.

They were at Stubbs Senior's country house at 3.50 p.m. Humph, exercising discretion, parked the decrepit Capri round the corner. Dryden walked in, round the camomile lawn and the magnolia tree, and up a sweeping gravel drive. The house was an old manor farm. To one side were stables topped off with a clock tower.

Who says crime doesn't pay, he thought.

A small fish pond was frozen solid. A large off-colour goldfish was lying belly-up just below the surface.

An elderly man appeared from the side of the house, two red setters at his heels, a third appearing from the lilac bushes.

Stubbs Senior stood his ground and waited for Dryden. Distinguished was the word. And tweed was the material. He had a head like a cannonball and no neck. His eyes were as dead cold as any in an identikit. He looked nothing like his son – except for the antiseptic cleanliness. Dryden guessed he was seventy – perhaps older.

'Mr Dryden?'

Stubbs carried two sticks but Dryden noticed he took both off the ground to point out the distant gallops on Newmarket Heath. Most surprising, in an ex-deputy chief constable, were the extravagant laughter lines around the eyes. His handshake was enthusiastic too, even warm. If this was an act, thought Dryden, it was the result of a lifetime's practice.

They sat in the conservatory amongst orchids, a vine, and a spreading fig tree. A grandfather clock ticked in one corner and the interior wall of the house supported thirty timepieces, mostly antique.

'Hobby?' said Dryden.

The former deputy chief constable looked through him. 'Was.'

On a marble table an intricate glass mechanism gurgled with flowing water. An elegant glass bowl fed water down a pipe to power a tiny gold mechanism which, through a series of flywheels and gears, turned the hands on a filigree clock face. Dryden examined the carved teak base. An engraved silver plaque said: 'To Deputy Chief Constable Bryan Stubbs on the occasion of his retirement. From his colleagues in the Cambridgeshire force.'

'Clepsydra,' said Stubbs. 'A water clock. The Egyptians had them.'

The heating was generous and all the ice and snow had melted from the roof and windows. The furniture was wicker with comfy cushions, striking unfortunate echoes of an old people's home. A woman, who remained nameless and unintroduced, brought tea and biscuits for Dryden, a small glass bucket of whisky for Stubbs.

'How can I help, Mr Dryden?'

Dryden eyed the whisky furtively. The curiosity he had heard in Stubbs's voice on the phone had evaporated. Some of the bonhomie of the introductions had evaporated too. He felt like an intruder on borrowed time. And the trickling water clock reminded him of the two pints of bitter he'd bolted down at Newmarket. He shifted uneasily in his chair.

As always in times of supreme insecurity he decided to attack, but Stubbs got there first. 'Where did they find the gypsy boy?'

Dryden sipped his tea, he was damned if he was going to be intimidated by an ex-copper. The clocks chimed four and he glanced at the water clock. The elegant face read four o'clock precisely. He saw now that the fretted metalwork picked out a picture. Dogs running with hounds.

'His body was found yesterday afternoon on the roof of the cathedral. It had probably been there since the summer of 1966. There wasn't much left but it appears he jumped from the West Tower. The detective leading the case . . .'

'My son.' Stubbs blinked slowly, blankly. Dryden read disappointment in the look, almost antipathy. He decided to fill the silence rather than let it be.

'What did you think had happened to Tommy Shepherd?'

'At that time we felt certain he was being protected by someone, someone able to send him away, or someone able to keep him hidden. Looks like we were wrong . . .'

'Yes. If it was suicide. Or it could be murder. Another member of the gang?'

Stubbs swallowed an inch of his neat malt whisky. 'Possible, but unlikely. In my experience the gang members would have separated after the robbery and kept well away from each other. They would have been in a state of panic anyway – they'd seen the injuries to that poor woman . . .'

Panic. Dryden looked at the old man's hands. One lay dead on the arm of the chair, the other gripped the whisky with easy practice. Stubbs gazed out into his garden. 'They, the robbers, must have presumed she would die of those injuries. At first, of course, they wouldn't have known that Tommy Shepherd had left his prints inside the Crossways. The plan would have been to split the money right after the robbery, possibly as they drove away. One of them would have had to keep the cups of course – but that could wait in the circumstances.'

For a crime that had happened more than thirty years ago his recall of the details was remarkably clear.

'Then they would have dumped the car and gone back to whatever alibis they had concocted – if they'd bothered at all. When we let the press know we wanted to interview Tommy Shepherd he might have tried to contact the rest of the gang, but they'd hardly be likely to welcome such an approach. They must have had some arrangement for keeping in touch, possibly a meeting place, and a prearranged time. My guess is that would have been several weeks later. In the meantime we felt he was holed up somewhere, and fed and clothed by someone.'

'You don't think he could have lived rough on the Fen?'

'A bit John Buchan, don't you think? We looked hard for Shepherd for nearly six months, right into the winter. There's no way he could have survived out there, let alone coped with the boredom. He wasn't the type to curl up with a good book, you know. He would have tried his luck at some point and made a break for it.'

'What about the rest of the camp at Belsar's Hill? Surely they could have hidden him. Got him out?'

Stubbs paused and inspected the contents of his glass. 'What exactly is the status of this interview, Mr Dryden?'

'Your ball game. Off the record – all for background.'

'You can have the information by all means – this is a case I would particularly like to see tied up. The reasons are my own but entirely professional. But nothing traceable, please. That's clear?'

'Yes. It is.'

Stubbs pressed a buzzer beside his chair. The unknown woman returned to refill the whisky bucket. This took a few minutes during which no word was spoken. Stubbs seemed to be in a world of his own, one apparently run on alcohol. As the woman filled the glass a sneer lingered on the former deputy chief constable's puffy face.

When he took up the story again his voice was heavier and oiled: 'We knew Tommy Shepherd was still in the area in the weeks after the A10 robbery. He sent us a letter. Or, to be exact, he dropped us a letter. By hand – but almost certainly not his hand.'

Dryden had lost the plot. 'A letter? Handwritten?'

'Yes. If you could call it that. Someone's education had been sorely neglected.' The disfiguring sneer again. 'It said that he would give himself up and provide us with the names of the rest of the gang if he could be assured of preferential treatment.'

Stubbs drifted off again into self-absorbed silence. So Tommy offered to shop the rest of the gang – that presented two decent motives for murder.

'And your reply?' prompted Dryden.

Stubbs's eyes swam back into focus. 'None. We planned a brief one at first. He asked us to make a statement to the press indicating publicly what the position would be. I was happy to do that. After all, according to the caravanette driver the man fitting Tommy's description was not in the Crossways when the raid began. We would certainly have cut him out of the GBH or murder charges. Plus his role in bringing the rest to book, due no doubt to his sense of remorse at the injuries inflicted on Mrs Ward, would have helped soften the judge.' The sneer reached theatrical proportions. 'We would have been happy to plead for leniency.'

'But?'

'Command of the operation had passed to the Yard. They wanted to review the case – it took them a few days. By the time they agreed with our original decision Tommy had gone. We never got a reply. Now we know why, do we not?'

He hoovered up some more malt.

'Where was the letter delivered?'

'To one of the village stations – house at Shippea Hill. Middle of nowhere. It was found in the postbox early one morning.'

'How do we know it was genuine?'

'He put a fingerprint on it, in coal dust. Very neat. My guess is that he had gone to ground locally. As I say we were sure someone was sheltering him. Sherlock Holmes might conclude a coal cellar was likely. Whatever. He was in the Fens.'

The heat in the conservatory had begun to steam the windows. Trickles of water ran down the green-tinted panes. Stubbs was lost in a haze of dreamy mellowness. Dryden guessed he had already said much more than he'd planned.

'So. How far had your enquiry got before the Yard arrived?'

Stubbs stood abruptly. Dryden stood too, expecting to be thrown out. But the former deputy chief constable was already out of the conservatory door and heading for a pine cabin at the foot of the open paddock behind the house. His gait was long and surprisingly steady. The dogs appeared from nowhere to circle their master.

By the time Dryden got to the cabin the door was wide open and Stubbs was sitting at a desk pulling open the drawers. The cabin was clearly a den. Books lined one wall and filing cabinets the other. A single word processor stood on the desktop with a printer attached. A paraffin heater was pumping out heat.

'Memoirs,' said Stubbs, by way of explanation. 'Here.' He handed Dryden a brown file marked with a reference number and the single word: CROSSWAYS.

Dryden looked inside.

'They're copies of course, they all are. An entire career. I'd like this one back. Don't show it to anyone else please. Especially my son. Anyway – he should be able to get the originals. Not that he'd know what to do with it. Good luck, Mr Dryden.'

'What do you want me to prove?'

'The truth. It would tie up a loose end.'

He patted what looked like a manuscript. His finger found a buzzer on the desktop while he tidied sheets of paper into neat piles. The silent woman appeared again with the inevitable refill. Dryden was ushered out wordlessly.

Humph asked no questions when he got back to the cab but flipped on the tape, bathing the cab in Catalan conversation. They sped back to Ely thinking of entirely different things: an intimacy they often shared and certainly enjoyed.

CHAPTER TEN

Dryden used his mobile to do emergency services calls. Fire, ambulance and police. Ely Police reported an incident at one of the town's two comprehensive schools – Friday night vandalism on a big scale, according to the officer on duty.

The noticeboard outside West Fen High was flecked with snow and said: 'This is a Community School'. The building itself had been an advert for trendy sixties architecture. But one winter had scarred the concrete with damp. A thousand aerosol cans had done the rest. Like all bad buildings it had won an award which was bronze, ugly, and set in the wall by reception. The architects still used a picture of West Fen High in their promotional material. An aerial photograph. It was its best side.

The main building was six storeys high and box-like

– a sugar cube on the landscape visible from fifteen miles. Four wings spread out from this central pile, prompting unfavourable comparisons with a modern prison. Set on the far side of the city's ring-road the school was surrounded by fields under snow with just the occasional wobbly goalpost coming up for air.

The uniform at West Fen High was navy blue but you'd never guess. A knot of kids was on the drive in front of reception carrying rolled-up swimming towels. Already the school lights were on – splashing lurid orange squares over the snow. Above the main doors hung a banner – 'East Anglia Regional Gala'. Dryden left Humph with his language tapes and struggled up the school's main drive in the dusk. The flapping black greatcoat made him look like a scarecrow on the march.

Inside the main doors two first-formers sat behind a 'welcome desk'. A ritual – even on a Saturday when the school was open to host sports events. The scandal of West Fen High's academic results had at least one benefit – designation as a 'sports college' and an extra £1 million to build new facilities.

One of the first-formers behind the desk was asleep, the other must have been trying to win a bet as she was wearing the school uniform. She looked up with barely concealed annoyance from a well-thumbed copy of *Hamlet*. Tiny notes in red biro littered the margins.

'Hi. Is the head around?'

'You here about the vandals? Amazing – guess what they did?'

The headmaster, Bernard Matthews, poked his head out of his office as Dryden produced his notebook.

Matthews had that haunted look any teacher would get in a school like West Fen High if they shared their name with East

Anglia's best known turkey farmer. The sound of poultry clucking had dogged him down the years.

'Dryden. Thank you, Gayle. I'll look after our unexpected guest.'

The Crow descended on West Fen High every year when the government published its league tables. Dryden's sympathy for Matthews's plight could not stop the resulting headlines. ROCK BOTTOM WEST FEN IS WORST IN EAST OF ENGLAND.

'Vigilant as ever,' said Matthews, grabbing a regulation corduroy jacket from the back of his door. 'You might as well follow me.'

They set off down one of the cavernous corridors that linked the central block to the outlying classes and the sports complex. Every window was open and snow had blown in onto the lino.

'Bastards got in late last night. Caretaker was away for the weekend – they must have known. The police made checks but only from the outside. Tell me. Coppers do have legs these days, do they?'

They passed a nature table in the corridor on which was a tank of tropical fish. Tropical no longer, they had suffocated thanks to a thin layer of ice above their heads.

Dryden walked on briskly, leading Matthews away from the nature table. 'And they just opened all the windows?'

'No. They started by opening all the windows. Then they got into the cellar and closed the heating system down. Then they did this.'

Matthews pushed open two double wooden doors into a tiled lobby – the entrance to the school's swimming pool. The pool itself was under a thin 'bubble' roof and surrounded by glass doors which could be opened in summer, the architects having

144

imagined well-behaved children lounging on the grass and taking an occasional dip between bouts of revision.

Every door was open and the pool's surface was frozen a milky sky-blue. The pool wasn't empty. Looking down through the thin ice into the unfrozen water below Dryden could see computer terminals. The vandals must have chucked them in and then opened the doors. Other oddities had been added to the soup.

'Isn't that a blow-up doll?' said Dryden eagerly.

Matthews slipped glasses on and studied the flotsam. ''Fraid not, Dryden. Nice try. It's an anatomical figure, taken from the biology lab.'

Other items included a desk, a basketball post, some wastepaper bins and a chemistry lab fume cupboard.

Dryden produced a banana from his coat pocket for tea and began to circle the pool. On the mobile he called Mitch, *The Crow*'s photographer, and told him the details. He'd just shut his shop up for the weekend and agreed to do the job.

At the far end of the building a retractable seating area had been rolled forward and a banner on the far wall proclaimed: 'West Fen High. The Best in Sport'. Scattered over the seats were some disappointed-looking parents and some of the local 'great and good' looking suitably outraged.

A hand touched Dryden's sleeve. Ben Thomas – Labour leader of the local council – was eager to see if his comments on the emergency work on the cathedral would make it into *The Express*. Dryden found it hard to believe it was only yesterday that they had discussed the story.

Thomas was also keen to get a quote in on school vandalism, but first he had a point to make. A party political point. 'I blame the Tories of course.'

'They broke in, did they?'

Thomas ploughed on, congenitally unable to spot irony. He was spindly tall and clever, disguising an Oxford education behind estuary English. Mid-thirties and serious, he taught in the city's special needs school – a fact that cropped up in every speech he made. He wore his heart on both sleeves.

'They've cut the school security bills. West Fen can only afford one caretaker – and he's got to have some time off.'

What's wrong with the school holidays? thought Dryden, but let the subject drop.

Thomas was a county councillor, and shadow education spokesman, as well as leader of the district council. His education brief had got him an invitation to the swimming gala. The Tories held a hefty majority on the county council – and therefore had control of the education authority budget as well. Thomas's personal ambitions had been cruelly thwarted by democracy.

Normally Dryden dealt with rent-a-quotes like Thomas by putting his notebook away. This time he spotted an opportunity to find out some useful inside knowledge on former Deputy Chief Constable Bryan Stubbs. Thomas was Labour's representative on the authority's police committee.

'So what do you reckon the damage is?'

Thomas looked around and failed to suppress a smile as Dryden flipped open the notebook.

'Got to be fifty thousand – biggest problem is unthawing the pipes. They can't do it quickly, they'll burst. We might have to close the school for a few days.'

'And you blame the tight budget? Surely the school got a million off the government – the Labour government – to set up the sports college?'

146

'Oh yeah. But what about running the thing? That's down to the council allocation of the government grant . . .'

Thomas set off, verbally losing himself in the maze which is local government finance. When he finally emerged Dryden closed his notebook.

'By the way . . . does the name Bryan Stubbs ring any bells? Police bells?'

'Retired two years ago? We voted through the terms – he went early, at sixty-one I think.'

'You didn't try to keep him?'

Thomas cast a theatrical glance around the pool and took a step closer to Dryden.

'Hardly. Bloke was bent.'

'Bent?'

'We reviewed the file. Over the years at least half a dozen complaints of fabricating evidence. He'd got to the top because he knew where the bodies were buried – it was that generation. The sixties – they all went up together. Most of them grew out of it, but Stubbs was an "old-fashioned" copper. Heroes and villains.'

'I'm looking at a case back then – in the sixties. Halfway through they called in Scotland Yard. Is that rare?'

'No. Before they set up regional crime squads the Yard had all the expertise. But I'd be careful – sometimes they called them in to clean up dirty tricks, especially if the case is high profile. They often ended up investigating the investigation – not the crime.'

'So you were happy to see him go?'

'He wanted out – doctor's report said cancer. Smelt more like cirrhosis to me. He had a reputation for boozing. We agreed terms – got him out. Best for everyone.'

'His son is up on a disciplinary charge now – know anything about that?'

'Not much. I read it in your paper in fact. Nothing to do with us really – down to the local tribunal unless someone appeals.'

'What's your guess?'

'With the papers watching – and plenty of his dad's enemies still around – he could get busted down a rank.'

Dryden couldn't resist a final blow below the belt. 'Your kids at West Fen?'

Thomas zipped up his leather jacket. 'Nope. Anyway – better be off.'

No, thought Dryden, letting him go. *They're at Ely's grammar school. Hypocritical bastard.*

The visiting school bus had left and the kids were now snowballing the school windows in the dusk. He met Mitch, the mad photographer, coming in: 'Fill your boots – it's like the set for *Titanic* in there.' The photographer was hardly visible behind a high-tech pyramid of photographic equipment.

'Great job,' said the Scot, as he swept past the welcome desk.

CHAPTER ELEVEN

Laura's room was no longer a mausoleum. A new box of electronic medical tricks had been installed by the bedside and linked to her arm and ankle by electrodes. The screens danced in vivid greens and blues, emitting comforting beeps. Laura looked whiter than ever. A printout chugged out a line of figures: a glacial waterfall of white paper, which had already reached the floor and begun to fold itself into a neat concertina of vital data.

Dryden poured two glasses of wine and settled down by the window. The snow had thickened during the day and was punctured by birds' feet. The monkey-puzzle tree sagged with the load. The day was ending, but as the gloom deepened, he let the darkness engulf the room. The white light streamed in softly from the snowfield.

'Humph sends his love, Laura.' He looked to the bed. 'I told him to come in but getting him out of that cab is like pulling a cork from a bottle of port. A rather morose, plump cork.'

Out under the monkey-puzzle tree Dryden again saw the tiny pin-point fire of a cigarette burning in the dark. It was the slightest of lights and danced and disappeared on the very edge of vision. He waited for the security guard with the Alsatian to appear from the shadows.

He sat and smoked the obligatory Greek cigarette. 'So, Laura, what's the story so far? I've been on *The Crow* two years and the biggest crime until the day before yesterday was a sub-post office robbery – unarmed – at Littleport. That turned out to be two juveniles. In the last forty-eight hours, by contrast, two bodies have turned up in grotesque, some would say bizarre, circumstances.

'The first has been shot in the back of the head and dumped in the River Lark inside the boot of a stolen car. After death he was hanged by rope causing traumatic injuries to the neck. He was drunk at the time of death but otherwise appears to have enjoyed a healthy lifestyle. Fifties, corn-blonde. Odd age to be a murder victim. Passions are normally spent. His prints were on the police computer. They'd been found at the scene of a robbery in 1966 at a roadhouse on the A10 – the Crossways. We don't know who he was then, and as yet we don't know now.

'The day after the body in the Lark is found another one turns up. He is found on the roof of the cathedral. He's probably been up there since shortly after the robbery. The body is that of Tommy Shepherd, a gypsy and petty thief, wanted at the time of his disappearance for his part in the Crossways robbery. Besides a half-eaten driving licence he has in his back pocket two winning betting slips for a meeting at Newmarket on the day of the robbery. More than £500. A small fortune then.'

He paused as a shadowy figure being led by an Alsatian on a lead crossed the lawns, then turned back to Laura: 'Theories? The link is clearly crucial but difficult to unravel. Did the Lark victim die because Tommy Shepherd's body was about to be found? Who knew it was about to turn up? Someone who knew Tommy was up there – probably the person who pushed him off more than three decades before. But why would the discovery of the body necessarily mean the Lark victim had to die?

'The police think Tommy Shepherd jumped – suicide. But then, how did anyone know he was on the roof? Witness? Suicide looks increasingly unlikely anyway. He'd have to get up there in daylight and if he'd jumped in daylight he would have hit the roof with a hell of a crash a hundred feet above the heads of hordes of tourists. My guess is that he was up there at night and was helped over the side. When he fetched up in the gutter he tried to stand. Why? Hardly the act of a man bent on suicide. And somewhere in the world he had £500 waiting for him – or perhaps he had it on him. He'd offered to tell the police the names of the rest of the gang. He could also count on at least his share of the haul from the Crossways robbery. Enough in 1966 to start a new life. My guess is he died a pauper and someone else got the money.'

There was a muffled knock at the door. 'Mr Dryden? There's a Mr Holt at the front counter.'

It was a stunning concept. Humph, standing up.

By the time Dryden got to reception the cabbie had beaten a retreat to the car, which was parked, engine running, in the floodlit forecourt. It was moving before Dryden closed the door.

'You got outta the car?' asked Dryden.

'It happens. Your mobile's turned off by the way. A bloke jumped the wall, over there, going in.'

'When?'

'Fifteen minutes ago. I walked round to the gates and saw him making his way to a ground-floor room. He stood with his back to the wall by a lit window. I think he saw me coming – so he bolted back over the wall. Then I heard a car set off. It passed the gates going east. The nurse at reception said it was Laura's room.'

They didn't need to discuss it. The Capri's bald tyres squealed as Humph swung out on the drove road. Ahead of them, about a mile across the fen, they could see retreating red tail-lights. Overhead a large full moon radiated white light over a frozen night landscape.

Dryden savoured the rush of adrenalin: 'Kill the lights. Let's see if we can catch him by moonlight.'

Humph flicked off the headlights and for the first few hundred yards Dryden navigated by leaning out of the passenger window. After that their eyes became accustomed to the night. They kept half a mile behind their quarry.

'Slow up. Let's keep him in sight but don't get any closer.' They were travelling east across the Great West Fen towards the River Ouse, running into a dead end, a network of droves, all of which ended at the river's high flood banks.

'We've got 'im,' said Humph, and the moonlight showed, for a second, the excitement in his eyes.

And then they lost him. The tail-lights winked out. Humph let the cab idle to a halt. Silence descended on them like a giant duvet.

'Reckon he heard us following?' asked Dryden.

Humph nodded. 'He's gone to earth.'

The sky was an astonishing planetarium of starlight with a single satellite traversing from eastern to western horizon. The earth was black and featureless but for the dim tracery of dykes and ditches with their wisps of mist. The only sound was that of water percolating through the peat. Across a vast field the ghost-like form of a badger trotted on a secret assignment.

Dryden stood by the cab. Humph got out as well. Twice in one day.

'What's that?' Humph pointed east towards the river. A single black chimney stood against the stars. 'Let's go.' It was the first time Humph had ever provided a destination.

It took them ten minutes of threading across country to arrive at Stretham Engine. The main building was in the shape of a tall brick cottage loaf with a slim chimney rising from one corner. It had been built in 1831 – one of ninety steam-driven pumping houses which replaced hundreds of windmills across the Fens. Stretham was one of the few to remain, largely because the engine was still in working order and had been designed and installed by James Watt himself, the father of steam. Dryden recalled writing a story that it was to open for the public in the spring after renovation with a grant from the Millennium Fund. But for the most part, since it had last pumped water from the Great West Fen up into the River Ouse in 1941, it was a forgotten landmark. A single needle of brick, which on low, cloudy days seemed to scratch the sky.

Humph was out of the cab before Dryden. On his feet he looked lighter, like a spinning top balanced precariously on two tiny feet so neat and close they looked, by comparison with his girth, like a single point. He bustled to the boot and produced two industrial-weight torches and an overcoat that could have covered a small horse.

Dryden, astonished by Humph's burst of mobility, took the torch without a word.

They circled the engine house once. There were two doors both bolted and padlocked from the outside. None of the narrow windows were at floor level and the wooden doors to the coal chutes were held fast by iron bars padlocked to the brickwork.

'It's a lock-out,' said Dryden.

They were standing by the main door when the otherwise still night was rustled by a faint breeze. The door before them swung open with a theatrical creak.

'Spooky,' said Dryden.

They examined the door. The padlock was locked and the bolt in place but the latch had been carefully detached from the wood of the door jamb. To the eye it would look shut but a good shove would detach the door, allowing it to swing inwards – a good shove being considerably more force than that applied by a midnight breeze.

'This is the bit in the film where I normally say something like: "No sane person would go in",' said Dryden.

'There's no car in sight,' said Humph.

'And if he's in there he's outnumbered.'

'And this isn't a late-night movie.'

They went in.

Inside they stood quietly in the dark and sensed the space around them. Their torch beams barely touched the joists fifty feet above – like Blitz-time searchlights rifling the clouds. James Watt's great steam engine took up the lower two-thirds of the void. The giant machinery glimmered dully with the polish applied by a thousand steam enthusiasts. To one side sat a squat diesel engine, a metallic Swiss-roll of beaten panels, which had replaced Watt's engine finally in the 1940s – only for it to be made redundant by the electricity pumping station further upriver.

The machinery creaked as the various metals cooled at different rates with the chill of the night.

'Let's stick together.'

Dryden considered this redundant sentence. 'Oh all right then.' He indicated a flight of brick steps leading down to the cellars.

'Can't we stick together up here?' Humph's euphoria was dissipating. Besides, he knew Dryden well and there was nothing as foolhardy as a dedicated coward.

Dryden led the way. One of the cellars was being used as a storeroom by builders preparing the engine house for its first season as a tourist attraction. They'd constructed wooden handrails for the stairs and begun building a tearoom in one of the coal cellars, which was bathed in the moonlight from a row of freshly cleaned skylights. Plumbing gear littered the floor in another, where the porcelain kit for a set of toilets had been stored.

Rats, Dryden thought, and he adopted a peculiar skipping walk designed to keep his feet off the ground as much as possible. They returned gratefully to the main floor and played their torch beams on the single metal corkscrew stairway which led up to the loft: fifty feet of cast iron tortured into a spiral.

'You stay here – I won't be a sec.' Dryden knew with sickening self-knowledge that his bravery was the product of a tremendous desire to show off. He took the stairs two at a time in a desperate attempt to postpone the onset of vertigo. Unfortunately he ran out of breath first, halfway up, and had to cling to the fragile metal banister for support. Below he could see Humph waiting like a pocket diving bell in an underwater movie, his torch beam sweeping the ocean floor around him.

He made the trapdoor to the loft in one more unbroken run, pushed it open with surprising ease, and tripped over the wooden lip in his hurry to find safety. He fell to the floor, producing a plume of dust which hung in the stale air.

When his breathing stilled he cast the torchlight around the loft. Unlike the floor below this was cluttered with Victorian flotsam: wooden buckets, coal shovels, winches, tackle, ropes, and pulleys. The walls were lined with storage cupboards – vertical lockers for the workforce which must have once been needed to keep the great engine pumping twenty-four hours a day. They were wooden with brass locks and hinges and looked like a row of vertical coffins.

A workbench ran one length of the room – its G-clamps, vices, and loose tools covered in a sedimentary layer of white dust. The floor was uneven, punctured by several closed trapdoors. Dryden guessed that these were used to raise and lower machinery for repairing and maintaining the engine directly below.

He stopped to examine the silence. He could hear Humph's nervous cough and nothing else. An owl hooted and he laughed without conviction. In the silence that followed he hoped to hear nothing but instead, from one of the lockers, he thought he imagined the shuffle of a foot. Before fear immobilised his muscles he walked noisily across the loft and pulled it open, his heartbeat crashing in his ears. A pair of moth-eaten overalls hung from a single nail and for a second he saw, by way of hallucination, a body inside it with the bloody snapped neck of the Lark victim.

The flood of relief when he realised his nerves had betrayed him had the effect of a swiftly administered malt whisky. He felt a flood of goodwill and laughed, this time making a decent job of it. A tarpaulin hung from the beams at the far end of the loft and he pulled it back with bravado to complete the search. It took at least a second to realise that this time he *was* looking at a real human face. Or rather a human head. The features, other than the eyes, were obscured by a black woollen balaclava. He saw the eyes and the fear in them. Then a crowbar caught him in the crotch. Fireworks went off in his eyes and a pain so pure seared his spine that for a second he was able to admire it before it shut down the rest of his nervous system.

He came to within a minute. The air sang with the echo of something. He was on his feet before he realised it was a gunshot, and at the trapdoor when he heard the second. At the foot of the stairs he could see Humph's body, sprawled flat on the stone-flagged floor.

'Humph!' He felt better for the yell.

He swung down the stairs and realised, guiltily, that he was already hoping he wouldn't have to try mouth-to-mouth resuscitation. He paused ten feet short of the lifeless figure to avoid the sight of blood.

'Humph?' A whisper this time.

'Yup.' The cabbie's voice was clipped, bored and slightly embarrassed. Outside they heard the distant sound of a car engine coughing into life and then accelerating across the fen.

'You're not hit?'

'Nope. Fucker pushed me over.'

'And you're not hit?'

Humph struggled onto one elbow and raised his head. He gave Dryden a look of pained annoyance.

'No. But you are.'

A warm trickle of blood was making its way down Dryden's neck. He felt his ear and examined the mushy red mess on his fingertips.

James Watt's great steam engine swam before his eyes in a perfect circle. He collapsed like a folding deckchair to the stone floor and dreamt of a criss-cross pattern on ice.

The losers dropped their betting slips surreptitiously, a snowfall of disappointment settling on the Newmarket terraces.

But they *had won. The snapshot proved that. There was more joy in that small square of photographic paper than in most of the rest of her life. A faded souvenir from a day she felt she'd stolen from someone else.*

Her writing on the back. 'Newmarket. August 65. With Gypsy.' He called her Amber for the earrings she'd worn the first time they'd met. The time she wouldn't tell him her name. And she called him the one thing only she could get away with: Gypsy.

He was at home at the racecourse, that's why he'd brought her. But she distrusted him, even there. The cigarette cupped in the hand, the easy charm that got him what he wanted. Why, she thought even then, had she gone this far?

'Nothing to lose,' he'd said, taking her money and his own. The horse was High Flyer. He'd studied the form. The Sporting Life *rolled into his jacket pocket. She knew his secret only later – that he could read the numbers, but not the words.*

'Nothing to lose,' he said. 'All of it – on the one chance.'

He said it again when he got back from the bookie's stand: 'All of it.'

She'd loved that. Loved the contrast with her own careful life in the new semi by the golf course. Loved the idea that she too had nothing to lose. The marriage she had was so hollow it echoed when she cried. A routine chore as spiritless as the jangling progress of the milkman's early morning round.

Gypsy had nothing. No bank account. No address. No worries. Perhaps that's what she loved. The footloose freedom. But she wanted him as well. He'd taken his shirt off in the queue for a drink before the big race. Wooden brown, bony, and painfully thin. Younger than his eighteen years. His hair looked expensive, blue-black like slate. It was that day, later, in the burnt brown grass he'd played in as a child, that she let him in to what was left of her life.

High Flyer. 33–1. A long shot. But he knew the form. Or knew something. She'd seen him talking to the men by the ring. She knew that way of talking, the sideways mouth, the eyes elsewhere. She didn't ask.

He'd smuggled her through the crowd to the rail. One man, drunk, picked a fight. Gypsy looked at him, smiled, said he'd fight him if he wanted. She saw his hands then, with the knuckles white and ready.

They got to the front. He told her the colours to watch. Gold and emerald green. But the horses went by in a pack racing for the line, and she'd been too stunned by the noise and the beauty of them moving to spot High Flyer.

Then he was picking her up, kissing her, and she smelt the cheap cigarettes and beer in his hair. They bought the first bottle at the bar on the grass. He'd wrapped his shirt round it and shot the cork over

160

the crowd. That was the joke about the snapshot. It wasn't rain that soaked them, it was champagne.

Then he'd taken her by the hand, up through the grandstand, to the terrace bar. It was cool and the shade seemed to swallow sound.

'Dress code,' said the flunkey on the door. So he'd put the shirt back on.

'Champagne,' he'd told the barman, handing over the winnings. Then they sat on the terrace and looked down, for once, on the losers.

The barman took the picture. It was her best day. She never knew if it was his.

SUNDAY, 4TH NOVEMBER

CHAPTER TWELVE

Dryden had climbed to the top of the cathedral's West Tower with ill-disguised vertigo and a pathetic sense of martyrdom. The bullet which had removed his ear lobe the night before had been fired directly upwards from the floor of Stretham Engine by the man in the black balaclava. Just his luck – to be hit by a warning shot. The bullet had passed through inch-thick wooden planking before finding its target. The casualty nurse who had tended to him said he would benefit from the bleeding.

Dryden had diverted suspicions about the incident by making Humph confess to a wayward shot with a fowling gun delivered on a post-drinking night hunt for ducks. For now Dryden wanted to keep the police out of it, at least until he'd worked out what his assailant had been doing outside Laura's window. The bruising to his crotch from the blow with the crowbar he kept to himself.

And now the West Tower – 215 feet of vertical anxiety leading to the kind of view that could prompt a seriously embarrassing evacuation of body fluids. But he climbed, not only motivated by the pursuit of a good story, but now by something much more personal – the atavistic desire to repay physical violence with retribution. He had no doubt the events of the last forty-eight hours or so were connected. He sensed that if he could find out why Tommy Shepherd fell to his death he would be closer to a solution. The key to the present was in the past. The problem was that someone from the past had shot him.

When he reached the top of the corkscrew stone staircase, the world opened out below him with breathtaking completeness. The general public had had access to the West Tower since the sixties and the final ascent was regulated by traffic lights operated from an office below. In the high season tourists climbed in batches of twenty past the green light, and once their arrival at the top had been confirmed on closed circuit TV, a batch of twenty would descend. The viewing platform itself was surrounded by a low stone wall and an iron safety railing. The view, priced at £1.80, encompassed a large part of southern England stretching from the university library at Cambridge to the giant grain silos at King's Lynn on the coast to the north. On a damp Fen day, when the mist crept up from the river, the view barely encompassed the stone parapet of the tower.

Josh Nene was already there. He had clearly seen the view enough times to take the edge off the novelty. He looked healthier than he had on the night he had led them up to find Tommy Shepherd's body. But no happier. He was kitted out yet again in the immaculate blue overalls, over what looked like several layers of jumper, and the NENE & SONS blue hard hat. The ditchwater eyes were slightly bloodshot. He was engrossed in a tightly folded architectural plan when Dryden stepped out, with beguiling authority, into the crisp Sunday morning air. Around them the world was white and preternaturally clear. He fixed his eyes on the distant horizon and breathed in the icy air in lungfuls. It helped to clear his head – still swimming from the painkillers they had given him at the hospital. The bells at the parish church of St Mary's below signalled the ten o'clock service. One of the ringers must have been a learner, his bell clipping the sound of the one that preceded it, providing an uneven soundtrack.

Nene looked up but didn't bother with a smile. 'Dryden.' His voice whistled like a set of deflating bagpipes. He crunched a cigarette against the stonework and, lighting another, stuffed the plan in a back pocket. Dryden wondered how long he'd been there. The pale blue of his lips was still vivid.

'Quite a climb,' said Dryden, fishing in his pocket and producing a wine gum flecked with fluff. He belted up the black overcoat and fingered the bandage on his ear.

Nene eyed it but showed no other interest. 'Occupational hazard. I've got a couple more years in me yet. Two sons waiting to run the business then.'

Dryden looked down the long Norman spine of the cathedral nave towards the central fifteenth-century Octagon Tower, built to replace the spire that had crashed to the ground during a Sunday service in 1426.

Dryden smiled to himself and turned ninety degrees to look out along the south-west transept. The spot where Tommy Shepherd's body had been found was directly below but too close

167

to the foot of the tower to be seen from the viewing platform. From the Octagon's central viewing gallery it was obscured by a stone pinnacle.

He was dealing with the vertigo easily. The screaming pain in his head probably helped. 'So he jumped from here? Was the safety fence up then?'

Nene casually put a foot up on the safety bar and leant over causing Dryden to suffer a wave of sympathetic nausea. 'When's then?'

'Nineteen sixty-six – August, September. At a guess.'

Nene flirted with an emotion Dryden had not yet seen on his face: interest perhaps, even surprise. He ran a pudgy hand through thinning white hair. 'No. Nothing here then but the stone parapet. We put the ironwork in around sixty-nine after a suicide attempt. Lassie passed out before she could get to the edge.'

They chuckled bleakly.

'Nobody checked visitors then?'

'Not really. Most people came up in tour parties with a guide. If someone came at any other time I think they just unlocked the door and let 'em. Cost 'em a few shillings of course – they were desperate for the money then with the West Tower and the Octagon on the move. But they wouldn't have been counted down. Why bother?'

'When were the video cameras put in?'

'Recent that. Early 1990s, I think. We were asked to tender for the work but a specialist firm got the contract – we don't get everything. There's plenty of competition.'

Dryden hadn't suggested otherwise. He pursued the point. 'But there can't be that many firms able to take on work like this?' He patted the stone parapet and imagined a slight swaying movement underfoot.

''S right. Skills are dying. But there's no fortune in it either – the cathedral knows we rely on the contract. They get their pound of flesh.'

'Do anything else?'

'Loads. Rebuilding. Specialist stone work. Water authority too – specialist stuff again. We used to do general building, but I've tried to focus on the high value-added stuff, that's where our name is known. Some export stuff as well, States mainly.' He patted the stonework. 'Craftsmanship. The diocesan work is our bread and butter. The contract runs on a ten-year cycle. We've just started a new one.'

'Nice position to be in.'

'Wasn't so nice six months ago when we didn't know for sure if we had a future. I employ sixty people. That's a lot of families. One of the biggest employers in the town.' Nene spread his short pudgy fingers over an ample belly.

Self-satisfied bastard, thought Dryden.

He produced a notebook, not as an aide memoire, but purely to intimidate. 'And it's been your firm doing the work for how long exactly?'

'Cork & Co. did the first modern restoration under the Victorians – eighteen eighties. I did my apprenticeship with them. Fifteen long years. I bought them out in seventy-six. Since then it's been Nene & Sons but it's the same outfit – just a lot bigger. Annual turnover . . .'

'Annual profits . . .'

Nene adjusted the lapels of the smart blue overalls. 'Private company, Dryden. Private information. But we do all right.'

'We?'

'My wife – Elizabeth – we own all the equity.'

'I see.' But Dryden didn't. He thought money was supposed to make you happy. Nene's face had thirty years of misery written over it in capital letters.

'It's difficult to believe that Tommy Shepherd's body could stay up here for thirty-five years without being found.'

Nene lit up and began to wheeze as he smoked. Dryden sensed his witness had become hostile.

'Why? There's plenty of spots on the roof that can't be seen easily from here or the Octagon. We do visual checks each year but most of the survey work is done from the ground by theodolite.'

'And that's your responsibility, is it?'

The bells stopped suddenly at St Mary's and they heard the mechanism of the West Tower's clock turning below them as it began to strike the quarter-hour.

'No. That's down to the diocese – the Master of the Fabric. They employ a firm of surveyors as well. But they're looking for structural weakness, movement and cracking. We rely on their reports to frame the restoration programme which the Dean and Chapter then have to pass.'

Snow began to fall and Dryden turned his face up to meet the flakes. He felt a warm trickle of blood set out from the bandage down the inside of his neck. He fingered the blood and examined it coolly.

Nene gave him a look reserved for runaway lunatics.

'Gunshot. Someone tried to kill me.' Dryden had always wanted to say that. He contrived a shrug which indicated this happened almost every day.

He had, at last, got Nene's full attention. 'Wha . . . ?'

'What about aerial photography?' Dryden enjoyed cutting Nene off, he wasn't as imperturbable as he liked to think.

Nene hastily lit a fresh cigarette. He took three attempts to light it. 'As I said t'other evening we get regular requests to overfly from commercial aircraft – the RAF boys and the Americans are banned from flight paths which go straight over the top. Not that you'd think it if you watch them line up to come into Mildenhall. Still, that's the official line.

'Most are for reproduction and sale. You know the kind of thing, aerial pictures of pubs and people's backgardens to stick on the wall. They don't have the kind of detail you'd need to spot a body from five hundred feet, not one mostly obscured by stonework. I've looked through a few we've got in the office and you can't see a thing without a magnifying glass, and then only what looks like a pile of leaves.'

Through his bones Dryden felt the deep vibration of the cathedral organ signalling the start of a service below. Out to the east they turned to a noise – the sound of a giant blanket being snapped in the wind. Instead they saw a vast flock of Canada geese rise from the reserve at Wicken Fen and head south.

'It seemed quite easy to get out on the roof where the body was found . . .'

''Tis now. The door was rusted in. Hadn't been opened in a lifetime. I crowbarred it open when I got out there Friday afternoon.'

Nene had relaxed again and rearranged his scarf against the cold. 'Thing is if you go out on the structure you don't see much – you're too close. The water outflow is measured to make sure the gutters are free. Modern survey work is based on precise measurements taken from the ground; the exact position of the pinnacle that shielded that poor sod from view will have been mapped to within a centimetre a hundred times. There's no need to go up there.'

'So why did you go up there?'

Nene eyed him flatly. 'Better ask the surveyors. Their decision.'

'So if it had been down to you nobody would have gone up to the south-west transept roof this year?'

'That's right. They said the gutters were blocked with leaves. I'd leave 'em. The leaves rot – the water forces its way through eventually. It's not like a domestic roof – there's a dozen outfalls on the south-west transept roof alone. We were below the roof last year, and we would have been back in five under the current programme of works. But they said it was an issue of public safety. Ask me someone scared 'em. Told 'em a big freeze would bring down the stonework. Rubbish.'

Dryden shut the notebook. 'Thanks very much, Mr Nene. You have been very helpful, very helpful indeed.' *That always gave them the jitters*, Dryden thought happily.

Nene looked at him through rheumy eyes. His lips had shaded to a pale lifeless red. Dryden decided he had a bad heart. He should chuck it in while he still could.

Dryden descended with shaking legs and made his way to a bench on Palace Green. It had a brass plaque: In Memoriam: Canon John Virtue Gillies. 1883–1960.

'Good age,' said Dryden of the long-dead canon, and rubbed his ear.

Two Japanese tourists took pictures of each other in the snow and a ginger tom wandered by, picking its way through Dryden's footprints. The cathedral's doors were shut against the cold but the sound of hymns seeped out.

Besides being shot the night before, he had woken up that morning in bed on *PK 122* to find Kathy's naked body beside him. It was a narrow bunk bed and their bodies were folded neatly together in a frictionless union of knees, crotches, elbows and breasts. A brief echo had come to Dryden of the Lark victim – the cold body crushed and distorted like meat in a can. But it was only an echo – Kathy's body was as warm as a radiator and a lot better designed. He had bathed in the heat and, equally as palpable, the guilt.

The fiery Ulsterwoman had been waiting in her car when Humph had dropped him home from the hospital at four that morning. She'd driven straight back to Ely from her night shift on Fleet Street.

She was wide awake by the time she'd seen the cathedral on the horizon. She'd planned a stroll on the riverbank by *PK 122*. She knew Dryden was a poor sleeper – perhaps she'd cadge a coffee, or more.

She'd taken over the patient and Humph, exhausted, had slipped into the night. Dryden had undressed and showered in the tiny bathroom in the bow while she'd made soup and poured the whiskies. He hadn't jumped when he felt her hand on his back, gently smoothing the soapsuds in lazy circles. It was a master stroke of seduction, taking them both beyond the point where his guilt lay, beyond logical abstraction and considerations of betrayal. They'd come to sex without passing any moral barriers. He hadn't thought of Laura until it was all over. Or not quite. He'd thought of her for that moment of release as he had in his dreams.

He smiled now in the icy morning air and blew out a plume of steam. The cloud of condensation hung around him in the still air. 'My wife,' he said soundlessly.

He had already begun to construct the layers of defence. Like a child he rubbed the wound on his head as if it alone were excuse enough. He winced as the pain brought water to his eyes, which he left to swell into tears.

'Self-pity,' he said, again to no one.

If she came out of the coma he would tell her everything.

He stood quickly, his knees cracking in the cold. He looked at the cathedral's blue and gold clock and saw that the hands were almost on eleven. Soon the bell would toll. He told himself that when it had finished he would never think of the night again. It was a childhood game which had never worked. Anxieties clung to him despite the passing of time. The bell tolled ahead of the hour. Then came the first tenor stroke of eleven o'clock.

Kathy had agreed. She'd sensed the guilt and left quickly, pulling on clothes and declining a cup of coffee.

He'd waved from the deck of the *PK 122* but she'd not looked back. The tyres of the red MG had squealed through the frosty gravel.

The last tenor stroke of eleven o'clock boomed out. Before the echo returned he'd thought of her again.

CHAPTER THIRTEEN

The Crow's offices were normally deserted on a Sunday but he met Henry coming out of his flat in full Scout commissioner's uniform and regalia. The editor was unnaturally and strangely excited. His bony throat pulsated with the bobbing of his Adam's apple.

'Scouts' sports day,' he explained breathlessly to Dryden as he rearranged his badges in front of the mirror.

'Goodo,' said Dryden, and got a vaguely suspicious glance in return.

He hit the phones. During his time with the *News* at Westminster he'd built up good contacts with a press officer at the Treasury. About the same age as Dryden, he'd lived close by in north London. He'd invited him and his wife to Laura's family cafe for lunch. They'd got on. He rang him at home.

Money was the key to the puzzle. A lot of cash, assuming the Crossways gang had flogged George Ward's silver, was still unaccounted for after more than thirty years. There was the £510 Tommy Shepherd had won, there was the £648 in cash and the silver – valued at £800–£1,000. More than £2,000.

He left a message on the answerphone. What would that £2,000 be worth today?

In *The Crow*'s darkroom Dryden emptied the paper's antique camera and put half a dozen prints in the fixer from those he had taken of the fire at the circus wintergrounds. Then he made a coffee and reminded himself that only sad fuckers worked on Sunday. He unlocked the drawer of his desk to retrieve the file Stubbs Senior had given him on the Crossways robbery. It was a résumé, presumably written for the incoming Scotland Yard detectives, of those interviewed in connection with Tommy's disappearance. It was sixty pages long, close-typed on A4, and it took him two hours to read. He was interrupted only once by the phone on his desk. He let it ring and listened to the message.

'Hi.' It was Kathy. 'You there?'

He picked up the phone just too late to stop her ringing off – and felt the guilty rush of relief.

Once he'd finished the file Stubbs Senior had given him he still had a Sunday afternoon to waste until Tommy's funeral. But now he had something to waste it on. The squad Stubbs had led had done a thorough job. More than thirty interviews had been conducted with what the police liked to call Tommy Shepherd's 'associates'. Two had caught Dryden's attention. In the first days of the investigation Stubbs had personally interviewed the Reverend John Tavanter, a newly installed vicar in his first parish at St John's, Little Ouse. Later, in the September of 1966, he had brought Liz Barnett, then a twenty-year-old housewife and local Labour Party activist, in for questioning. Both had what the files coyly called a 'romantic' attachment to the suspect.

But Dryden decided to start with Gladstone Roberts, then a local hoodlum, interviewed within hours of the Crossways robbery. His links with the suspect were more business-like.

Dryden locked up and walked out of the town centre, now swaddled in a foot of unblemished Sabbath snow. Cathedral Motors stood just off a roundabout on the ring-road about a mile from *The Crow*'s offices. It was a new garage, built when the by-pass was completed in the late 1970s, and it included a car wash, shop, and a spacious showroom. The pumps were automatic but an attendant sat behind a computer in a Perspex booth. Suspicious of anyone on foot, he eyed Dryden with open distrust. Dryden beamed. 'Hi. Howya doing? Mr Roberts about? Gladstone Roberts.'

The attendant, a teenager of obvious timidity only emphasised by a daring silver earring, reached for the phone on the till. He wore a baseball cap marked 'Cathedral Motors' and the kind of large brash wristwatch that can tell you the time under fifty fathoms of water.

'Name?'

'Dryden. Philip Dryden. *The Crow*. Tell him it's about Tommy Shepherd.'

There was a short conversation during which the would-be deep-sea diver failed to take his eyes off Dryden's face. He replaced the receiver with exaggerated care as if it might go off with a bang.

Dryden got the impression he was trying to memorise his lines.

'Mr Roberts will be down in a few minutes, Mr Dryden. Sorry we don't have a seat. Mr Roberts is off to church so he said to mention that he would only have a few seconds to spare.'

'Church?' said Dryden, and smiled. He recalled the police résumé on Gladstone Roberts: the words 'vicious', 'petty', and 'crook' had stood out along with 'educationally sub-normal'. He didn't recall 'devout'.

Looking around, Dryden felt subnormal might have been a bit wide of the mark as well.

The car showroom was full of waxed BMWs and two Bentleys polished to the point where they seemed to have gained an extra, translucent skin. The piped-in Muzak was classical, had a rock 'n' roll beat, and was at that annoying sound level known as discreet. He counted a long five minutes.

Roberts bustled in looking preoccupied. He was immaculate in white shirt, floral tie, gold Rotary Club tie-pin, dark blue suit, and polished slip-on black leather shoes. This was dress as performance art. It shouted respectability.

It was immediately obvious why the police file may have been slightly unkind to Gladstone Roberts – he was black. Ely was not famous for its melting-pot society. The town was insular and insulated. A multicultural event in the Fens was a phone call from London.

'Mr Dryden?' The natural deep tone of Roberts's Trinidadian skin had weathered badly over the last forty years. But the lilting joyful voice was just discernible below the flat East Anglian accent.

It was a question, and looking into the pained dark brown

178

eyes he saw that it needed a bloody good answer.

'Tommy Shepherd.'

Roberts shook his head slightly and screwed up his eyes – a performance designed to ask: 'Do I know that name?' But he said nothing.

'His body was found on Friday. He'd . . .'

Roberts looked at the floor. He seemed weighed down by the effort of pretending he didn't know what Dryden was talking about.

Then he nodded. 'Of course. The suicide.' He fished in his pockets for a packet of Hamlet cigars and lit up without offering one. Dryden wondered if the greyness in the dark wrinkles was ash.

'I'm just doing a piece on Tommy Shepherd – you probably remember the robbery at Crossways in 1966?'

'Why would I remember that, Mr Dryden?'

Dryden recognised he had arrived at the dividing line between being a reporter and a detective. He was reluctant to cross it due to a combination of innate cowardice and the lack of a blue uniform covered in comforting buttons and insignia. Also Roberts was the last person he wanted to insult. He imagined that years of racial discrimination had been insult enough.

He stepped in close and felt a surge of power as Roberts rocked back on his heels. 'I've seen the police file, Mr Roberts. On Thomas Shepherd and those associated with him between 1964 and 1966. I wanted a brief word – in private.'

They found somewhere private. The office was above the showroom with an internal picture window looking down on the cars. With the snowfall the lights had come on to counter the gloom. The cars sparkled in that depressing way reserved for impossibly expensive merchandise.

Roberts didn't offer Dryden a seat.

'Are you aware of the penalties associated with breaching the Rehabilitation of Offenders Act, Mr Dryden?'

Good line, thought Dryden.

Roberts sat perched on a ridiculously large walnut desk. Gilt-edged picture frames covered the leather surface: wife, children, car, house, holiday, golf club. Dryden felt less sorry for him. For a 1950s immigrant he had done well for himself. Dryden could only imagine how hard that had been in a community which saw the world in two halves. The Fens were 'home' and the rest of the world was simply 'away'.

What was clear, however, was that he didn't feel sorry for Dryden. There was a carefully constructed edge of menace in Roberts's performance so far.

'What offences?'

A masterstroke. He saw Roberts struggling to find an answer that wasn't self-incriminating.

He sighed again. He looked uncomfortable despite being firmly on home ground. 'Look. I wasn't at the Crossways. Sure I knew Tommy Shepherd. So did half the petty crooks in the county. So what?'

'So . . . the police at the time thought you might have been harbouring him. I've seen the file. Yes, they thought you might have been at the Crossways – but you had an alibi. A good one. There was a lot of money taken. It's never been found. They think Tommy committed suicide. I think he was pushed. Any ideas?'

It was Roberts's turn to take a step closer. Dryden felt the inevitable urge to back off. He resisted it with a commendable effort not unassociated with an inability to move his legs.

'Mr Dryden. Slander is a serious business. How can I put this? I have a choice – recourse to the law or my own devices. I use the second reluctantly, but expertly. Do I make myself clear?'

Dryden went for another question. 'Where'd you get the money for this place?' He took the opportunity to step back and look out at the showroom below.

Roberts composed himself by smoothing down his suit with exaggerated care. He stubbed out his Hamlet and took an overcoat from a brass peg. 'I can't help you any further, Mr Dryden. I have to be in church. Can I give you a lift home?'

'Sure,' said Dryden, with commendable bravado. It was a Rolls of course. Powder blue with the walnut finish. Registration plate: BOB 99. *Nice touch that*, thought Dryden. *Very classy*.

The doors locked with a soundless miniature thud. Roberts was doing 60 mph by the time they crossed the forecourt and swung out onto the by-pass. They sped south and then took the corner into Barham's Farm with a screech of burning rubber. Parked in sight of *PK 122* they sat in an uncomfortable silence. Just time for Dryden to realise he'd given Roberts no directions. How many people knew he lived on the boat? Twenty? Fewer?

Roberts slipped the locks and they sprang up. Dryden felt his nerve waver. He cursed his motto: *There's always one more question.*

But Roberts got in first. Only it wasn't a question. He sighed again, and his chin, briefly, sagged down on his chest: 'It's a Yale.'

Dryden knew he shouldn't ask. 'What is?'

181

'The lock on the cabin door. Then there's two bolts inside. But the coal chute's only got one. No telephone. Gas cooker. Nice picture over the bunk bed. Pretty girl. Your wife?'

Roberts had been aboard *PK 122*. But why? And when? Dryden was pretty sure he wasn't the man he'd chased to Stretham Engine the night before. But clearly Roberts saw Dryden as a threat, and was prepared to stop him investigating Tommy Shepherd's death.

Dryden climbed out of the Rolls but leant back in to invade Roberts's personal space. A personal space about as attractive right now as an inner-city playground. He was close enough to smell the ash in his wrinkles.

'Fuck you.' First lesson with bullies. Never show them you're afraid. Roberts didn't move an eyelash.

Dryden walked to the boat without looking back. He heard the Rolls purr away a few minutes later. By that time he was in the loo with a large malt whisky. He had the mobile with him so he rang his voice box at work. There was a message to ring Andy Stubbs. Stubbs answered immediately. The connection was astonishingly clear. Dryden could hear a light wind blowing in the background and the call of crows.

'Where are you?'

'Cathedral roof – checking if anything else came out of his pockets on the way down.'

Dryden heard the sound of shoes slipping on lead. It added to a growing sense of sickness. His stomach was still churning with fear from the encounter with Roberts. He gulped some more Talisker. 'I want something.'

He virtually heard Stubbs's patience snap. 'Look. You've got the exclusive on the link between Shepherd and the Lark victim – and much more. I want the story on the photofit to run. That's it. Do we have a deal or not?'

'No. I think I met our killer last night. He shot at me. And I think I know where the Lark victim died. All this is yours. What I need is a file.'

Dryden heard a long leaden slide and the hefty thud of a body meeting stonework.

Stubbs wheezed. 'Great timing. What file?'

'My wife Laura. The car accident. There's a file – classified apparently. They won't let me see it. Get it.'

There was a long silence in which decisions were being made.

Dryden rang off before he got an answer. Then he called the lumberjack-shirted idiot at Feltwell Marina. In the background he could hear the saliva-dribbling Alsatian tearing something apart. He was told what he knew, that until 1st April next year it was closed while engineering work was underway. Dryden said he wanted a temporary berth on the riverbank for a week – downriver of the new bridge. The sluices had been opened and the river was clear of ice. He said he'd be docked by dusk the next day.

The Merlin engine fired first time, cracking the silence on the snow-clad fen. A wisp of oily black exhaust trailed from behind *PK 122* as he nosed her towards the city wharf downstream. He tied up by the Cutter Inn and walked to the office to clear his head. The newsroom was Sunday teatime quiet. He checked his watch – Tommy's cremation was at 3.30. He had time to knock out some copy for Monday's early deadline for *The Express*.

Heartless vandals burnt two circus ponies to death in an attack at dead of night, Ely Police revealed at the weekend.

Circus wintergrounds manager Joe Smith said thousands of pounds worth of damage had been caused by the vandals who struck on Friday night.

Police are trying to trace a white van seen speeding from the scene of the incident at The Pools, near Ely. They later made extensive house-to-house enquiries in the Jubilee Estate, but without success.

The horses, a piebald called Horatio and a black pony called Beauty, were trapped in the stables. The fire also caused extensive damage to dodgems and a wooden merry-go-round.

'We were lucky to get out alive,' said Mr Smith. 'I am concerned that the local police take this incident seriously.'

Det. Sgt John Adams, of Ely CID, said: 'We take all such incidents very seriously. We have appealed for witnesses.'

It is understood that several caravans, which were slightly damaged, and the livestock and machinery are all fully insured.

The Pools have been used as a circus wintergrounds for more than a century. This is the first serious incident of vandalism in living memory.

Dryden was rereading the story on screen when he heard Gary coming up Market Street – his heels crashing down through the snow to the pavement below. He often popped in on a Sunday to check his stories for *The Express* – or to catch a quick nap with his feet up before trudging off home to his parents. The junior reporter had just had a pub lunch and as he sat down he patted a distended stomach and smacked his lips. He farted loudly.

Dryden decided to ruin his digestion. 'You doing a round-up on the snow? The subs will want it early tomorrow to lay out with pix. What you got?'

Gary went red and turned on the pleading eyes.

Dryden was merciless. 'Have you got the out-of-hours number for social services?'

Gary flipped desperately through his contact book. 'Yup!' He looked triumphant.

'Well ring 'em then!' Dryden snapped. 'Old biddies cut off. Newborn babies delivered on the farm. RTAs. Skating accidents. Frozen pipes. Schoolkids stranded. Anything. And plenty of human interest – this is supposed to be a downmarket free tabloid. But keep the details for a round-up in *The Crow* on Thursday.'

Gary nodded excitedly. He pulled out a packet of cigarettes and inexpertly ripped off the cellophane. He stuck one in his mouth, unlit, and cradled the phone between chin and neck: a position from which he was unable to reach the telephone directory.

Dryden couldn't watch. He transferred the circus story off his PC screen to his own electronic basket – he'd check it through one more time on Monday morning before filing it to the newsdesk. Then he looked at the prints of the circus fire and picked out half a dozen for the insurance company and put them in a brown envelope. He put the best shot of the kids posing on the burnt-out merry-go-round on the news editor's keyboard where it couldn't be missed. Just one print: golden rule – never give the subs a choice.

Half a yard of paper was trailing out of the office's only fax. Dryden ripped it off.

Hi.

So you're alive. Steph is well. We sent a card after the accident. Sorry. What can we say?

Your questions are typically oblique if I may say so. You always were a mysterious bastard. Just to get things straight . . .

This is a background note and not for quotation.
Your question . . . to reiterate.

If you were given £2,000 in 1966 what would it be worth today – if it had been wisely invested?

I passed this to the state people. They use an inflation table and then they have to make some assumptions about the investment. 'Wisely' is a tricky one to evaluate. Typically they gave me three answers. The lowest is based on sticking the money in a building society, the second on a decently performing investment portfolio, and the third based on putting it all in a goldmine like rental property. Your three answers are therefore . . .

£32,000

£115,000

£265,000

As the wise man said: there are three kinds of lies. Lies, damned lies, and statistics.

Hope this helps but suspect it won't.

Cheers from everyone.

Guy

Money, thought Dryden, grabbing his black greatcoat, scarf, and a pair of oversized insulated gloves which appeared to be nobody's but were always available on the newsdesk. 'Funerals,' he said to himself. 'Nothing as cold.'

CHAPTER FOURTEEN

The Victorians were good at crematoria. It must have been the combination of utilitarianism and worship. For once they had a good reason to be vulgar. Ely's was a model of its kind – red-brick and stucco friezes topped off with a campanile which could have graced any London railway station.

Another fine quality was its position – well out of the way. Built on waste ground by the water meadows its dignity had been undermined by the arrival of the Bury Co. sugar beet factory in the sixties. The smell of gently roasting vegetables mingled with the wisp of white smoke trailing up from the crematorium's furnace.

The sun was failing fast, a watery circle of pale yellow obscured by mist rising from the snow. As Dryden walked through the wrought-iron gates a flock of crows rose from the roof and relocated to a bare magnolia. There were five cars in the car park. The sound of organ music was just audible. Bach. It was so well played it had to be a tape.

The congregation was four-strong and he knew them all. The young woman from the circus wintergrounds, presumably Joe Smith's daughter, was in the back row. She ducked her blonde bobbed head when she recognised Dryden. The mayoress, Liz Barnett, was in the front row. Having found her 'romantic' link with Tommy Shepherd in the file Dryden wasn't surprised, but he admired her loyalty. A lot was still at stake even if the passage of time had lessened the risk to reputations. Dryden had spotted the civic limo outside with the chauffeur asleep under his peaked cap. She sat still, and rigidly upright, and didn't turn when Dryden closed the chapel door. The last time he'd seen her she'd been calmly finishing her drink at the Maltings while her husband had been rushed off to the Tower. He'd checked on Roy's condition on Saturday afternoon. The mayor had discharged himself and refused a twenty-four-hour heart monitor.

Former Deputy Chief Constable Bryan Stubbs was in the second row. He turned to see Dryden slip into the third row behind him. He was welcomed with a weak smile. No guilt, no embarrassment, no discomfort. Stubbs Senior returned to the *Book of Common Prayer*.

Beside him sat Dr John Mitchell, the district coroner. Dryden had seen Mitchell at funeral services before; he seemed to make a point of attending if there was any chance nobody else would. For a coroner Mitchell had the wrong face: he always looked like he'd been treated to a good joke

189

and the punchline was just about to be delivered. Jovial expectancy. Perhaps it was job satisfaction. Mitchell's head was back and he was studying the Victorian painted ceiling – a sickly arrangement of blue sky, stars, and fat angels. Dryden caught a thin whiff of whisky on the air. Mitchell and Stubbs clearly had something in common. It was a good job it wasn't a Catholic service, one candle and they could have both gone up in a ball of fire.

With only a mild shock, Dryden realised he was wrong, he knew five people at the funeral of Tommy Shepherd. The presiding priest was the Reverend John Tavanter of Little Ouse. He stood from seated silent prayer and his dove-grey eyes swept the congregation. There was no need to wait for silence. He made a brief fuss with his simple vestments and placed a modest wreath on the coffin which stood in plain pine on a draped trestle. A brass plate had been engraved *Thomas Shepherd: born 1947, disappeared 1966.*

The service was like Tommy Shepherd's life: short and bleak. The congregation seemed uninterested, each lost in a private world of memories. Dr Mitchell stuck with the ceiling. There may have been some snuffling in the back row, but everyone had the good British manners not to look. Otherwise there wasn't a wet eye in the house.

Dryden sneaked a miniature pork pie into his mouth. He thought, not for the first time, that religious ceremonies brought out the worst in him. It was one of the few good things about a Catholic education. Finally the great moment of comedy arrived. Dryden could never watch the end of a cremation without wondering how everybody else kept a straight face. The Reverend Tavanter pressed a button by the pulpit lectern and the coffin began to slide electronically towards some parted purple curtains. The music was insipid, pastoral, and piped. When it ended there was a silence in which the sound of a gas furnace was distinctly audible. Dryden suppressed the image of some superannuated gravedigger frantically ramming 10p bits into a gas meter. Then the music returned, upbeat, hopeful, and entirely inappropriate. It was worth making a will, thought Dryden, just to make sure that it didn't end like this.

Tavanter, hands together around his slightly rounded frame, moved towards the tiny congregation, but almost everyone was too quick for him. The woman from the travellers' site bolted for the door and the mayoress was halfway down the aisle before he'd got to the front row. She had failed to dim her usual patchwork of colours for the funeral – save for a jet brooch at her neck. She gave Dryden a look which mixed a lot of anger with just a little self-pity.

But Bryan Stubbs and Dr Mitchell were slowed down by infirmity and alcohol. Tavanter helped them into the aisle and they processed on, arm-in-arm, like old comrades. Swaying like a couple of stage drunks in an end-of-the-pier show they weaved towards the door. The coroner gave Dryden a nod. Stubbs paused, effortlessly guiding Dr Mitchell on towards the west end, as though he'd launched a toy sailing boat across a pond. He met Dryden's question before it was asked.

'Just tying up loose ends.'

'You take a very personal interest in your old cases.'

Tavanter joined them. Up close he looked ill, as if he'd lost a lot of weight in a very short space of time. His skin was too big for him.

Stubbs unsnapped a silver-topped collapsible walking stick. 'Great believer in being there in person. Allows the intuition to flow freely. Know what it's telling me now?'

Opening time? thought Dryden, but shook his head.

'It's telling me you're going to find out who killed that young man. You've certainly got a better chance than my son.'

He sailed off on an ocean of whisky.

Tavanter leant on the pew end and slipped into the seat beside the reporter. He looked exhausted and closed his eyes as if in prayer.

Dryden had planned the question: 'What would Tommy have thought?' It invited self-incrimination, self-justification.

Tavanter took the question seriously as Dryden knew he would. He placed his fingers together in a little steeple of thought. 'Not much.' The voice was languid and modulated, like a priest's during confession. 'Tommy's faith was rooted, if at all, in rural ignorance. He knew no better. Not an excuse that could be called upon by those here today.'

'I'm sorry. This isn't the right place for questions.'

'Quite wrong!' It was nearly a shout. Tavanter opened his eyes as though seeing the inside of the chapel for the first time. He cast them up to Dr Mitchell's sickly ceiling. 'The very place, Dryden. I've asked all my best questions in front of God. My tragedy is that it appears to be a lousy place to expect answers.'

Dryden wondered where to start. But Tavanter saved him the trouble. The priest of St John's had been interviewed three times by the detectives in the Tommy Shepherd case in 1966.

'I didn't see Tommy again after he went missing that summer. It wasn't through lack of trying. We were very close. I went to

192

Belsar's Hill but they said he was in Ireland. They were lying of course, but they must have thought I'd go to the police.'

'Tommy never tried to use your relationship to get help, money, a place to hide?' Dryden was fishing, the file had been circumspect, but reading between the lines had been easy enough.

'That would presume our relationship was physical, which it wasn't. For the record, that is actually a matter of regret to me. Especially today. But no, Tommy had no basis for blackmail.'

Dryden thought of the hunched decaying remains on the cathedral roof. He'd never thought of Tommy as a human being, let alone a lover. In his experience murder wasn't something that happened to real people, people whose going left other lives empty. Murder happened to cardboard cutouts who appeared on police WANTED posters. Chalk outlines on the pavement.

'Tommy could have lied. The circumstantial evidence of your relationship would have been enough to raise questions. It could have been very damaging.' Tavanter was lost in the past. Dryden brought him back by touching the hem of his cassock: 'Did he try?'

'That's all true. But frankly Tommy was no fool. Far from it. He knew exactly where he had me, in the palm of his delicate hand. He knew I'd do almost anything for him anyway, he didn't need to resort to blackmail. I was looking for him.'

'So you've no idea who was capable of killing him?'

'Oh, I've got lots of ideas. Take our esteemed deputy chief constable. What if Tommy hadn't been at the Crossways that day?'

'But he offered to tell the police who was. He sent them a letter.'

Tavanter let his eyes rest on Dryden's. 'But did he say he was there himself? If he had turned in his friends – an act of betrayal he was more than capable of, by the way – any one of them could have cleared Tommy. Where would that have left Stubbs? As the detective in charge of the case he was responsible for verifying the fingerprints. They could have lied to take Tommy down with them, but that would have required a collective act of revenge. Unlikely I think. If Stubbs faked the evidence and Tommy gave himself up, the future deputy chief constable's career was over. What about that for a motive?'

'Is it as good as money?'

Tavanter smiled. 'My fortune?'

'Certainly a fortune spent on good deeds, but a fortune nonetheless. And spent. The AIDS centre in Cambridge was built with your money I believe, and is still run with it. Quarter of a million? Half a million?'

'Yes. Oh yes. More. And we sceptics know that all charitable giving is selfish. I enjoy running the centre. It has given me a purpose in life. Status. Friends. A place of my own. So you think I killed Tommy to get the money?'

'No. No, I don't. But, for the sake of the argument, the money wouldn't have had to be the reason for his death. It's just that whoever did it would have got the money anyway, and faced the problem of finding somewhere to spend it. It was no small amount – if he got a share from the Crossways and his winnings, it was a small fortune. Well invested, a large fortune.'

'You've turned detective? Don't the police do these things better? But then they might be suspects too?'

Tavanter tugged at his collar. 'I was lucky. Lucky to the tune of seven hundred and fifty thousand. I bought some land in London. It was worthless then, except for a youth club. I sold it when developers moved in and the youth club needed it no longer. I gave the money to the diocese here, they asked for the details before accepting. I'm sure they can confirm if . . .'

Dryden raised his hand. He knew the story but would check it anyway. They stood and walked to the chapel doors, left open by the departing deputy chief constable. Out in the garden of remembrance the mayoress sat with her back to them on a cast-iron bench.

'And then there's jealousy,' said Tavanter, smoothing down his ash-white cassock. 'She could tell you about that.'

Dryden's golden rule: you can always ask one more question.

'Did Roy Barnett know?' The police file had been clear about Liz Barnett's relationship with the young, handsome gypsy boy.

Tavanter shrugged. 'They went away a lot, she had some money. But he may have guessed.'

'If Tommy was on the run and needed help why do you think he didn't come to you? Wasn't Little Ouse the perfect place to hide? St John's was remote, he was unknown.'

Tavanter's grey eyes swam. 'An astute question, Dryden. One I have asked myself many times. We've just consigned to God's mercy the only soul on earth who could have given you an answer. Perhaps I don't want that answer. Perhaps he used me. I gave him some money, not much, but some. God knows. We don't.'

Dryden found Liz Barnett in the rose garden. The mayoress had recovered what little of her composure had been lost. She was smoking, sucking in lungfuls of nicotine in the bitter cold air. She wore a full-length suede coat, and a brilliantly coloured scarf, held fast by the jet stone. The make-up was applied with an audience in mind – circle rather than stalls. The hands, fine but muscular, were decked out in silver rings. On the whole the effect was diverting and worked a treat. She was angry still, and spitting self-justification.

She answered a question he hadn't asked. 'He wasn't a bit like they said, you know.'

'They?'

'The police. Old Stubbs. He looks dreadful by the way, made my day. Pity Tommy wasn't here to see it.'

She turned and walked down the snow-covered path between ranks of memorial urns. Above, thin white smoke from the crematorium chimney thickened to grey and drifted up into the low clouds.

'Low-life, scum, that's what Stubbs said. They showed me pictures of that poor woman from the Crossways. Made me sick in a bucket. Said they'd have to interview Roy. They said Tommy was an animal. But I tell you what he wasn't, Dryden.'

They faced each other between two bare rose bushes. 'He wasn't at the Crossways.'

She fished inside the suede coat, produced a small leather snapshot holder and flipped it open. Inside was a picture of two people laughing, drenched in sunshine after a rainstorm. One was Liz Barnett, hair a bright red, twenty years old, no make-up, in a white linen blouse. She looked fabulous. High cheekbones, flashing green eyes, and a perfect wide smile revealing flawless white teeth.

The boy looked a lot younger than eighteen. The blue-black hair lay in rich curves over a fine narrow face. The eyes dominated the neat features, black and wide and slightly watery. He looked unsure, nervous even, but happy, his hair and shirt damped down from a shower, his bony shoulders showing through.

Dryden flipped the snapshot over. *Newmarket. August 65. With Gypsy.* She took the picture back and slipped it carefully into the holder.

'Got one of Roy?' It was a cheap shot but she laughed.

'Just for the dartboard. We all make mistakes. Tragedy is when you make one that ruins your life.'

'He's a good socialist.'

She didn't laugh. 'Yes. Yes, he was. That must have been it.' Her eyes searched the fen beyond the river.

'But it wasn't politics with Tommy?'

She gave him an old-fashioned look. 'No, Dryden. It wasn't politics. But it was a lot more than sex. All right?' She looked back at the waiting car as if uncertain whether to go on. 'He wasn't at the Crossways. He was with me.'

Dryden considered this alibi. 'Wouldn't it have been helpful to have said that at the time? You might have saved his life.'

She took a step back and Dryden thought she'd decided to walk off but she rocked back on her heels and delivered a full-handed slap across his face before he'd even thought of ducking. His eyes swam for a second and he felt tears well.

'I'm sorry,' she said.

Dryden managed to suppress the surge of adrenalin. 'That's all right then.' He placed his cold palm against the stinging skin.

She didn't look sorry. 'This isn't a game, you know. A newspaper story. It's about two ruined lives – three.'

Dryden, having overcome the urge to punch her in the face, now fought back the urge to apologise. 'So why didn't you tell the police?'

197

She ignored the question. 'We were at the coast. We went to Newmarket on the way, Tommy won, he wouldn't say how much but he was flush. Then we went to the beach. We had a radio and Tommy listened for the news all afternoon. I guess he knew the job was on.

'He paid for the B&B at Orford. God knows what they thought. I was married, twenty. He was eighteen. Sounds a bit sordid, doesn't it? Actually it was rather romantic. I'd been married eighteen months, things weren't working out. Tommy was fun. He'd never been to the cinema. He'd never sat down to eat a meal unless it was at home. He'd never been on holiday. He'd certainly not been to school, none of the kids at Belsar's Hill could muster an attendance record. Illiterate.'

She paused and changed tack. 'Sensitive. He was the youngest in the family, spoilt I suppose. He'd been in trouble a few times, but no more than a lot of kids. But he'd done a fraction of the things they said he had. He'd been set up a few times for things he couldn't have done. They planted evidence, drummed up witnesses, basic stuff. But with his record he didn't stand a chance in front of the bench in a town like this. Gyppo. The family couldn't pay fines.

'We were away that night at the B&B when they raided Belsar's Hill. We'd given false names so there was no need to run. They took his brother, Billy, in for questioning, along with the father – Old John. Then they put out the statement, on the morning news, saying they'd found Tommy's fingerprints at the Crossways. Billy said they'd picked up the prints from Tommy's caravan.

'After that there was no point in coming forward with an alibi. The people at the B&B couldn't swear Tommy was on the coast that afternoon. Anyway the police were hardly likely to let it stand in the way of forensic evidence they'd planted themselves. And we knew they'd planted it.'

The mayoress drifted off into a memory as she started a fresh cigarette.

Dryden smuggled a wine gum from his jacket pocket into his mouth. 'And then?'

'Billy phoned the B&B. Tommy trusted him. Left him the number. He said to stay away but they cooked up some place for Tommy to hide. Billy was like him, coarser, knew a bit more about the world, but he loved Tommy. Billy said the police would charge him with murder if the Ward woman died, even if they were claiming he was the third man, the one outside on the forecourt.

'And he didn't want to hurt me with the alibi anyway. Roy still had a chance of the parliamentary nomination then. Wouldn't have looked very good, would it? Family values weren't an issue in the 1960s, they were taken for granted. It was a basic requirement: wife, family, and church. He wouldn't have got on the parish council if the papers had said his wife was having an affair with an eighteen-year-old boy, let alone a gypsy.'

'Did Roy ever know? Does he know?'

Dryden took half a step back by way of precaution.

'Does he care? Don't ask me. He guessed the basics I think – but no details.'

'Jealous man?'

'Indifferent man. Our marriage had broken very quickly. He'd been the first to find someone else. He paid for his.'

Dryden bit his tongue.

'And I didn't,' she said, answering the question anyway.

'But he had ambitions. You too?'

She ignored the question in the best traditions of New Labour's media training.

'I dropped Tommy off near Belsar's Hill to meet Billy on the day after the robbery. Some old pumphouse down by the river, I . . .'

'The one at Stretham?' But Dryden knew the answer.

'Yes. How did . . . ?'

It was Dryden's turn not to answer the question. 'Could he have killed himself? The police had enough evidence to hang him. He must have thought the Ward woman would die.'

'Tommy? Never. He could do desperate things, Dryden. *Had* done desperate things. But there was no room for despair. Cornered he might have been dangerous, but only to someone else.'

They walked back towards the car. She leant forward and lightly touched Dryden's stinging cheek. 'Sorry about that, a woman scorned . . .'

Dryden smiled. One last question, the golden rule: 'When did you know the work on the cathedral would be extended to the roof of the south-west transept?'

Liz Barnett's eyes narrowed in the effort to remember. 'Last Tuesday – just after Roy authorised the money to be paid out. Why?'

Two days before the discovery of the Lark victim, thought Dryden. 'Fate, I guess. If you believe in it. Tommy's body would still be up there otherwise.'

She offered him a lift back to town but Dryden needed the walk to clear his head. His footsteps in the snow were regular and purposeful – unlike the disconnected and jumbled thoughts in his mind. Could Roy Barnett have killed the gypsy boy to save his marriage and his career? Or did Bryan Stubbs, facing the prospect of disgrace if Tommy testified that he was on the coast at the time of the robbery, decide to remove a deadly witness?

His steps took him to the Tower. The joyless history of the Crossways was beginning to undermine his own fragile good humour. It was an event which seemed to have wrecked the lives of everyone involved. All except one, of course. Whoever had kept the money.

For the first time Laura's room felt like a morgue. The cold white clinical tiles seemed to suck the warmth from the air. He sat, silently, for an hour knowing it was a betrayal. He felt abandoned and lonely, leaning his forehead against the cold windowpane and feeling the despair flood to his eyes. Outside, in the gloom, the monkey-puzzle tree sagged under its load of snow.

He found Humph waiting just beyond the gates. The latest snowfall had accumulated on the roof. Inside, the cab driver had abandoned Catalan for the evening and was happily working his way through his collection of miniature spirit bottles. He'd had three and had just turned the cap on the fourth. Dryden joined him, picking a Campari from the selection Humph had amassed in his regular runs to Stansted Airport. They drank in silence. Trappist monks on a night out.

Humph drove carefully to the town centre and dropped him off. Then Dryden walked to Kathy's flat and stood under a street light looking up at the darkened bedroom window.

It was part of a Victorian villa split into four units. He'd walked her home after the last office Christmas party – an act of gallantry that had ended in a confused attempt at a goodnight kiss. He watched for an hour as the snow fell. Then he crossed the street and knocked once. She opened the door a minute later, brushing her hair back from a smile, and they climbed silently to the flat above. 'Have you got a typewriter?'

Kathy disappeared into a cupboard under the stairs and emerged with a battered Imperial her father had given her when she first joined the local paper in Derry.

'Drink?'

'Coffee. Black.' He sat drunkenly on the sofa with the typewriter perched on his knees. He fed in a leaf of clean A4 and wrote – in capital letters – WHAT DO I KNOW?

– That Tommy wasn't at the Crossways – but that the gypsy boy knew who was.

– That Tommy offered to name the members of the Crossways gang to win his freedom.

– That the Lark victim – a member of the Crossways gang – died two days before Tommy's body was found.

– That the money, neither the haul from the Crossways nor Tommy's winnings, had ever come to light.

– That Gladstone Roberts, according to the police file, was suspected of being the fence who had sold the silver from the Crossways robbery.

– That Roberts had set out to intimidate him and make him drop the case.

– That Liz Barnett had loved Tommy.

– That John Tavanter had loved him too.

– That Roy Barnett had probably hated him.

– That Deputy Chief Constable Bryan Stubbs planted his fingerprints at the Crossways.

And that Laura's never coming out of the coma . . .
Kathy returned with two cups of coffee which they never drank.

The Reverend John Tavanter had conducted many paupers' funerals in his years at St John's. Disappointment had undermined this, his first, ministry in small, but cumulative, instalments. Now the weight of failure was almost insupportable: each new sign of God's uninterest an insurmountable barrier to the regeneration of his faith. The paupers' funerals were the milestones in this long journey from scepticism into cynicism: biblical in their bleak denial of the joys of life, they offered none of the comforts which he preached would lay in death. John Tavanter was for the first time aware of the possibility that his life could be a failure. Worse. That it could end in the annihilation of death without salvation.

His faith, a wisp of smoke now compared to the fire which had burned when he left Oxford, was no longer a defence against the despair he felt. Paupers' funerals marked the nadir of what faith was left. So low was his reservoir of belief that when the day of a funeral dawned he would open his eyes to the high Victorian ceiling and its cobwebbed corners and think only of that which the pagan gods could bring: the symbols of light and darkness, of burning shadeless sun or enveloping mist and rain, the overpowering presence of the Fen weather.

He would rise early, at 5.30, in the Victorian manse. He would shuffle, barefoot, to the shutters in the parlour and throwing them back to the new dawn he would close his eyes and pray for sympathy from the sky. Rain, clouds, grey skies, and sleet were his friends. These would save him from a sunny graveside and provide, instead, a fitting backdrop to a lonely burial. Buffeted and soaked, he felt at least that he had the sympathy of the elements.

But this morning, in that last summer of 1976, he had prayed hard and long because he could feel even at that early hour the warmth beyond the bay windows of the manse. He opened his eyes to see a clear sky, purple in the west, shading to a cobalt blue in the east. Venus, the morning star, was rising over St John's. It was a perfect day: a day indifferent to the ceremony he was about to perform. He felt his heart crush a little more.

The body of Martha Jane Elliott, spinster, was delivered at 10 a.m. by a Co-operative Society hearse paid for by the parish. Her body had lain for three days in the mortuary at the Princess of Wales Hospital. During this time she had been visited by no one. Tavanter had known her for all the years of his ministry and saw in her the petty insecurity which seemed a blight on this tiny community. She'd lived her life in a world still coming to terms with the arrival of the motorcar and the independence and affluence of youth, ill at ease with both technical progress and social change. Her cottage so closely resembled the kind of house drawn by a child that Tavanter always expected to see a pencil-thin line of smoke snaking up from the chimney stack. Built on the peats of the southern fenland, it had been undermined by the shrinkage that had followed the systematic draining during the nineteenth century. As a result it stood crazily at variance to the horizon: a worthless hovel which creaked in the wind.

She died on a brass bedstead in a bedroom so damp he could push his fingers into the plaster. In that last bitter winter rats had nibbled at the rugs downstairs. She lasted until the summer when, on a day weighted down by the vast sky above the fen, she clutched her family Bible to her chest and asked her confessor finally what she had asked him constantly throughout her long, final illness. 'Has no one come?'

No one came. The landlords of the cottage prepared to repossess: the bailiffs, mindful at least of the villagers' acute sense of sacrilege, made discreet requests of the vicar on behalf of debtors afraid they were about to be cheated by death. Martha directed him to a wooden chest beneath the bed which on inspection yielded some costume jewellery, a badly corroded silver picture frame, and a brass candlestick. Wrapped in tissue paper there were four china cups, perfectly intact, but nearly worthless.

He'd been with her when she died. A moment marked by the chattering of her rotten teeth.

The bailiffs came in through the back door as her body left through the front. The villagers watched in silence as her chipboard coffin slid with a thin veneer of pine and decorum into the back of the Co-op hearse. Then they melted back into the fields.

Today they would stay in the fields, not because they had little respect for the dead, but because they had no respect for him.

He stood now alone at the edge of her grave. His white cassock soaked up the great blast of sunlight that had fallen on St John's — mocking the burial. They would not come. They had rejected him for many reasons: but largely because he had brought no wife. He had come as a herald of the modern world but they had expected God's representative of the past. He wanted to understand them; they wanted him to preach to them from the stunted pulpit in the damp chapel. He wanted to sympathise with them and their lives; they expected that he would remain aloof as his predecessors had done. They wanted the vicarage to be a symbol in brick of the set order; he wanted it to be home to a social revolution. They wanted their children to work there, cleaning and gardening and answering the door. He wanted it to be a modern world.

And he wanted it to be an honest one. There had been other men after Tommy. His life was fractured by the pretence he was forced to maintain. Public opinion in the wider world had changed. He felt it was best for his parish to tell them, from the pulpit one Sunday, that his sexuality was not conventional. A fatal error.

And this was their revenge. His cassock flapped in the sunshine and wind like the flag of surrender it was. The pall-bearers, hired from the Co-op along with the hearse, had seen the coffin lowered into a wet Fen grave – they were always wet whatever the summer – and had then retreated beyond the churchyard wall to smoke and chat. He was alone to say the rite. Standing there he knew it would be his last. A week earlier the letter had come by registered post. A new position in London, lost in the teeming millions. By the time the last clods of earth had been placed over the grave he'd packed his first case.

MONDAY, 5TH NOVEMBER

CHAPTER FIFTEEN

Detective Sergeant Stubbs had left a message on Dryden's mobile. He'd meet him at nine on the riverbank outside Camm's boatyard. He didn't mention the file on Laura's accident. Dryden had made up his mind: no file, no more information. Which would mean he was on his own.

He stood on the towpath and the icy damp enveloped him far more effectively than the black greatcoat. He stood for several minutes, a painfully thin figure cut by the north wind. He fingered the bandage at his ear, the injured lobe throbbed with a sharp pain only partly deadened by the sub-zero temperatures and a hangover.

He walked the towpath to Camm House. Why had Stubbs's investigation led here?

He shivered at the sight of the damp which had spread in an ugly scar across the pebble-dashed exterior of the house. Tilting his head back he smelt the rotting wood, the stagnant water, and the keen aroma of failure. A long narrowboat dock ran beside the Victorian villa, the stagnant bottle-green water held back from the river by a dripping wooden lock. A crow strutted along the apex of the roof holding a pebble in its beak. It dropped it and watched as it rattled down the corrugated-iron roof and lodged in the ice-filled gutter. Then it shrieked once, the echo bouncing off the low ceiling of snowcloud.

He decided to pre-empt his appointment with Stubbs. He knocked on the front door and shivered again. He rubbed his eyes in an attempt to expunge the echo of the late-night drinking session. The vivid image of Kathy was more difficult to remove: he saw her breasts swaying above him, the nipples just within reach of his lips. As his body warmed beneath the greatcoat he could smell her too, a novel combination of soap and a perfume he would soon be able to recognise. And the sounds: sounds which even now made him feel less alone.

He knocked again on the front door. Few skills were a reporter's by second nature but knowing a house was empty from the sound of a hollow echo was one of them. He might as well have been tapping on a coffin lid. He peered in through the letterbox. Hatstand, Axminster (threadbare), hall table with a pile of unopened letters, and stairs leading up into gloom. He stood back and gave the frontage one more look. He thought a net curtain twitched, but then he always thought a net curtain twitched. They had a life of their own, net curtains.

The crow returned to the corrugated roof and after a brief scramble of birds' feet on rusty iron it reconquered the apex. It looked at him with one eye. Much of a reporter's life was pointless. Dryden rather enjoyed it. It was like having a licence for being idle. He dug his hands deeper into the greatcoat pockets and fished for some food. Then he heard the voices – recognising with a dim sense of irritation the monotone of Andy Stubbs.

He walked round Camm House past a freshly repainted sign: OFFICE – HOLIDAY BOOKINGS, and crossed a yard strewn with discarded maritime flotsam to a grubby Portakabin. His knees, ever-sensitive to the damp, cracked with each step.

Not surprisingly they heard him coming. Stubbs was interviewing Paul Camm, the owner's son, and Dryden's eyewitness to the sinking of the pleasure boat *Sally Anne* on the night of the Maltings' opening. The story would be in tomorrow's *Express*, with picture.

Five days ago. Already it seemed like a long winter.

The Portakabin served as the boatyard's office. Stubbs was making small neat notes in a small neat notebook. He clipped it shut and slipped an elastic band around it to hold it closed when he saw Dryden.

'Keep in touch, Mr Camm. As soon as you hear anything. In the meantime we'll start a search, along the banks by the boats, just a precaution. Anywhere else your father might have gone?'

Camm glanced briefly at Dryden but seemed to disregard him, or failed to recognise him. Dryden recalled now his distraction on the night of the sinking of the *Sally Anne*, the constant worried glances across to the flooded water meadows. If Camm's father had been missing that night he had already been gone five days. Stubbs's professional optimism couldn't disguise the fact that there was little hope unless he'd run away. Suicide, murder, or accident – the other options all led to death.

'He liked his own company. Anywhere out on the Fen you can get by boat. Anywhere. What spare time he had he spent fowling.'

'We'll find him,' said Stubbs, already looking at Dryden and seeing the bandaged ear for the first time: 'Can I help?'

Dryden ignored the detective's question and shook Camm by the hand. 'Lost any more boats?'

Camm registered recognition. 'Oh, hi. Nope. Just the one. We only lost that coz Dad, well, coz he'd gone missing. He did the narrowboats.'

Past tense, thought Dryden. *Even he knows it's beyond hope.*

Camm looked at Stubbs and seemed to know then, finally, that his father had indeed gone. Five days. Freezing temperatures.

Dryden took his chance. 'Did your father receive any messages before he disappeared, an unusual letter perhaps, a telephone call . . . ?'

Dryden took Stubbs's silence as an indication that the detective had not yet asked the same question.

'Mum thinks he got a note – that night.'

'That night?'

'Yes, last Wednesday.'

The Portakabin had two offices – one beyond a thin partition through which came the sound of a single, stifled sob. They all pretended not to hear it. A dog barked and scratched at the door.

Stubbs reopened his notebook. 'Could we?'

Camm slipped through the door. After a brief muffled conversation his mother appeared, dabbing at blurred mascara.

'Detective Sergeant?' She was in her early sixties. A patina of the respectable middle-class housewife she had been after her marriage to Reg Camm had survived decades of hard work and genteel poverty. She wore a cameo brooch pinned to a scarf held tight at the neck.

Dryden knew her then, despite the passage of twenty years. The day his own father had gone missing she had come to comfort his mother. She had been a teacher too, she'd been a friend, but not a good enough friend to make comfort a reality. He recalled sharply the confusion he'd felt as she had taken him, aged eleven, to play in the garden at Burnt Fen while his mother had talked to the police. It was an odd coincidence that they should meet again like this, the kind that convinced him that there was no great plan to life, just the aimless collision of scattered snooker balls.

Stubbs tried to regain control of the interview. 'I'm sorry, your son mentioned that your husband may have received a note on the night he disappeared. Is that true?'

She clutched at the brooch. 'Yes. Yes it is. I, I didn't think . . .' She looked helplessly to her son and clutched his arm.

'It may be nothing. Did you see it?'

'No. Well, yes, but only as a folded note on the mat. A white envelope, with his name on the front in capitals. REG, that was all. I took it to him down by the dock, he was working on one of the for-hire launches.'

'Did he tell you what it said?'

She clutched again at the brooch: 'He said it was a letter from an old friend.'

'Did he seem upset at all?'

'Surprised, Detective Sergeant. Surprised – and a bit relieved? Perhaps . . . it's difficult.'

'What did he do with the note?'

She closed her eyes and conjured up the scene. 'He folded it, carefully, and put it in his overalls' pocket. Then he got on with his work . . . He seemed angry, he'd been less patient recently anyway. So I left him to it. That was the last time . . . the last time I . . .'

'Yes.' Stubbs closed his notebook. They smiled at her stupidly. 'We must get on with the search. We're confident he's out there.'

She smiled for the first time. A travesty of hope dispelling certainty. She looked at Dryden with glazed eyes and a whisper of recognition clouded them further.

Camm showed them out and turned the sign on the glass front door to CLOSED.

Dryden fell in beside Stubbs, catching a brief whiff of Old Spice on the breeze.

Out of earshot Dryden asked the obvious question. 'When are you going to let them identify the body?'

'This afternoon. They only called us last night. We'll finish a search, and check the bank account to make sure he isn't a runner. No point putting them through it if he's done a bunk with a dolly bird to Benidorm. But it's him, got to be. He's the Lark victim. Hair's right, age – if he's her generation – lifestyle, clothes. The lot.'

Stubbs nodded at Dryden's wound. 'And the ear?'

'Details later.'

Stubbs stopped but Dryden continued to walk. 'Withholding

evidence is a criminal offence, Dryden. We could continue this conversation at the nick.'

Dryden turned. 'I don't think so. No photofit story. And you won't get anything out of me until Friday, when *The Crow* comes out with the full story. Make you look a bit stupid that.'

The day was stillborn, killed by the gloom of the snowclouds.

Stubbs turned on him, the merest hint of a bead of sweat at his temple: 'You've got no right shadowing a police investigation like this. Or for that matter withholding vital evidence.'

'You've got no right expecting the press to print misleading statements about the progress of your enquiries.'

They walked in uncomfortable silence the mile along the quayside to the Cutter Inn. It was still only 9.30 and the riverside walk, a lively spot in summer, was deserted. *PK 122* was moored just opposite the pub. Dryden stepped aboard and offered Stubbs his hand. He brewed coffee while the detective nosed around.

'I thought this was out at Barham Dock.'

Dryden stopped pouring milk into coffee mugs. 'How d'you know that . . . ?'

Stubbs shrugged. They sat either side of the galley table. Dryden felt happier on home ground. 'Where's the file?'

The detective sergeant teased at the starched white collar of his shirt. 'I want the story on the photofit in tomorrow's paper, giving the clear impression that we have a decent ID of the driver of the car found in the Lark.'

Dryden nodded.

But Stubbs wanted more. 'You can also mention that we are poised to make an arrest in the case. An arrest that will bring us close to finding the Lark killer.'

Dryden considered this unlikely development. 'An arrest which will help impress the disciplinary tribunal even further?'

Stubbs studied a packet of extra-strong mints. 'You don't need to know any more.'

'No details? Timing?'

'You could speculate that it is a development linked to a painstaking forensic examination of the Nissan Spectre pulled out of the Lark. It could take place as early as this evening.'

Dryden didn't believe for a moment that Stubbs was close to finding the killer. 'I'll print the story. And you can have everything I know about the Crossways – information which will get you very close to the real killer. But first I want the file. Have you got it?'

Dryden produced a paper bag from his pocket and sprinkled the remaining wine gums on the tabletop. Selecting one he sucked it noisily.

'The file is classified. I've requested it. It takes time – twenty-four hours.'

Dryden would have to trust him. It meant he would have to print the story first, but he still had plenty to bargain with if Stubbs tried to welsh on the deal.

A river agency boat sped past, its wake rocking them. They listened in silence to the sound of its engines fading.

'Talk to your father much?'

Stubbs stiffened and slipped a mint between dry lips. 'Meaning?'

'Meaning your father may have planted Tommy Shepherd's prints. Which must have been a bit tricky when Tommy got in touch offering to shop the gang. Can't have been a pleasant prospect, can it? Tommy Shepherd as star witness for the prosecution but claiming he was never at the scene of the crime.'

'So how did he know who was there?'

'My guess is he was asked to join them. May even have been in on the planning – but then something better turned up.' He pictured Liz Barnett on a carefree beach and Tommy's winning horses crossing the line at Newmarket.

Stubbs neatly folded the silver paper over the top of the tube of mints and returned it to his pocket. The detective lowered his head as if in a confessional. 'It wouldn't surprise me if the prints had been planted.'

'Would it surprise you if your father had killed Tommy to stop the truth coming out?'

Stubbs pushed out his bottom lip and returned Dryden's gaze.

Dryden looked out through the porthole over the snow-covered water meadows. 'We're still lost. If Camm was at the Crossways we still don't know the identity of the other two members of the gang, the young buck out on the forecourt with the GI cap, and the man Amy Ward described as the leader. My guess is, one of them is the killer.'

'Who was the letter from?'

'That I don't know. But I think I know who Camm *thought* it was from. I'll fill you in – when I get the file.'

Dryden set out up Forehill into town. Shopkeepers were opening up and shovelling the night's snow from pavements.

The Crow's newsroom was in full press-day swing. Dryden had arrived at an absolutely key moment in the production of *The Express*. Kathy was standing on her chair putting a new neon light up: Gary was helping by holding the chair and trying to look up her skirt. Bill Bracken, *The Crow*'s ineffectual news editor, was directing operations from his captain's chair.

Bill was a striking illustration of the editor's ability to award jobs on the basis of inverse qualification. Dryden had been assigned to cover personal finances on the basis that his own were in complete disarray. Kathy had been given housing and mortgages to cover on the grounds that she lived in a flat and paid rent. Jean, born with badly impaired hearing, was telephonist and copytaker. Bill, in line with this innovative policy of positive discrimination, had got the news editor's job on the grounds that he was unable to deal with stress.

Bill had purchased the new neon light and assured everyone that it was the correct appliance. Gary flipped the switch while Kathy was still trying to fit the tube. There was a loud bang and a flash of light.

By the time Dryden's pupils had returned to normal Kathy was standing in front of Bill's desk She leant across it, presenting Bill with her cleavage, and put her face very close to his.

'Bollock brain.'

Respect for superiors, that was what Dryden admired. The news desk phone rang and Bill grabbed it gratefully.

Kathy gave Dryden a smile and then disappeared behind her PC to tap out her feature on surviving the blizzard with the help of the WRVS. The smile was intercepted by Gary. He leered horribly at Dryden, revealing snippets of breakfast between tombstone teeth. Dryden sent him out to get coffees. Then he flicked on his screen, waited for the prompt to appear, and began, immediately, to knock out his story.

Murder squad detectives are close to making an arrest in the hunt for the killer of the man found butchered in

220

the boot of a car dragged from the frozen River Lark late last week.

Police are closing in on the man last seen driving the Nissan Spectre in which the body was stashed. An accurate photofit will be issued later today while vital forensic evidence has also been recovered from the car.

Detectives have now also linked the murder to the bizarre discovery of a body on the roof of Ely Cathedral on Friday. Detectives think that body had lain undetected for more than thirty years.

It was found by a stonemason in the guttering of the cathedral's south-west transept and has been identified as that of Mr Thomas Shepherd – who went missing in 1966 suspected of being involved in an armed robbery at the Crossways filling station.

The Ely coroner, Dr John Mitchell, recorded a verdict of death by misadventure at an inquest on Saturday. Police believe Shepherd fell to his death from the cathedral's West Tower soon after the robbery.

The murder squad is now convinced that the man whose body was dragged from the River Lark was also at the Crossways. They were expected to make a positive identification late last night. (MONDAY).

While the police would not comment officially on suggestions that the Crossways robbery provided the motive for the killings, detectives are working on the theory the killer could be another member of the gang.

The robbery – timed by the gang to coincide with the World Cup Final of 1966 – is one of the most notorious unsolved crimes on the records of the Cambridgeshire force.

A woman was shot and received horrific head injuries during the raid.

Forensic experts are trying to formally identify the body recovered from the Lark with the help of dental and other medical records.

For *The Crow*, out on Friday, he would need to get interviews with the Camm family, and pictures once the identification had been made.

The editor poked his head round the newsroom door. Henry's thin frame, like a vision in a fairground mirror, enabled him to project his head around corners without revealing any other part of his body.

'Philip. A second.' The rest of the newsroom went dead quiet. Dryden tried to suppress the irrational guilt always attendant on the use of his full first name. He followed Henry behind the frosted glass partition into his office.

The editor's room smelt strongly of carbolic and fag ash. The last aroma was provided by Gladstone Roberts, proprietor of Cathedral Motors, who was sitting stiffly in one of the two comfy chairs. He didn't get up. Dryden took the wooden window seat and let his feet hang a few inches above the carpet. It was a regular perch and he knew it annoyed Henry intensely. The editor sat and adopted his hanging-judge face.

Dryden decided, as always, that attack was the best form of defence. 'Mr Roberts.' He beamed. 'While we're here. Are you a member of the cathedral fundraising committee set up by the Chamber of Trade?'

Roberts looked too surprised to object. 'Why?'

'So you would have heard about the emergency work on the

south-west transept which is going to cost council-tax payers thirty thousand pounds?'

'I . . . ?' Roberts looked to Henry for help.

'Philip. If I might. Mr Roberts has a complaint, which I think we should deal with first.'

Dryden contrived to look overjoyed at this turn of events.

'Mr Roberts says you gained access to his office under false pretences and accused him of several, er, serious offences. He wishes to know whether any such accusations are to appear in print and tells me that his lawyers are prepared to seek an injunction if that is the case. Now we will obviously discuss this in private but in view of the lack of time perhaps you could, er, put our minds at ease?'

'I asked questions. I'm not sure what false pretences are in this case. I've met Mr Roberts before – he knows I'm a reporter for *The Crow* – what did he think I wanted to see him about, a new Datsun Cherry?

'And as I didn't get any answers I'm not planning to write anything about it. But for the record, so that we all understand each other, I've passed the questions on to the police involved in the enquiry into the death of Tommy Shepherd. And that of Reg Camm . . .'

Roberts jerked visibly in his chair.

'. . . Along with a complaint concerning a threat Mr Roberts made against me, and my wife. I think he can expect a visit concerning that matter from the police.'

For effect Dryden fingered the head bandage. Henry was a sucker for the correct channels – one of the reasons he was such a lousy journalist.

The editor nodded judicially, a movement which changed

223

to a shake of the head as Roberts rose to his feet. He looked genuinely shocked. The question was, did the news about Camm shock him, or the fact that Dryden knew it? He grabbed a heavy overcoat from the hatstand and placed his hands, palms down, on Henry's desk: 'You know the score, Henry. If the story goes in and I'm in it then I pull the advertising for the year. And you hear from the lawyers with a charge of racial discrimination thrown in.'

Henry had half risen as his guest departed. His small stick-insect body seemed to dwindle. His head glistened slightly with sweat.

He turned wearily to Dryden. 'You have notified the police?'

'Sort of.'

'And the relevance of the questions about the cathedral?'

'Anyone who knew the emergency restoration work was being extended would have known that the gutters of the south-west transept would be cleared. If that person was also the killer of Tommy Shepherd then they had something like twenty-four hours to cover their tracks. Common sense says that Camm was killed and dumped in the Lark because Tommy's body was about to be found. What we do not know is why.'

As the editor was down Dryden decided to give him a good last kick. 'Henry. How do you know Gladstone Roberts exactly?'

Henry attempted to draw himself up to his full height; always a mistake for someone sitting down. 'The cathedral fundraising committee. *The Crow* makes a substantial donation. I'm an ex-officio member.'

'Ah. I see. Now, if you'll, er . . .'

'Yes, yes. Of course. Clearly I am not intimidated by Mr

Roberts's threats. However, if you are going to name him you will let me know . . .' He waited for an answer in silence. 'We understand each other, Philip?'

'We are a model of communication, Henry.'

Back in the newsroom Bill Bracken was panic-struck. He held out a fax in Dryden's direction with a quivering hand.

The annual Queen's Awards for Industry.
Embargoed for midnight Monday.
Special award to Nene & Sons for an export order to the US
and excellence in training schemes.

Dryden read it quickly. 'Good story. Have we got a pic of the Nene yard on file?'

'Yup.' It was Kathy's voice and it came out of the darkroom where she was checking the picture files.

'Right. I'll get down there. Get some quotes and a bit of colour and I'll phone you two hundred words by three, OK? Kathy can do the body of the story here – just tack my bit on the end. Got it?'

By the time Humph had driven him down to the stoneyard, dusk was in the wings. The snow was still falling but a south wind was now blowing it into drifts. The yard was on the edge of the Jubilee Estate and kept the vandals out with an eight-foot-high wall topped with razor wire. The entrance was flanked by two large whitewashed pillars with NENE in foot-high letters on one and & SONS on the other.

The business had been built around an open courtyard. To one side was the Nenes' house, a thirties villa with double bay windows. An off-white flagstaff held a threadbare Union Jack. The sound of power tools and Radio One came from a set of corrugated-iron workshops. A group of three workmen in blue overalls stood smoking beside a flaming brazier.

It was a hostile, male environment, but the first person Dryden met was a woman. She was in her fifties – possibly older – short, and weathered. Wisps of grey hair with just a hint of an original red lined the edges of a floral headscarf. Her eyes were intelligent, quick, and suggested stoicism.

'Can I help?' She pressed a rag between her hands and saw no reason to apologise for the mud-clogged boots or the paint-spattered overalls. She radiated proprietorial assurance.

'Hi. Philip Dryden, *The Crow*. I wanted a few words with Mr Nene. Queen's Awards, I understand congratulations are in order.'

'Yes. I'm his wife. He's out on a job I'm afraid, in Cambridge. An estimate on a college chimney. He'll be back about three – perhaps a bit later.'

'Too late, I'm afraid. We'd like to get something in *The Express*. Local employer. Boost for the town. As it's for training, could I have a word with the apprentices?'

She brushed some hair back from her forehead and pinned it under the headscarf. 'Go ahead. Look, I'll get Josh on the mobile as well. Get a quote, that's what you want?'

'Yes. Thanks.' She took him over to the yard where the apprentices, sensing either extra work or contact with the outside world, had melted away – except for one, left tending the open fire.

'This is Darren. Darren Shaw. One of our star apprentices, he's just finishing his modern apprenticeship – that's the

226

government's new programme. Then he plans to do a foundation degree in stonecraft. Most of it will be taught here, but it will be awarded by Cambridge. We're very proud of Darren. Perhaps you can help Mr Dryden, Darren. The firm has won an award.'

She left them. Darren was fluent, unabashed, and, out of earshot of his fellow apprentices, an enthusiastic trainee. Dryden wrapped up the story in ten minutes.

Darren offered him a Silk Cut, which he took. The apprentice was twenty-two and looked eighteen, but for his hands, which were weathered and several sizes too big. He wore a single silver earring and a crisp white shirt. Despite the sub-zero temperatures he was dressed in the regulation blue overalls, but his looked like they'd been to work.

'Tea?' Darren nodded to a timber store where a kettle, mugs, and biscuit tin were neatly laid out on a white ceramic tray.

'Thanks – I'll file first.' Dryden rang Jean at *The Crow* offices and gave her the story. Mrs Nene had agreed a quote with her husband on behalf of the business – so he tacked that on the end. It was the best free advertising they'd get for years. He had to shout for Jean's benefit so Darren got to hear himself praising his employers, and so did everyone else.

Finished, Dryden sat on a workbench with his tea and watched the softly falling snow: the light was now fading and Darren stood to switch on a single hundred-watt bulb. Dryden ostentatiously stowed his notebook away. ''Nother paper gone,' he said, to drive the point home.

Darren nodded happily, enjoying his fifteen minutes of fame. He'd get copies for his parents. Girlfriend.

'What's old Nene like to work for?' Dryden looked around the

227

yard. A group of workers were making their way home towards the gate chatting happily.

'OK. He knows his stuff. She runs a lot of it a' course.'

'The wife?'

'Yeah. Bit scary. Really wears the boots.'

Dryden nodded. 'And the old man?'

'Like I said – knows his stuff.' He seemed reluctant to go on.

'Tidy business.'

'Yeah. He bought it in the seventies – least my old man said he did. They worked together, just apprentices. Pretty grim by all accounts; mind you, you know what old codgers are like.'

'Grim?'

'Sweatshop. They got a pittance too. The boss got the worst of it apparently. He wasn't local, came in off the Fen somewhere. Must have been sweet, buying them out. Her money, but still, who cares?'

'Her money?'

'Her aunt. Wealthy family, the Elliotts. Out from the sticks. Left her a small fortune in her will, they'd been married ten years. Used it to buy the business in seventy-six.'

'So he's under the thumb a bit?'

'A bit. She doesn't let him forget where it all comes from.'

Back at the cab, Humph was asleep. His torso resembled a large Ipswich Town duvet. Dryden fished in the glove compartment and found a Campari miniature which he sipped.

Around them the water-laden breath of the fields was gathering. The mist had weight. It was rising now, lifting itself with an effort from the snowfields and the riverbanks. Within the mist lurked silhouettes, fence posts, cattle standing and dropping dung, a house on the dyke.

He nudged Humph. 'Little Ouse. Pronto.'

They were there in twenty minutes. The mist here was thicker, so wet it slumped in the ditches with the effort of rising.

He knocked at the vicarage and the Reverend Tavanter answered the door. In the background Dryden heard laughter, the clatter of cutlery and plates. Despite the practice of a lifetime Tavanter failed to disguise the death of the smile which had been on his lips.

'Sorry, you said we could have a picture for the paper. The gravestones.'

A head poked out into the corridor behind Tavanter. A middle-aged man with a crisp white shirt, tie and dull, badly cut hair. Behind him another head appeared, bleached blonde and cut short. Dryden had spoilt a party.

'Don't be long. The food's ready,' said the first.

They walked to the paupers' graveyard without talking. Dryden used the flash on the ancient camera in the failing dusk. It looked like a good shot in the viewfinder, but then they always did. He took twenty – one might work.

He let Tavanter get back to his meal. No questions. He found Humph asleep again. Dryden retrieved another miniature, Campari again, and turned the cab's interior lights off. He sat watching the mist creep towards the house, perfectly lit by the vicarage's security light. A fox trotted across the snow leaving a double line of ink-black tracks. From the house he heard the just-discernible strains of music and a burst of laughter. The lights looked warm, and they danced with shadows.

When he saw the figure on the riverbank he knew it immediately. The walk betrayed him: Joe Smith, the gypsy from the camp at The Pools. The man with the giant wrench and the Bronx accent. The missing arm unbalanced his posture giving him a distinctive lilt as he paced up and down. The right arm rose occasionally in the mist to check the face of a wristwatch.

Smith turned south on the riverbank, breaking into a long easy lope of a run. Dryden cursed, grabbed the mobile, and followed him into the thick white light. To the east the sickly orange rim of the sun appeared at its death above the spirit-level horizon. In the ridged snowfields swans sat in the furrows, their necks raised like question marks. They too were listening, and they too heard nothing.

Ahead Smith stopped his run and slid down the bank. Dryden also dropped to the water's edge. They were half a mile short of the point where the Lark finally meets the Great Ouse. Smith had gone, swallowed by the river mist. It clung to the swirling water in miniature stormclouds. In the midst of one he saw Smith's head, to his left a single oar rose in a circular motion, the boat below obscured. Clear of the bank, Smith's head dipped, an arm rose out of the mist, and the sound of an outboard motor chainsawed the air. He was heading east. Dryden knew now where he was going. If he turned downriver he would pass Ely in the dark and reach the village of Aldreth within an hour. Here a short drove leads out across the fen to the ancient site of a pre-Christian encampment – a low circular dyke being all that remained of this ancient place of worship. This was the misnamed Belsar's Hill, a travellers' camp for centuries, and the place where Tommy Shepherd had lived his short, but eventful, life. Tommy, and his brother, Billy.

Dryden strolled back to Humph's cab. The cabbie was awake. Dryden was in need of a good meal and a drink. 'Let's eat. The Peking I think – all expenses spared.'

CHAPTER SIXTEEN

The Jubilee Estate stood on the edge of town and most of its streets petered out into the fen. Built by the Victorians it had been abandoned by the New Elizabethans in the 1950s. Now it was a sink estate – a concrete cesspit for the people society couldn't flush away. In bad weather wild ponies wandered in off the fields to nuzzle the warm air vents at the council waste disposal unit. It was the kind of place that the statistics said didn't exist.

The Peking House Chinese restaurant stood in a shopping parade alongside a newsagent, washeteria, ladies' hairdressers, pet shop, a corner minimarket, with its windows obscured by Day-Glo posters advertising cut-price everything, and a pub called the Merry Monk, which enjoyed a reputation for civil disorder of Wild West proportions.

Humph parked outside – right outside, with Dryden's passenger door aligned exactly with the restaurant's plate-glass entrance. Humph was a symphony in time and motion – other people's.

Dryden didn't even ask if Humph was coming in. He turned to his friend. 'It's rude you know – sitting outside. He's a friend of yours too.'

Humph pressed the tape-deck button and the silky voice asked him what the weather was like in Barcelona. Humph told the silky voice.

Sia Yew, proprietor of the Peking, was a one-time Hong Kong short-order chef. He'd spent the last five years of colonial rule in the kitchens of the officers' mess – Royal Artillery. He emigrated to the UK equipped with a letter of recommendation from the governor general and a perfectly modulated upper-middle-class English accent. He had adapted this into pidgin English to meet the prejudices of his new clientele.

Dryden took his usual table by the window – an honour he had never been denied largely due to lack of demand. He folded his legs beneath the plastic bucket seat and began to fiddle with the toothpicks. Gary, summoned to the free meal by mobile, fingered his spots and the plastic menu card.

'Yo, people,' said Sia. He had two teenage sons and enjoyed picking up the latest slang. He swung a bloodstained cleaver with one hand while the other held a cordless white telephone. The high-pitched tin voice of a hungry customer could just be heard.

He finished taking down the takeaway order. 'Ya. 14. 27. Two 58s. Fangyou – yes. Chop chop. Express. Burrbye.'

Tucking the cordless into his smock pocket he stuck the

order on a metal spike on the hob. He made no attempt to start cooking but took ostentatious care in extricating three beers from the cold cabinet and bringing them to Dryden's table.

He opened his own, took an impressive draught and burped. 'Wicked,' he said, making a mental note to ask his eldest what it meant. 'Humph well?' he asked, as if the cab driver wasn't sitting ten feet away, double-glazed against the world of personal contact. They watched him holding a long conversation with his cousin Manuel who didn't exist.

Dryden sniffed. They sat in easy silence. Gary shook his beer and directed the plume of spray when he pulled the tab into the back of his mouth. Dryden idly pictured Sia's customer expecting the feverish activity normally associated with the expression 'Chop, chop, express'.

He scanned the dark street outside and watched a yellow plastic child's football roll past in the east wind followed by a few pages from last week's edition of *The Crow*.

Without turning his head he asked the usual question: 'Any luck?'

Sia was a regular gambler, a pastime he had picked up from the officers' mess rather than from his forebears, a fact he was sensitive about. For Gary's sake he made the point. 'There is a difference between being born with a genetic disposition to gambling and enjoying the intellectual challenge of betting on horses.'

'What's the difference?' asked Dryden.

'About ten thousand a year.'

Gary wasn't listening. His jaw, normally slack, had become dislocated in a spectacular slump. He raised a single hesitant finger of alarm.

Cherry Street, a cul-de-sac, was directly opposite the facade of the Peking. It ran out towards the fen where bollards stood preventing incursions by marauding gypsies who had been on the land several generations longer than the residents. Despite this, the locals delighted in telling them to 'fuck off home where they came from'.

The local council mirrored the sentiment if not the precise wording.

But there was no gypsy in sight. What was in sight, advancing steadily up Cherry Street towards the Peking, was a platoon of riot police. The street lighting glinted on their black Perspex helmets.

Dryden stood and squinted through the Peking's steamy windows.

The police, in full public disorder gear, held their plastic shields expertly in an unbroken wall at the front while those behind held them aloft to form what any Roman general would have recognised as a perfect illustration of the defensive stratagem known as the 'tortoise'. A sublime comic effect had been achieved by an order to advance in silence. They were tiptoeing up Cherry Street like the chorus line from some modern military ballet.

Dryden took his seat and placed it closer to the window. It looked like Stubbs was going to get his arrest in time to impress the disciplinary tribunal. Presumably the fact that the Lark victim had been shot justified the military response. But the body language indicated a certain lack of tension. It looked more like a training exercise than the arrest of an armed killer.

A police car, with standard jam-sandwich markings, drew

up and blocked off the top end of the street. Its blue light flashed silently.

Meanwhile, in the back kitchen of No. 29 Cherry Street, George Parker Warren was placing his second egg in the frying pan and considering with some satisfaction the fact that the teapot had now been brewing for nearly eight minutes. Perfect. Or nearly so. Another minute perhaps? The local water was hard and the tea needed time to brew. He lit a cigarette.

The tiptoeing police tortoise had stopped immediately outside.

In the kitchen George Parker Warren, retired car thief and occasional mechanic, poured his tea and reflected that despite the recent death of his beloved wife, Rebecca – there had been little hope after she had started drinking the Brasso – he could still look after himself.

It was just the loneliness really. Company. That's what he missed. Nobody ever seemed to drop round now Rebecca had gone. He'd had a few days in hospital recently to fix his bladder and he'd rather enjoyed it. Surrounded by people, even if they were sick people. He stared at the clock they'd bought together on their honeymoon at Skegness. It ticked and echoed in the empty house.

'Company,' he said out loud, and sipped his tea. He even missed prison – at least the food was good.

The phalanx of padded policemen wheeled expertly with miniature Japanese steps to face George's front door.

There was a silence in which George sensed something. Had someone knocked? He went out into the hall. Silence. Imagination was a funny thing, he thought, feeling better.

The order to make a forced entry into No. 29 was given

by hand signal and by the time they hit George's front door they really had built up quite a speed. They saw the splinters fly from the Peking.

Dryden winced. 'Hope they got the right address.'

After a brief attempt to break the world record for the number of uniformed police officers crammed into a terraced house, a group of three PCs appeared with George. He had been restrained – a procedure that had broken both his china teacup and his nose in about the same number of places.

'Here we go,' said Dryden, ripping the ring-pull off another can of beer. 'They've been watching those repeats of *The Sweeney* again.'

Sia placed two plates of chicken chow mein on the table. The usual.

Dryden deployed chopsticks for the meal. 'Hard luck, Gary.'

Gary didn't even look at his. It was one of the eternal verities of life as a junior reporter that when shit did happen – it happened to you.

'Talk to the neighbours before the coppers get to 'em. Then get down to the station to see what the story is. My guess is he's been arrested in connection with the Lark killing. We've got a line in tomorrow's paper already – but get any details for *The Crow*. It's too late to update now.'

Gary's shoes banged noisily out of the Peking.

A small crowd had already begun to gather outside No. 29. Nobody was as excited as Gary. Dryden reflected that despite some serious handicaps, including phonetic spelling and Olympic stupidity, Gary was probably a born reporter.

Humph flashed the lights on the Capri. Dryden bolted his food, a bad habit he enjoyed, and jumped in.

'Radio News,' said Humph. 'An accident at the fireworks display by the cathedral. Some kids hurt.'

The thought of blood and burns turned Dryden's stomach. They both jumped as a rocket exploded overhead and silver rain fell on the dreary streets of the Jubilee Estate.

CHAPTER SEVENTEEN

A crowd of about 8,000 had filled Cherry Hill Park – an open field that boasted one of the few gradients steep enough in the Fens for tobogganing. It provided a natural grandstand to view the display in the cathedral meadow opposite. Humph parked up at the Porta, the massive medieval gateway to the cathedral grounds. Dryden left his friend heroically attempting to extricate himself from the cab and ran through into the crowds.

The police had decided to let the display restart – the best way of keeping the crowd in the park and not fouling up the emergency services. In the cathedral meadow a Catherine wheel whirled while acrid smoke drifted off to be caught up in the cathedral's pinnacles. The great oaks and alders of the meadow cast black flickering shadows; beneath each stood a volunteer with stirrup pump and fire bucket.

Two fire engines and three ambulances had come in through the lower gates and were parked up behind the small row of mobile fish and chip shops, burger bars and hot soup sellers. Laid out on the grass or sitting on the ground were about twenty children, surrounded by a knot of parents and St John's Ambulance Brigade volunteers.

There were plenty of noisy tears but no sign of blood – both good signs.

Dryden headed straight for the fireman in the bright yellow jacket: the incident controller. He recognised him – one of the bonuses of local newspapers.

'Wondered when you'd turn up. Good news is that the kids are going to be fine. Scared stiff most of 'em but all superficial burns – although a couple actually took a glancing blow off the thing. They've got some nasty bruises.'

The fireman turned round and picked a large burnt-out firework from a metal box. What was left of it was about three foot long and about as thick as the core of a toilet roll. It appeared to be smeared with blood.

Dryden felt the earth tilt. Scared of blood. Just scared. He concentrated on a point between the fireman's eyes. 'And the bad news?'

'The first one to get in the way of this charming object was your colleague. Kathy Wilde. Over there.' He pointed to the ambulances.

Dryden found himself analysing his feelings as he walked across the grass, winding his way through knots of happy smiling families. Happy smiling families didn't seem to be his

240

destiny. The women in his life seemed to be exposed to bizarre life-threatening dangers. He half expected to find Kathy in a coma. He wondered, not for the first time, if he brought them bad luck. He felt a pang of guilt, but not a very strong one.

Kathy was sitting in a wheelchair wrapped in a blanket beside an ambulance. She had a patch over a swab on the right eye and a bandage, wrapped around her head, above the left.

He stood in front of her without speaking. Her one good eye looked skywards. 'This is so fucking embarrassing.'

Dryden had removed his ear bandage. A plaster hung like a cheap earring. He took her hand. It was an oddly parental reaction and he felt she looked sadder as a result.

'Oh, I'm all right,' she said, answering a question that hadn't been asked. 'Just don't let me anywhere near that tosspot of a lord mayor.'

There was a loud bang and a cheer as the display moved towards its climax. Kathy jerked in her seat and shouted out with the pain. A St John's Ambulance volunteer appeared out of the dark. He was two sizes too small for a uniform that was three sizes too big. He had to roll his sleeves up to take Kathy's pulse, an operation hampered by a sudden explosion of firecrackers.

Dryden let the echoes die away over the park. The crowd 'ahhhhhhhed' as a rocket showered them with golden snowflakes.

'And what did the worshipful mayor do?'

'It was the first sodding firework. All he had to do was light the blue touch paper and retire. Retire! Too bloody right. Let's have a whip-round now.'

Dryden brushed his hand across her cheek. A sign of intimacy a minute too late.

'He got his chain tangled up with the rocket, pulled it over when he walked off. Next thing I knew it was headed straight for me. It hit me here.' She pointed to her eye.

'I was wondering.'

Kathy started to laugh, which brought on tears.

Two orderlies arrived to lift her into the ambulance. Dryden promised to come and see her later. Then he collared a medic who appeared to be in charge. 'She gonna be OK?'

'Eyesight should be fine. Luckily the rocket was so large it couldn't penetrate the socket. But the bruising is nasty and the force of the rocket may have cracked her skull. The eye filled up with mucus from the impact and the fumes. She'll just need to rest and let it clear, then we'll know for sure. And she's going to go into shock soon.'

Dryden caught up with Roy Barnett in the VIPs' enclosure with a large whisky in one hand and a cigarette in the other. His Bobby Charlton hairstyle had flopped badly over his left ear. He had been released from the Tower on Saturday and advised to rest and avoid alcohol. He was due back for a check-up in forty-eight hours. Dryden felt the appointment might be immaterial, he could be dead by then.

As Dryden approached he was just finishing an anecdote. '. . . So I said to the headmistress: Can I come too!' There was a dutiful peal of laughter. Then he spotted Dryden advancing across the grass and tried to make a break for the civic Daimler.

The reporter expertly cut him off, flipping open his notebook as he did so.

Barnett rearranged the offending chain. 'Nasty business, Dryden, very nasty.'

'She's going to be fine by the way, so are the kids. Thought you'd want to know.'

'Oh. Yes. Good. Wonderful work by the emergency services. You can quote me.'

'Thanks. Perhaps you can tell me what happened.'

Over the mayor's shoulder Dryden could see some of his Labour Party colleagues. Most were smirking. Barnett had got to the ceremonial top in local politics thanks to his money. He'd made a £50,000 donation to the party in the mid-1960s – a bribe that secured three terms in the Mansion House and a nameplate on the party's town centre HQ which read 'Barnett House'. He was well aware he had no friends. He was even aware he wasn't the sharpest tool in the box, a level of self-knowledge that made him easy to underestimate. Dryden noticed, not for the first time, his eyes. The rest of his face was crowded with a bigger person's features. But the eyes were doll-like, black, and oddly threatening.

'Simple accident. I bent down to light the fireworks and the chain of office slipped round the rocket. The fuse was very bright so I jumped back and the rocket fell over. Frankly – and this is off the record – I blame the organisers. It wasn't very secure.'

'Then what?'

'I ran.'

'And then what?'

'It went off. Straight at the crowd. Pure fluke. Total accident. One in a million, etcetera.'

Dryden closed his notebook and Barnett breathed easier. He considered offering Dryden a drink but thought better of it.

'A word about Tommy Shepherd.'

The rest of the guests had moved off to see the climax of

243

the display outside. Dryden attacked the drinks table. He mixed some vodka, blackcurrant, Pernod, and lemonade. The resulting drink glowed with a sickly incandescence like an indoor firework.

Barnett watched uneasily. He considered his answer as he looked out at the last of the fireworks breaking over the cathedral. They fell, lighting his face alternatively green, gold, red, and blue.

'I've been expecting someone to ask.'

'Why?'

The mayor grabbed a bottle of malt whisky and poured a three-inch slug. Then he mixed it, to Dryden's horror, with an equal measure of R White's lemonade. Some things, if not many, were sacred.

'Why d'you think?'

'Because he had an affair with your wife – which you probably knew about at the time. Because someone threw him off the top of the West Tower and killed him. Because someone knew his body was going to be found last Thursday, someone with links to either the cathedral or the council, or both.'

'You're way ahead of me. I knew all right – about Tommy and Liz. The marriage wasn't in very good shape then. She wasn't the only one shopping around. I just didn't appreciate her choice. A bloody gypsy, for Christ's sake.' He looked disgusted still, after more than thirty years.

'Who do you think killed Tommy?'

Barnett laughed and gulped some whisky. 'Not me. I could have done, cheerfully. I probably came as close as I ever will. But I wouldn't have pushed him off a two-hundred-foot tower. I'd have strangled the little shit with my own hands. And nobody would ever have found the body – I can promise you that.'

Dryden could see the logic in Barnett's answers, a logic that seemed too readily at hand.

'I wanted to know what Tommy was like. Did you ever meet him?'

'Once. The first time we went out to Belsar's Hill with the council. He was a kid. Good-looking. Gabby. Bright.' Barnett looked out at a dying firework: 'Innocent.'

'So you don't think he was at the Crossways?'

'I don't think so. If he was he had nothing to do with injuring that woman. I thought he was a bit of a coward. He wouldn't face me. I went out again, to Belsar's Hill. This was shortly after they – after it – began. I knew he was there but they sent out his brother – Billy. Same stock. Bit older. He brought his dog with him. I brought a shotgun. But what could I do?'

The last fireworks exploded: a necklace of brilliant chrysanthemums strung across the night sky.

'Gladstone Roberts, owner of Cathedral Motors – you're old friends I believe?' Dryden knew that Roberts and Barnett were business partners. The mayor's newsagents had found outlets at Roberts's garages. Roberts also provided the van fleet for Barnett's deliveries.

'Yes. Why?'

'Good business.' Dryden let his face set in stone.

Barnett cast around for escape.

Dryden persisted. 'How'd he get started?'

'Long time ago. I think at the start there was another partner in the business – a silent partner. The late sixties. That's where the money came from, and the town council gave him a grant to clear the ground – it used to be a landfill site, toxic waste, chemicals, mainly from the beet factory. It was a ratepayers' liability. So we gave him some money to make it safe and then he got the land for a decent price. All above board, it's called planning gain.'

Dryden didn't move a single muscle.

'And I didn't take part in the debate – if that's what you're thinking.'

Gary raced up with impeccable bad timing. He'd brought the office antique camera.

Dryden clapped him on the shoulder. 'Just in time. Perhaps my colleague could take a picture of you with the children.'

On his way back to the cab Dryden met Humph puffing down the path. 'Next stop, the Tower,' said Dryden, walking briskly the other way.

Humph looked skywards. It had taken him twenty minutes to get out of the cab.

While Dryden waited for him he fished out the Ordnance Survey map from the glove compartment. Belsar's Hill was marked as a historic site, a stippled circle with the lettering in a Gothic typeface. He'd need to go, to see the gypsies. Which meant dogs.

'Dogs,' he said, out loud. But it didn't help.

As soon as they got to the Tower, Dryden knew Laura had moved again. He was ushered into a consulting room and given the regulation pea-green teacup. It was the consultant with the horse's face again: Mr Horatio Bloom. He looked mildly excited as he bustled in with a clipboard. He wore a silver-grey suit and polka-dot bow tie. Standard registrar's uniform.

'Good news,' he said, addressing Form 1A on the first day of term.

Dryden tilted his head to one side. He was irritated at being sidelined onto Bloom's territory and away from Laura.

'The sensors picked it up at 2.07 this morning.' Bloom checked the clipboard to make sure he had the time right. 'We didn't call you at the time – I wanted to check the equipment and make sure there was no mistake. And we've done tests.'

'And?'

'And she moved. There's no doubt. It's very encouraging. Some movement both of the . . .' The clipboard again. 'Upper right arm and lower right leg and a slight tilting of the cranium. That's very good news. Spinal articulation.'

'But nobody actually *saw* her move?'

'No. That's what the sensors are for.' Bloom removed his glasses as though preparing for a long explanation to the village idiot.

Dryden got in first. 'But presumably the sensors are simply that, electronic pads which detect movement. Fit them to a clock on the wall and they'd detect movement – that doesn't mean the clock's alive, let alone conscious. Surely the key question is whether Laura moved, or someone moved her?'

The consultant gave him a long hard look designed to intimidate. Dryden returned it with topspin.

'Are you suggesting that a member of the medical staff here is so incompetent . . . ?'

'No. Although a little more scepticism might not go amiss. I'm suggesting that before you invite me to dance a jig at the news I think all the other possibilities should be discounted. False hope, Doctor, is something I can live without. I'm asking you to humour a sceptic. So: what next, Doc?'

Bloom reddened. 'It's Mr actually. Mr Bloom. I'm a surgeon.'

Dryden contrived to look like someone who had just forgotten the one thing they have been told to remember at all costs.

Bloom placed his fingers together in a neat lattice. 'Too early. We must wait for the results of some of the tests. So far we have nothing dramatic. Some extra brain activity, perhaps.'

'What are we looking for?'

'Clear evidence of biological changes in muscle and nervous tissue. We would expect the occasional large limb movement to be accompanied by many more micro-movements within the muscle and tissue system; that's what we're looking for. And continued higher brain activity.'

'And that's what we haven't found?'

'So far we have found no such evidence. It's my opinion that we will.'

Dryden ended the interview. 'I'd like to see my wife. Alone.'

Bloom's eyes glazed over. It was like being eyeballed by a dead fish.

Laura's body had been rearranged. She lay absolutely straight in the bed with her head raised slightly on two shallow pillows. The bedclothes had been smoothed flat and perfectly replaced. He sat beside her, watching the very slight rising, and falling, of the chest.

He saw it then, and knew why Laura had moved. A single corner of paper showed between the flattened pillowcases. He eased it out, and, putting it on the bedside table, turned on the reading light. It was a single half-mile square cut from a river chart. It showed a short stretch of the Lark, and Feltwell Marina, where Dryden planned to move *PK 122* that night.

Later, as Dryden lay on Kathy's couch, he considered the implications. Clearly someone had moved Laura and placed the map under the pillow. Whoever it was wanted Dryden to know that they could strike at any time. They knew his plan to leave the boat at Feltwell. Roberts, he knew, had been aboard his floating home when it was moored at Barham Dock. They could get to Laura, and they could get to him. He must be close to the killer – or killers. Would they give him the luxury of another warning?

After the Tower Humph had dropped him outside the Cutter Inn on the riverbank at midnight. Two drunks were arguing on the towpath but otherwise the world was white and silent. He'd slipped *PK 122*'s moorings and set off by moonlight upriver to the confluence with the Lark.

The sluices at Denver had been opened the day before and both rivers now ran freely between frozen reed banks. Instead of turning into the Lark he slipped further north on the main river until it met Brandon Creek. He swung upstream to the Ship Inn where there were moorings. He tied up at 2 a.m. and left a note on the boat saying he would phone to confirm the mooring and the fee. Humph picked him up on the main road an hour later.

He'd let himself into the flat with Kathy's key.

He found the couch and was almost immediately asleep but not before he saw again the loping figure of Joe Smith blending into the mist.

'Belsar's Hill,' he said to the empty room.

Over Stretham Mere, Telstar makes another hyperactive orbit of the earth across a clear night sky. Somewhere in mid-Atlantic Francis Chichester, on the first leg of his round-the-world solo voyage, looks up and sees it too. And from their prison cells Myra Hindley and Ian Brady watch the stars as the first summer of their life sentence for the Moors Murders drags slowly by.

One month after the Crossways robbery three men make their way to Stretham Engine but, their minds on other things, they fail to notice the speeding pin-point star.

Tommy Shepherd waited happily for them to arrive. On the run for four weeks he now had within his reach escape and a new life. He wanted to whistle but kept his silence. The engine shed was a childhood haunt and he was comfortably hidden in the lumber store. Illiteracy had saved him from the news that day. A campaign was mounting in the press for the reintroduction of the death penalty. The depravity of the Moors Murders had shocked the public. But for now, at least, the Homicide Act reserved the death penalty for five specific offences. Destroying an innocent woman's face with a shotgun was not one of them.

That night Amy Ward lay sublimely unconscious in a hospital bed at King's Lynn Royal Infirmary. She had undergone her eighth operation, tissue from her back and thigh being used to mask the deep gash which had partly destroyed her jaw and right cheekbone. The shock of the gunshot wound had severely undermined her health and she had only narrowly survived two bouts of pneumonia. Her heart was weak and had acquired an irregular tremor that would kill her – but not soon enough.

Her husband, George, was not at her side. That evening, as the Crossways gang headed for Stretham Engine, he could be found pawing a barmaid in the lounge bar of the King's Arms at Southery. George loved life and Amy in that order. They would divorce within two years on the grounds of his adultery.

Billy Shepherd arrived early, by rowboat from Belsar's Hill, and lit a fire in the cellar. It was vaulted and arched in the form of a crypt. The smoke looped through the coal chutes which led up into the engine room. The river damp, trapped in the walls, seeped out in moist waves as the fire warmed the room. At one end of the cellar was a lead-black pile of coal sacks – rustled occasionally by the movement of mice and rats. Billy placed the note he had got his grandfather to write on a stool in the light beside the fire. He put two bottles of whisky on the stone-flagged floor and three tin mugs beside it. He poured himself a measure.

He settled down to wait. His appetite, always voracious, nagged. He smoked to kill it. Like Tommy he had been a thin and delicate child – but their resemblance would not last long. Billy was thickening out in a layer of honed muscle which had already obscured the bones beneath his face. It was taking on the beaten look of newly rolled sheet steel – a chassis for life.

Billy timed ten minutes on the Timex he had stolen from

252

Woolworth's that Christmas. Then he began to whistle. It was their signal; and above, in the engine shed, Tommy edged closer to the coal chute to listen. A bat flitted in and out of the broken windows as dusk fell. The silence creaked and overhead Telstar completed another orbit.

He heard Reg Camm's Ford Anglia park carefully on the drove road by the river. His tentative steps stopped just outside the cellar door.

'It's OK,' said Billy, knowing it wasn't.

Reg Camm stood in the shadows. 'You can see the smoke,' he said. Even in the half-light he radiated stress – the voice dancing on the edge of panic; his fingers flickering as he massaged his corn-blonde hair. Billy pointed to the stool.

Camm read the note and looked around in disbelief, then he read it out loud.

'I need money and I know who my friends are. I'll go away with it and not come back. I can't get away without the money. Give it to Billy. All of it. Tommy.'

He looked at Billy.

The door opened. The light of a torch died in the stairwell. It was Peter. It was always just Peter. Reg knew his real name, not Billy.

They never knew why Peter needed the money. Reg had met him at Newmarket, in Tattersalls, studying form the way the professionals do. Up close. Reg owed the bookies nearly £10,000 – that's why he needed the money. Peter owed them nothing. Peter had a plan, a purpose, a secret future. That's why he needed the money. And he couldn't wait for it to arrive.

Reg knew why they had to wear the balaclavas – to cover Peter's face. Amy Ward was right, she did know the leader of the Crossways gang.

Peter came forward to the edge of the firelight and it gave his normally pallid face a rich warmth, something it never enjoyed in life. He carried a holdall, a holdall they recognised now with a mixture of excitement and resignation.

He picked up the note and read it. He wasn't surprised. 'All of it?' he asked.

The Crossways gang considered each other. Billy was the only pro. For him crime was a way of making a living not an adjunct to it. He'd been involved in petty crime since the age of ten, adept at stealing cars in a school uniform, a primary school uniform. By the time he reached secondary school he was as used to crime as most children are to the Saturday morning cinema. He brought to it the blasé attitude of the professional, an attitude which made him the ideal lookout and driver. And he wanted the money for a purpose too, a one-way ticket to America and a new life.

Little brother Tommy had joined in on some of the jobs when they needed an extra pair of eyes. Big brown eyes. They'd asked him to come on the Crossways but he'd other plans: better plans, at the coast. So they made do with the single lookout.

Both the brothers had the gift of the gab; an amiable country-boy talkativeness which was just short of charming, but effective nonetheless. For them crime was just like the pranks they'd always pulled – victimless.

But now Tommy was a victim. They would have to buy Tommy's freedom. And his silence.

They deserved the money – all of them. All of them except Peter. 'Attempted murder,' the papers said. 'She can't live,' they'd said.

Peter had dismissed it: 'Silly cow, why did she go for me?'

The gun had gone off in the struggle, that was the line, but Reg and Billy knew the unspoken truth. In the weeks since the robbery they'd rewritten many things about that day: imagined it all as it had

254

not been, but that fact could not be dissolved: Peter had maimed Amy Ward with a shotgun cartridge to the face.

'Bitch.' He'd spat it out.

An hour after the robbery the gunshot was still ringing in their ears. They'd driven by the droves to Belsar's Hill. They sat in the car, sweating. Screaming. Reg had circled the car, kicking the bodywork, hugging himself in a fit of desperate grief — grief for the life he knew he'd ruined. His own.

They didn't want the money then, or the gun, or the car, or the silver. Peter, calmer, had taken them all. Later; they'd meet later. At the engine house — the old place.

Then they'd seen the papers. The police, impossibly, had Tommy's prints. But Tommy would run.

Then they'd been elated. Each, alone, worked out the sums. The cash and the silver. A life-changing haul.

But Tommy wouldn't run. Tommy wanted the money. They had to give it to Tommy. All of it.

Peter unzipped the holdall and turned it upside down. The money fell in rubber-banded wads to the straw-covered floor.

'The silver's safe.' His voice, even then, was reedy and whistled slightly in the sinuses. 'I reckon I'll get eight hundred for it. I'll have it tomorrow, perhaps the weekend. That's twelve hundred.'

Peter stood in front of Billy, an inch too close. 'You Mr Postman, are you? Thicker than water. Better that than let him turn you in, eh? He'd have done that, would he? After you'd skipped back to Ireland perhaps . . . back where you belong.'

Billy got off his haunches and stood. He was just over six foot tall. He lacked menace but he had courage. 'We're all in trouble. Coz you pulled the trigger'.

Peter pushed one of the wads of money with his foot. He took an apple from his pocket and began to skin it expertly with a thin-bladed flick-knife.

Reg Camm had taken a mug and poured himself a couple of inches of whisky. 'What's he gonna do if we don't give him the money?'

Billy shrugged. 'Work it out.'

Tommy, listening above, smiled sweetly.

Peter pocketed the knife. 'I've heard he's made an offer already, Billy. Pal of mine at the nick, business associate. Shop the lot of us, coz we were inside the cafe. Leniency for him coz he was outside. If he was outside you weren't there. Neat innit? Very.'

Billy stared into the fire. 'How's the Ward woman?'

They all looked at Peter, an elegant allocation of responsibility. 'She'll live.'

Camm sat with his back to the wall close to the fire. Now he sank his head into his lap. Trembling fingers ran through his hair.

'Give him the money then,' he said, self-pity welling up like water from a blocked drain.

Billy brushed the coal dust from his hands: 'I'll . . .'

'Oh no, Billy. You won't . . .' Peter stood now with his back to the door. 'We'll draw lots. Reg and I.'

Peter put the money back in the holdall. Then he took a straw from the fire and cut it into two pieces, one short. 'Short straw takes the stuff to Tommy.'

They drew. Peter took the short stick. 'Where's the next meeting place?'

Camm raised his head. His eyes were liquid and flashed in the firelight. 'Newmarket . . .' It came out as a sob. 'This Saturday. The usual pitch.'

Peter nodded. 'I'll see you all there.' He turned to Billy. 'Tell Tommy I'll meet him first. Palace Green, in front of the cathedral. Dusk, day after tomorrow. I'll have everything in cash. Tell him it's OK. The deal's simple: I give him the money and we never see him again. Ever.'

They all nodded.

'Ever,' said Peter.

Billy stood across the door. 'Just so we all understand. Once Tommy's got the money he's gone for good. But there's a signal. Once he's free – with the money. So no mistakes, Peter. No sudden changes of plan. If he doesn't get the money I'll know. And I'll come looking for it.'

TUESDAY, 6TH NOVEMBER

CHAPTER EIGHTEEN

Dryden loathed the doorsteps of the recently bereaved. He knew that as he knocked on the door of Camm House it would, this time, not be empty. The night's search parties along the river had found no trace of Reg Camm. The pathologist had meanwhile matched his dental records to the corpse retrieved from the Lark. In the morgue at eight o'clock the previous night Paul Camm had formally identified the body of his father. And here, twelve hours later, was Dryden. His professional objectives were clear: a brief interview with the widow and – the main priority – a picture of the deceased. He knocked again and saw the net curtains twitch.

Peggy Camm answered the door. The cameo brooch this time held a silk scarf in place. Otherwise she was in black; a deep velvet black which sucked in what little light the house enjoyed. The dismal hallway reeked of white lilies. Dryden was mystified by the use of such a flower to witness death, it radiated a sickly sweet medicinal aroma. From a back room came the gentle tinkling of the teacups of condolence. Upstairs a child cried in that confused way reserved for the first encounter with death.

They sat in the front room, an old-fashioned parlour in perfect keeping with the house's post-war gloom.

She looked at him kindly. 'I remember now. Your father. I'm sorry about your mother. Last year, wasn't it?'

'Yes. Thanks. You've got a good memory. I was eleven when Dad died. You haven't changed.'

She smiled. 'She was a good friend. I'm afraid I wasn't. I faded away after your father died. I'm sorry.'

Dryden shook his head. It didn't matter now.

'And I'm sorry about having to sit in this antiques shop,' she said, brushing down her black velvet skirt. 'Reg loved this room – he remembered it from childhood of course. I think he saw it as a representation of continuity. The children hate it, too stuffy and you can't run round can you, not with all this stuff just waiting to topple to the floor.' She adjusted a small porcelain figurine by her elbow.

The accent was more finishing school than Fens.

'Frankly, that's why we're in here. The children – the boys – don't think I should be speaking to you. I think they are angry about Reg's death, confused perhaps. But Reg rather liked *The Crow*, I think he'd want me to talk to you.'

Thanks a million, thought Dryden, feeling unclean. Did he have some horribly apparent disease? He wanted to ask a few questions and put Reg Camm's picture in the paper; the family would be ringing up later that week to pay for an obituary notice. He was doing them a bloody favour.

Her hand twitched again at the brooch. 'We imagined you'd like a picture as well.' She touched a brown envelope stiffened with cardboard on the table between them. Inside was a large black and white print of a man at the wheel of a pleasure cruiser. He had a shock of corn-blonde hair and the slightly ruddy skin of someone who has spent a lifetime out of doors. Dryden suppressed the image of the body of the Lark victim, and the blood-dripped corn-blonde head which had looked out with a fish-dead eye.

'Thank you. I am really very sorry to be butting in just now, it must have been a shock.'

She fiddled absent-mindedly with the brooch. 'No. No. I wouldn't have said a shock. Murder we didn't expect of course . . . I'd rather you didn't put this in the paper . . .'

Dryden hoped the tabloids didn't get to her, they'd eat her alive.

'Reg had been unhappy for several years and had, well, tried to take his own life as a result. It's not nice but there it is. I think failing to succeed, even in that, made it even worse. The last attempt was quite serious and we were all rather fearful of the future. He was a determined man.'

Dryden looked suitably confused.

'Debts,' she said.

Money, thought Dryden, but said: 'I thought he inherited the boatyard from his father? It's a well-established business . . .'

'It could be a thriving one. But Reg mortgaged it in 1980. My husband could run a boatyard, Mr Dryden, but he couldn't run a business. I'm afraid he panicked. We needed money rather

263

quickly you see. Our first son, Paul, had leukaemia as a baby and the doctors said he'd have a much better chance going to a specialist at a London clinic – the Princess Grace. Rather expensive even then. A fortune in fact, and no credit accepted, at least not the kind we could offer.

'Reg had friends, rather bad friends as it turned out, and he went to one of them to organise everything. He was duped: quite blatantly in fact. There's no way that this business will ever make enough money to meet the repayments. But then we have our son. So who can say if he made that much of a hash of things. I think Reg thought he had failed his family, not just us, but his parents and grandparents. The boatyard was his inheritance and he felt that all he was leaving for Paul and James was a burden.'

Dryden leant forward in the old armchair, his knees cracking loudly in the silent parlour. 'Can I ask you a question about your husband's past? About the time before he met you?'

Was that fear in her eyes? 'Yes. Yes, of course. There were no secrets you know, not between us. Reg had rather a wild youth – letting off steam. He was very lucky: he was the only child and the business was very lucrative. He went to a private school in Cambridge, foreign holidays, everything he wanted really. I often think he felt he lived the rest of his life in penance for having wasted such opportunities. He had no need. But there it is.'

'You met?'

'In 1968. Our first date was at the Picture Palace. *A Man For All Seasons*. It had won an Oscar.'

Dryden cut the reminiscences. 'Did he ever mention friends from his past – Tommy Shepherd?'

'That was the man they found on the cathedral roof, wasn't it?' She took silence for yes. 'He knew Tommy I think. Reg was a modest teenage rebel: Mods and Rockers, that kind of thing. There was a whole crowd of them. I think Reg's money helped – otherwise I don't think they would have given him the time of day. I got the impression that they did a lot of betting, horse racing. Reg got an allowance but when he was in trouble, which was pretty often, it was stopped. That's when he needed another source of income. It was all over by the time we met, but I think it had been a bit of a, well, passion.'

She blushed. Perhaps not the only passion.

'Reg was, in some ways, quite a weak person. Easily led is too trite – but it can't be far from the truth. Perhaps they went a bit far. Anyway he dropped them, all the old crowd. He said he wanted to start again – that was good enough for me. His father paid off his debts. It was a difficult time for both of them – but it was a new beginning.

'His reputation wasn't good though. My parents tried to stop the marriage. I met Reg at night school – at the college. I was doing teacher training. Your mother was a lecturer in fact. Reg was doing business accounting, trying to show his father that he was serious about taking on the yard.'

'Have you any idea who killed your husband, Mrs Camm?'

She shook her head and stood.

'You said there were no secrets, Mrs Camm, none at all do you think? Tommy was involved in a robbery before he disappeared. Could your husband have got involved in that?'

'I think . . . I believe, that my husband told me everything. Nothing he told me would warrant his murder. That is enough for me.'

Within thirty seconds Dryden was standing on the doorstep. Would she, he wondered, have married someone involved in the Crossways robbery? If she found out, what would have been her reaction? Betrayal perhaps. Anger.

He paused on the doorstep. 'Was Mr Camm insured, Mrs Camm?'

She didn't miss a heartbeat. 'I think that's a family matter, Mr Dryden. Will you drop the photograph back?'

'Of course. Thank you.'

He was talking to a closed door.

CHAPTER NINETEEN

Belsar's Hill – the travellers' site that had been the home of Tommy Shepherd at the time of the Crossways robbery – had been an encampment for more than a thousand years. A ten-foot-high earthwork in a perfect circle surrounded a hollow corral. Through the site ran an old drove road, cutting in half a landscape already a thousand years old when the Normans landed at Hastings. The earth couldn't be farmed, and the site couldn't be levelled, because of its status as an Ancient Monument. The rampart provided natural protection from the elements and for animals – with wide gates closing off both ends of the drove road after dark. In the sixties the county council had put in a waterpipe and a toilet block on the basis that a gypsy site at Belsar's Hill was in very few people's backyards. Protests from the few local farms had been vociferous, then bitter, then resigned and now folklore.

As Humph's Capri clattered through the open gate the dull percussion of barking dogs rose to greet them. An unruly pack strained from a set of leashes tied to an iron stake in the centre of the clearing. Half a dozen shiny aluminium caravan trailers stood neatly in the lee of the western half of the ramparts. The snow was dotted with dogshit and paw prints.

Dryden put a leg outside the car. He dangled it as if fishing for a Dobermann pinscher. He caught an Alsatian instead, which came bounding out from beneath one of the caravans and left four feet of bubbling slobber along the nearside cab window.

A caravan door opened and Joe Smith appeared.

Why am I not surprised? thought Dryden. *And he's got that bloody wrench again.*

Humph switched his latest language tape back on and closed his eyes. The sound of the sea filled the cab as Manuel described a day on the beach at Tarragona.

'Thanks. A friend in need,' said Dryden.

Smith ambled up to the car with the calm assurance of ownership. The dogs orbited the vehicle like satellites. He wore a heavy quilted jacket against the cold, the empty left arm pinned up across the chest. Dryden inched the window down and fed a brown envelope through the crack. It held large photographic prints of the circus winterground's fire. Smith examined them slowly, nodding.

'Coincidence, you here,' offered Dryden, looking around the encampment as if for the first time. 'I was looking for Billy Shepherd. Tommy's brother.'

Smith crouched down on his haunches. 'You've seen him, mister.'

Dryden noted that the accent was stronger, more streetwise, less forgiving. He wasn't surprised by the answer but he contrived to look it. Smith bore so little resemblance to the one picture Dryden had seen of Tommy that it was difficult to believe they shared a mother, let alone that they had been born less than a year apart. Only the cobalt blue-black hair provided a link across four decades.

'Any chance of talking to him as well?'

Shepherd stood in answer and walked away towards one of the caravans with the Alsatian at his heels. Both disappeared inside. Dryden followed after a decent interval.

The trailer's interior was immaculate: a museum of trinkets and mementos of dubious taste. The Alsatian had metamorphosed into a family pet and was curled under the table. China figurines crowded the shelves and the walls were all but obscured by heavy gilt-edged frames around prints and photographs. Lace fringed the net curtains, cushions, and tablecloth. The smell of furniture polish was so strong it hurt Dryden's throat. It seemed colder inside the caravan than out, the cosiness of the heavy snow being replaced by an almost antiseptic, over-polished cleanliness. Billy Shepherd lit a gas heater with a pop, its warmth creeping out to reawaken the dairy.

Dryden sat at a glass-topped table and Shepherd offered him a cigarette – Lucky Strike. Dryden took one and examined it carefully. Billy answered the unspoken question. 'US air base at Mildenhall. Old habits.'

Under the glass tabletop was a large black and white print of Houdini's successful attempt to go over Niagara Falls in a barrel.

'America?' asked Dryden. It was as good a place to start as any.

Shepherd drew deeply on the Lucky Strike. 'Nineteen sixty-eight. After Tommy went missing.'

Dryden wondered, if Tommy had lived would he look like this? Smith's face was hard and unforgiving, the facets meeting in sharp cheekbones below the bottle-green eyes.

'We'd dreamt about it as kids. Grandad had been.' He tapped the glass top over the print. 'Full of stories. Kids' dreams. So I went.'

Dryden's silence enticed him on.

'There was an uncle in Jersey City – Mum's brother. I worked in a car breakers in Washington Heights. Married a local girl. Family. Then this . . .'

He nodded at the empty sleeve pinned to his overalls. 'Accident?'

'Car crusher.' They winced together. 'Came back last Christmas. Left the wife – we're separated. Brought the daughter. That's my life, anything else while you're here?'

'I'm trying to find out who killed your brother. I need some help.'

Shepherd fixed his extraordinary green eyes on Dryden. The Alsatian growled in his sleep.

Dryden pressed on. 'The police thought Tommy had killed himself when they found his body. Now they're not so sure. The body pulled out of the Lark last week was Reg Camm, who left his prints at the Crossways. Something he had in common with Tommy. The only difference being that they already had Tommy's on file. Did you see your brother after the robbery?'

Shepherd put a finger into his eye and appeared to remove his pupil. He examined the contact lens while Dryden's stomach did a somersault.

'I don't want to be involved with the police.'

Dryden decided, bizarrely, on honesty. 'This is more than a story for me. I need to know because I have to help the police, and I have to help them because I want something in return. I need it very badly.'

A masterstroke. The inference was plain, they were both on the same side.

'And I need it very quickly.'

Shepherd mumbled a command to the dog, which slunk out from under the table and slid under a bunk bed. He took a long time to take a single drag from the Lucky Strike.

'Tommy and I did meet after the Crossways. We were brothers, like all brothers we had a secret place.'

'Stretham Engine?'

Shepherd began to tear the packet of Lucky Strike into thin shreds of cardboard. 'I met Tommy the day after the robbery. He'd been away at the coast. The boardwalk. He'd been with – a friend.'

'Liz Barnett.'

'Do you need me to tell this story?'

There was plenty Dryden didn't know. And he wanted to cross-check the mayoress's version of events that day. 'Tommy was on the run; how did he know the police had found his prints at the Crossways?'

'Radio. Idiots put out a description. If they'd sat it out for twenty-four hours he would have walked straight into their arms. But then that would have made it damn clear he'd never been there in the first place. They wanted him to run. And they knew he would. They'd raided the camp here that night – straight after the robbery. They hadn't found the prints then of course, they popped up overnight. They picked them up here, his caravan's gone now. Smashed the place up a bit in fact, got us all out in the dark around the fire. Like a prisoner of war camp . . .'

He expelled a square yard of acrid smoke: 'Like yesterday . . . the memory.' Shepherd blinked and the cat-green eyes were filled with water. 'They had the local copper with 'em so they could spot Tommy. We looked like twins then; they knew we'd try to pull something. We all looked the same, that's the problem with gyppos of course . . . Ask anyone.'

Dryden laughed with his eyes. 'Was Stubbs there that night? The detective inspector in charge of the case, head like a cannonball?'

'Yup. Mean man. He was gonna solve it all right. One way or another. History's written by the victors, right? He won. Tommy did it.'

'Did he?'

No answer. Billy traced with his finger the image of Niagara Falls under the glass tabletop. 'We were allies.'

'Against?'

'Everyone. Old man mainly.'

'Was he alive then?'

'Just. He died the following year . . . liver . . . or what was left of it. It was a long slow death. It's a pity Tommy missed it.'

The bitterness took a couple more degrees off what warmth there was in the air.

'This was his caravan. Grandad's before. No one's lived in it since.'

'He was . . . violent?' Dryden was fishing.

'He was what the shrinks call an abuser . . . and that's answer enough. If he'd lived we'd have killed him one day.' He looked out

272

of the trailer's window at a sudden squall of snow. 'We planned it enough times.'

'So when you met, what did Tommy say?'

'He wanted to know what the police had on him, other than the fingerprints. I said they might have a description from a passing driver of a caravanette. It sounded like him, an ID parade would have got Stubbs the final nail in the coffin.'

'Because the man on the forecourt, the man with the US-style cap, was Tommy's image?'

Billy just looked through him.

'So Stubbs planted the prints. Why did he pick Tommy? If his prints weren't at the scene, why did he go for him?'

Billy shrugged. 'The woman was gonna die. There was loads of pressure. The witness description fitted Tommy. Tommy had a record. Tommy was in the frame, simple. But I know Tommy wasn't there.'

They looked at each other for slightly longer than is normal in any kind of society.

'They didn't have your prints on record?'

Billy shook his head. 'I was smarter. Tommy was a fall guy. They always went for him.'

'How did you keep him alive?'

Billy laughed, the cat-green eyes brightening up a few volts. 'They put surveillance on this place. Two cars. Plain as daylight. I'd go out on the river to fish. They didn't bother to keep me in sight. The food was in the tackle box, plus what I caught. He even put on weight.'

The sky outside was darkening and the trailer was unlit. They sat in an inky gloom which made Dryden feel suddenly exhausted. His pursuit of the Lark killer seemed to be sucking the life out of him. He pressed his fingertips into his eye sockets to expel the weariness.

'I think Tommy was killed for money. He wrote a note to the police offering to give himself up and name the Crossways robbers.'

'Grandad wrote it.'

'The aim?'

'Tommy wanted the money, all the money. Reg was attached to it, or at least his share. He planned . . .'

'And the third man? The man Mrs Ward said was the leader?'

'*Was* the leader. Fired the shot. Yeah, he wanted the money too. But they both saw Tommy's point of view.'

'Dangerous tactics.'

Billy shrugged. 'They had no idea where he was. Townies, both of 'em. They wouldn't go looking on the Fen. Tommy was safe, at least from them.'

'Why did they think Tommy would shop his own brother?'

'They knew Tommy could have done a deal, for both of us.'

Dryden let the implicit confession pass.

'Until yesterday, when you told me they'd found the body on the roof, I thought he'd got the money. And lived to spend it.'

'You presumed Tommy got all the money. Everyone's share?'

'I was sure he had. The last time I saw Tommy he was off to pick up the money. Then he was going Stateside.'

Billy stood and opened an ornate wooden chest which doubled up as a seat. He took out a box of old photographs. Selecting three he set them out neatly on the glass tabletop. They were postcards, identical, of Niagara Falls. They neatly matched the black and white print of Houdini beneath the tabletop. Each was graced with an elaborate stamp – a series marking great moments in American history.

'This was the signal. That he'd got the money and was OK. I told him to send a card when he felt he was clear. I got these around Christmas the year he went missing. US postmarks – all Boston.'

Shepherd flicked them over. The address was printed in ink. There was no message but a small hand-printed 'T'.

'That was the best Tommy could do on the writing front – T was his mark.'

'Why didn't you meet up in the States? Wouldn't he have gone to your aunt's in Jersey City?'

'We talked about that. But what's the point of starting a new life when the police could turn up at any moment? They could have traced the family, especially after I went. There was too much at stake. We thought we'd meet one day. But there were no plans. I just thought he'd started again. He was trying to lose the past – and I was part of that too.'

By the time Tommy's postcards arrived in Ely his body was already rotting on the cathedral roof. Why would Tommy have given away his secret signal? Dryden remembered the pathologist's report on his body. The oddity of the neatly broken fingers on the otherwise unharmed right hand.

He shivered and buttoned up the black greatcoat. 'The police think Tommy may have tried to blackmail someone. It's possible, isn't it? A new life doesn't come cheap.'

'He tried to call in a few favours. One of them came round here to get him off their backs.'

'Gladstone Roberts?' He took silence for assent.

Billy laughed. 'Fifty quid. I told him Tommy would be disappointed.'

'And was he?'

'He wasn't overjoyed. He owed him much more than that. A fence. A good one. But he kept more than his fair share. And not just Tommy's fair share.'

'Do you think he tried to get it?'

'Tommy didn't tell me everything.'

'Did you know who the third man was? The leader?'

He shook his head. 'Reg fixed the job. They were both desperate. Debts in Reg's case. I'd never seen him before. Fens somewhere, but not our patch. I never knew his name – just Peter. Plain Peter.'

'But Reg knew. Is that why Reg is dead?'

Billy put his hand flat on the glass tabletop. 'Perhaps it's why I'm alive. But I'll find him,' he said, rising.

'Because he killed Tommy?'

The gypsy switched off the gas heater. 'We're both on the trail. I'll get there first.'

Dryden saw again the right arm rising out of the mist of the River Lark. Did Billy know about Tommy's friendship with John Tavanter at Little Ouse? Is that why he'd gone there?

The morning light was going and they stood, bathed in the thin reflection of the snow.

'I'll get there first,' said Billy.

Humph's cab slid across the lightless fen towards the warm marmalade orange glow of Ely's shop windows. On the Jubilee Estate the lamps sparkled above the snow like glitterballs in a downmarket nightclub.

Outside the Peking House a large stainless steel fish-and-chip fryer stood on the pavement. It was immaculately shiny and boasted a sunburst motif in red, green, and blue chrome with fish, trawlers and following seagulls picked out in zinc. Four workmen were trying to negotiate it through the open double doors. Inside a couple who had planned a romantic lunch were sat in their overcoats cradling dishes of spicy wonton soup.

Sia was directing operations. A role enhanced by the ever-present bloodstained meat cleaver.

'Unbelievable. They're three hours late. I'm losing custom here.'

Dryden helped himself to beers from the fridge and redistributed them to Sia and Humph who, in a clear effort to atone for his previous immobility, had struggled out of the cab and was availing himself of the open double doors to get to a table. He brushed both sides on the way in.

The three sat drinking beers at minus 5 degrees centigrade.

'This is nice,' said Dryden, juggling the ice-cold can from one frozen hand to the other.

The last two customers ran out shivering, jumped into their car, and sat morosely waiting for the on-board heating to restore their circulation.

'How's Laura?' asked Sia.

'The doctors think she's coming out of the coma.'

Sia nodded vigorously. 'Good?'

Humph stopped reading the menu, put down his beer can, and looked at Dryden. 'That's great. Isn't it?'

'She's moved. Twice now. But I think someone's moving her. Well, I know they are. It's a warning.'

Sia tipped what was left of the beer down his throat. 'A warning about what?' he asked.

'The Shepherd case, the body on the cathedral roof. I'm helping the police, helping one detective to be precise. I've got close to finding the killer. Too close. Humph'll tell you. They want me to stop. They can get to Laura. They've been on the *PK 122*. I think they're running out of patience.'

Humph burped, achieving a volume that managed to startle the customers outside in their car.

'Why not stop?'

'I want something from the police. From this copper. He's going to get me the file on the accident, our accident. I want to know what happened that night, and why they wouldn't let me see the file two years ago.'

Sia and Humph exchanged glances. They took Dryden's persistent paranoia about the Harrimere Drain accident as a symptom of guilt. Guilt about the fact that he'd been left to enjoy the warmth of life, even in a freezing Chinese restaurant, while Laura had been consigned to a state of cold, clinical marble.

'I need to get the file before they get me. Call me paranoid if you like,' said Dryden.

'Paranoid,' they said in unison, and drank.

Dryden's dark mood failed to lift, despite the Chinese beer. In his deepening self-pity he even managed to think of someone else – Kathy. He hadn't checked her condition since the accident at the firework display.

He left Humph and Sia starting their fourth can of beer and trudged back to the office. The mood at *The Crow* was icy – despite the throbbing radiators and the steamed-up windows. He asked Henry how Kathy was.

'Well, it's most unfortunate.'

Dryden looked at Gary for a straight answer.

'They think her skull's cracked. She's still seeing double.'

'Shit.' Dryden felt a wave of emotion and recognised it immediately as guilt. More guilt.

Henry coughed. 'And . . .'

'She's gonna sue the town council,' finished Gary.

'Good for her.'

Henry extended his neck obscenely from his collar. Dryden imagined his head turning through 360 degrees.

'The Lord Mayor is distraught as well, Dryden. He has personally paid for her treatment at the Tower,' said Henry.

'Bollocks. He thinks that'll look good in court.'

Dryden pulled his desk open and retrieved a packet of cigarettes he kept for emergencies. He lit up despite Henry's non-smoking rule, and glared at them. 'I hope she takes them for a fortune.'

Dryden picked up a copy of *The Express*. Stubbs had got his story, but there was still no sign of the file. Now he really needed something else to bargain with, not just theories. He needed evidence. His mood lifted, pumped up by anger. One loose end was bothering Dryden – the identity of the man arrested on the Jubilee Estate in connection with the Lark killing.

Gary checked his notebook. 'George Parker Warren. Apparently an old lag. His prints were all over the car they pulled out the river. But according to the police briefing he isn't the killer. Just a petty thief.'

Dryden retrieved from his desk the photocopies he'd made of the cuttings from *The Crow* in 1966 on the Crossways robbery. It made the lead story that first week, with a blurred snapshot of Amy Ward across three columns. It had already been christened 'The World Cup Robbery'. For *The Crow* the layout was sensational and it was clear the paper thought she'd die as a result of the gunshot wounds. The headline screamed:

A10 ROBBERY VICTIM FIGHTS FOR LIFE

There was also a picture of the Crossways. Dryden felt it was time to visit the scene of the crime. But first he had to indulge a favourite pastime, baiting bureaucrats. He rang Horace Catchpole, town clerk. The officious official said he couldn't see Dryden for a fortnight. Ten minutes later Dryden was in his office.

Catchpole's office was a time warp. No computer, just a single black telephone. A large green leather blotter with a sheet of paper, face down, set exactly in the middle. The walls were unmarked except by a framed certificate proclaiming Horace Catchpole a solicitor able to take oaths. There was a single family photograph of an attractive woman with a disappointed smile.

Dryden put a copy of the Local Government Access to Information Act on the desk. 'It's apparent you haven't seen one,' he explained.

Catchpole tried a smile – a horrible error. Dryden felt his lunch shift.

'Do you want me to find the relevant clause for you?'

'That's not necessary, Mr Dryden. Please continue.' Dryden hated it when officials turned nice on him.

'How, exactly,' he said, savouring the e-word, 'is the council involved in funding the cathedral restoration works?'

Catchpole sniffed. 'The council has been involved in helping to finance the restoration of the cathedral for almost twenty-five years. The programme is agreed by the Dean and Chapter every quarter based on reports from the Master of the Fabric, the surveyors, and the building contractors.'

'Last meeting?'

Catchpole checked a small council diary. 'October 22nd. The

minutes of that meeting were entered into the minutes of the council's planning and resources committee when it voted the money on 29th October. Then . . .'

'But the extra money requested at that meeting had already been paid out?'

Catchpole clearly loved being interrupted. Dryden made a note to do it again.

'Yes. Yes, that is right. Under standing orders. The Lord Mayor signed the authorisation which was later ratified by the planning and resources committee.'

'Roy Barnett?'

'Well done.' It was the first sign Catchpole had given of the bitter, but limited, virtues required to become town clerk.

'He's the one who sets off fireworks which take out people's eyes.'

Catchpole looked at his desktop and slipped the single piece of paper into an open drawer. He doubled up, like many town clerks, as district solicitor.

Dryden grinned hugely and fished a Brazil nut out of his pocket. 'Fine. And the P and R committee minutes contain the relevant minutes from the Dean and Chapter?'

'Indeed.' Catchpole glanced at the clock.

'Nice clock,' said Dryden. 'I'd like to see those minutes for the last two years, where they refer to the cathedral works.'

Catchpole nodded and consulted his diary. 'I'll let the committee secretary know. Perhaps you could ring in about ten days?'

'I could. Somewhat pointless. I need to know today. I think the Act . . .' Dryden leant forward and touched the document before him, '. . . mentions a reasonable time period. I guess we could ask the local ombudsman to adjudicate. Or just run a story in *The Crow*?'

Dryden was led by a minion to a room in the basement with a Formica table and no heating. There was a payphone in the corridor. While he waited he rang the Office of Land Registry for the London Borough of Stepney and the Probate Registry for East Cambridgeshire.

An hour later there was a pile of papers on the table three feet high. It took him three hours to find what he was looking for – the reason why the gutters of the south-west transept had been left untouched for three decades. Then he rang Humph on the mobile, and met him opposite the Town Hall steps. Night had fallen and frost glittered on the cab's roof.

They parked the Ford Capri just outside the gates of the Tower. The grounds, extensive and thickly wooded, were swaddled in a fresh fall of snow. In the centre of the only lawn stood the monkey-puzzle tree, loaded with so much snow it appeared to bend down and pray to the ground. Dryden crunched up the drive for about a hundred yards, following the tyre tracks left by visitors, and then cut off to the right towards Laura's room. He traced his path without error to her window. He'd spent so many hours looking out that it was like spying on a looking-glass world. He examined the snow under the window. There were no signs of footprints now save for the inky splay of blackbirds' feet. He looked at the window, no signs of chisel or knife. He pushed his ungloved fingers against the wooden frame and it rose smoothly without noise or effort.

'Security,' he said. He peered in and let his eyes become accustomed to the night light beside the bed. He dropped into the room with an inexpert thud and stood a while to let the silence settle. Laura's heart monitor bleeped regularly and the paper printout, from the electric sensors on her body to detect movement, shuffled to the floor in a whisper.

Then he saw the paper – in the same place, tucked under the pillow. He marched to the table, allowing his shoes to make too much noise. He checked his watch with the bedside alarm clock: 11.32. He was a punctual person. Most nights he visited between half past and quarter to ten. He retrieved the paper. It was from the same map. A square half-mile. This time the Tower was in the middle. He turned it over. Two words. STOP NOW.

He saw himself die in the mirror.

Could he have seen the blood? Was that possible? The sudden arterial gush flying towards the silvered glass. Or was it the first memory of hell?

And behind him, Peter. Peter pulling the trigger. Reg Camm saw him for the last time in the mirror, and admired the dull gunmetal sheen of the revolver which touched his exuberant shock of hair as softly as a butterfly.

In the second before it was too late to care he saw his sons, from the bank of his memory, that summer, on the river, in their boat. And then he was gone, carried away by the blast which burnt his hair, and bore effortlessly through his neck to shatter his teeth on its way to the mirror.

Suicide – at least the attempts he had made – had been far worse. The tentative strokes of the razor across his shaking wrist, the fumbled bottle of pills and the agonising vacuum of the stomach pump.

Perhaps it was the drugs that Peter had slipped into the whisky. He hadn't seen him do it of course. But he knew just too late what

285

was happening. The world stood back and Peter's voice came to him like the shouts of his sons across the water meadows.

He tried to stand then but his legs buckled and his mouth, tortured by the drugs, had grappled with the words he wanted to shout, like a nightmare's call for help. He'd become resigned then, not by his immobility, but by the thought he looked undignified, pathetic, a loser. That he couldn't live with any more.

And it had started so well. Just another Wednesday. October 31st. But then the note from 'T' had promised so much. He'd got to Stretham Engine early. It was empty, waiting, the soundtrack still to be applied. He'd not been since the last time, the time they'd given it all to Tommy. All to 'T'.

The note had specified the cellar, but even then he had caught the disappointing scent of betrayal. So he'd climbed to the pulley loft above the great engine. Looking down he'd waited for 'T', half expecting him to be an eighteen-year-old still. Would youth have been disfigured? A gentle man, he'd hoped not, for Tommy's sake.

He'd recognised Peter immediately. He'd seen him many times since of course. They'd nodded, then not bothered, then crossed the road to avoid the memory.

Reg had called down into the great space – 'Peter.' He knew his real name now but it made them laugh amongst the echoes. Then he'd called him up the giddy twisted stairs to the pulley loft.

Peter began the story even before they'd touched hands. 'T' wasn't coming back, but he'd sent some money for all of them. All of them except Billy. He'd gone as well, they were together in the States. In business. Grocery. Reg lapped it up, nodding stupidly, feeling life turn another darkened corner.

What did the money matter now? So late. But they'd drunk to the money anyway. Gulped to fortune.

'How much?' he asked, the single electric light bulb reflected in the amber whisky, a pale imprisoned moon in the glass.

And in the theatrical silence Peter provided his own echo: 'How much . . . ? Fifty . . . each. Fifty thousand.'

Even if it was true it was too late. Reg's life had been ruined for the lack of it. Getting it now would be an ugly joke. So he'd drunk some more and took the seat Peter offered him. Then he closed his eyes for a second – or a lifetime. Almost the same thing now.

He opened them at the click of the safety catch. In the dusted mirror the workmen had used he saw Peter, behind him, with the gun.

Then it was over at last. He was dead before his forehead crashed against the wooden floor.

WEDNESDAY, 7TH NOVEMBER

CHAPTER TWENTY

Humph's mobile bleeped to answerphone mode: 'Magical Mystery Tour begins 10 a.m. The Ship Inn mooring – bring a bacon sarnie.' Dryden slid his mobile into his rucksack and made coffee in the stern of *PK 122*. The sun was already high over Brandon Creek. Frost melted and dripped from the heads of the reeds. He had slept well and late, confident that whoever was tracking him would take time to find his new berth. He had decided to avoid Kathy's flat. He'd phoned the district hospital that morning to check her condition. The cracked skull was causing discomfort but they hoped her vision would clear soon. Until then she was confined to bed.

There was still snow on the roof of the Capri when Humph pulled up. He'd slept in a lay-by half a mile down the main road after dropping Dryden off the night before. He was minus the bacon sarnies.

The sky overhead had filled with cloud, replacing the pin-sharp sunlight. A wind was blowing from the north and on it was the scent of the sea. The snow had lost its sharp crunch. There was colour in the landscape again, and, faintly now, the first tricklings of water.

'Where first?' Humph played his foot on what he laughingly referred to as the accelerator. His angelic face beamed.

'The Crossways,' said Dryden. 'And brunch.'

They pulled off the A10 about fifteen miles north of Ely at the sign of the Happy Eater. The restaurant itself was a new building in plate glass and corporate colours. Beside it was a nine-pump garage with three lanes under a wide white canopy.

Dryden thought the old buildings had been demolished until he left Humph to find the loo. He followed the arrows to the rear and there it was: a model of 1960s modernity with CROSSWAYS picked out in angular script in the concrete cornice. Below was the builders' date: 1965.

And behind it was the bungalow in which the Wards had lived. Dryden guessed it had never been used after the robbery. The wood of the window frames and the door jambs had rotted away. The concrete floors were cracked and a large giant hogweed grew from the corner of what must have been the sitting room. Most empty homes leave an emotion hanging in the air, the result of long happy childhoods or even longer bickering marriages. But here Dryden sensed only the shock that ended their lives, or at least ended the life they had. It was a house that still remembered that single moment when a shotgun blast had interrupted the World Cup Final.

Dryden stood and listened for the shot. He retraced George Ward's steps to the front door and out under the short covered walkway towards the back door of the old garage. The door hung from one hinge and dripped fungus. He stepped through into a short corridor which led to the back of the counter. Here George would have seen his wife on the floor; the cordite still in the air, the vivid splash of blood across the concrete, the disfigured face and the ringing echo of the shot circling the room for escape.

To Dryden's right was the door of what must have been the strongroom. The plaster had fallen from the walls with the years and he could see that it had been built with double-thick brick walls and the door jamb was steel. The door itself had gone, probably stripped along with anything else of value. Perhaps it too had been steel. Inside the six foot by eight foot box the wooden shelves still stood, each covered in the vestiges of green felt baize. George Ward's silver cups had lined the room. A thousand pounds' worth according to the original police file. A tiny, purpose-built strongroom for a small fortune.

Dryden imagined Billy Shepherd out on the forecourt on that hot July day in 1966. Sleek, black-oiled hair, US Army jeans and long-peaked cap. Inside Camm, nervous and frantic. And the third man: the man Mrs Ward may have recognised. The man she did recognise. He knew that now clearer than she ever did.

He jumped as the snow on the roof relinquished its frosty grip on the corrugated iron and slid to the eaves, finally thudding to the ground in a slushy heap.

Thaw, he thought. He found Humph in the restaurant about to attack a fluffy three-egg omelette.

They sped south then, only temporarily thwarted by a diversion around Littleport Bridge – a sunken road which slipped under the main line to King's Lynn. Here the first tricklings of the thaw had created a wash six feet deep in as many hours. They backtracked and took the Fen roads to Stretham. The engine house, where Dryden had so recently been shot by the man in the balaclava, was open to the public. For five days each year enthusiasts ran the great steam engine of James Watt. A small crowd had struggled along the winter droves and were now dutifully arranged in a miniature amphitheatre around a guide. Train driver's cap, lapel badges, and the unmistakable flat nasal delivery of the enthusiast proclaimed him for what he was proud to be: a steam nerd.

'The two pistons of Watt's Stretham Engine of 1823 are the longest, at sixteen feet nine inches, of any of the machines he designed after the accident at Sheffield in the summer of 1819 – an accident which you will no doubt already know resulted in the government enquiry of 1820 . . .' The amphitheatre shuffled uneasily. A small child asked loudly when he could go home.

The basement was still in the throes of conversion in readiness for the first summer of all-day opening. Beyond the toilets and the snack bar Dryden found a single door marked 'Curator'. He knocked and introduced himself. The curator was young and bald with the tetchy manner which betrays that all human contact is considerably less enjoyable than reading a book.

Yes, he'd heard that burglary was becoming more common in the villages. He understood why *The Crow* wanted to do a special feature on the subject.

'It's in the public interest,' said Dryden, hating himself. He'd heard that someone had broken into the engine house only this month. True?

The curator blinked. 'Twice.'

A large book was consulted. 'Last time was four nights ago. I found the doors open in the morning, and a bloodstain on the engine-room floor. Police said one of them must have cut themselves breaking in, not that they did really. Nothing missing that time.'

Dryden had the decency to blush mildly. 'That time?'

'The first time was . . .' The pages of the ledger flicked expertly backwards.

'The night of October 31st. They broke in that time, left a half-finished bottle of whisky and some cigarettes.'

'Where?'

The curator pointed skywards. 'Pulley loft.'

'And they took?'

'Rope. About forty yards of it, cut it off and left the rest. You can see where. They left a real mess.'

'And that was reported to the police?'

'They didn't ask.'

'Pardon?' Dryden pulled up a seat and sat down uninvited. The curator edged his chair back an inch.

'We didn't report the earlier incident. The building work was still underway then. The place was chaos, there was no real security. It just looked like petty theft.'

'And the second?'

'That was more worrying, we had the doors locked by then, so I called the police the next day. They came out this morning and I showed them the bloodstain.'

'And you didn't tell them about the first?'

'No. As I say, they didn't ask.'

Back in town the snow had turned to a steady icy drizzle. It still clung in tenacious patterns to the roofs around the market square

295

but everywhere the drains gurgled with meltwater. Nobody talked in the streets. A gale was beginning to blow and the wind battered at the ears and left the vast Union flag flying from the cathedral's West Tower stiff and cracking at its pole.

Outside the newsagents in the High Street stood a billboard for the *Cambridge Evening News*. It had been attached to the railings with wire: FLOOD WARNINGS.

Floods. Dryden dashed from Humph's cab into the front office of *The Crow*. Jean broadcast a stage whisper for his benefit: 'Henry's called a meeting. You're late.'

The editor had adopted wing-commander mode. He'd dragged the giant map of *The Crow*'s circulation area out of his office and it was now propped up in the bay window of the newsroom. He was still pushing red pins into it when Dryden burst through the door.

'Philip . . .' The editor ostentatiously checked his watch. Even by Dryden's standards noon constituted a late start.

Gary, Mitch, and Bill sat dutifully taking notes. It was newspaper time in Toy Town.

'Just in time,' added Henry, with menace. 'There's a press conference at the Three Rivers Water Authority headquarters in Lynn this afternoon. Bill's got the release. If they have any graphic material, maps and such, please collect it.'

Henry was keen on reporters picking up non-copyright pictures and illustrations as it trimmed what he considered an inflated editorial budget. He'd worked out a run for the photographer to take in all the most likely spots for early flooding, making sure all of *The Crow*'s circulation area was well covered.

Gary was detailed to ride with Mitch. 'Human interest

stories,' said Dryden. 'Talk to everyone. Plenty of names. Get their ages. Get their stories, this flood, the last one. Got it?'

The junior reporter nodded happily. 'I can't swim,' he said, still smiling.

'You won't get the chance,' said Dryden, unhelpfully.

Humph was parked up outside *The Crow* on a double yellow line. He found him sharing a small 2lb bag of mixed sweets with a plump traffic warden. They had an hour to get to the press conference at Lynn – thirty miles north on the coast of the Wash. Normally the time would have been ample but the weather was deteriorating by the minute. But first Dryden needed to make sure Laura was safe. He needed one more day.

Her condition was unchanged. There had been no further movement. The nurse who showed him in radiated that almost telepathic signal which tries to dampen false hopes. They exchanged brave smiles.

Dryden asked to see Kathy.

She was sitting up in bed in a red and white striped nightshirt. Dryden felt acutely embarrassed to find himself sitting on the bedside. They held hands awkwardly when the nurse left them alone.

Dryden was clutching a bunch of insipid winter flowers. 'I bought these at the shop at reception at the last minute. They're crap.'

This was the crucial point, thought Dryden. Either this was a personal visit and they talked about them or he cut straight to their lives as they were before.

He blew it. 'So you're going to sue the bastards. Well done.'

Kathy had expected no more. 'Bloody right I am. This doesn't hurt by the way.' She touched the eyepatch.

'Henry thinks you should drop it. His OBE may be in danger. Services to arse-licking.'

Kathy laughed and grimaced with the pain.

'Doesn't hurt, eh?'

Kathy's face was blotched red and purple with bruising and her upper lip was dotted with butterfly stitching.

'You look great,' said Dryden.

Kathy looked at her hands.

Dryden coughed. He was just aware enough of his own awkwardness to know he was making a total hash of the visit. 'I need your help.' He knew he was making a mistake but he ploughed ahead anyway, regardless of all feelings, but mostly Kathy's. 'Laura could be in danger. Someone is trying to stop me covering the Lark murder story. She's in Flat 8. I've let the nursing staff know you're an old friend of the family. When you have time, and they let you out of bed, I'd appreciate it if you'd sit with her. Watching brief.'

The silence told him he'd taken too much for granted. He realised now how inappropriate the request was. He tried to recover the situation: 'I'm . . .'

'No. It's OK. Let's just get through this, eh? Then talk . . .'

Dryden brightened, that was nearly never. 'Yup. Then.' He stood. 'Whoever it is has been pretty discreet so far. They want to frighten me: only me. Frankly, they've succeeded. I've got twenty-four hours at most. I'd feel better if you were watching out for me.

'Don't bother with anyone here, they think the Tower is Fort Knox and Laura's about to make medical history by doing the comeback coma cha-cha. I'll have a word, but it'll make little difference.'

He went straight to Bloom's office. He didn't knock.

'Mr Dryden, I must protest . . .' Bloom was entering figures into a PC. They looked like accounts.

'Just listen. I'm reporting an incident to the police. Someone has got into Laura's room – twice.'

Dryden held his hand up as Bloom stood to argue.

'I'm sorry. I don't care if you can't believe me. The police will call. I want it on the record now – at two o'clock – that I'm asking you to improve the security at this hospital. The windows need to be locked and the grounds properly patrolled. In particular I want a watch kept on my wife. If anything happens to her between now and the arrival of the police I shall hold you personally responsible. Is that clear?'

'Don't you want your wife to make a recovery, Mr Dryden?'

Dryden thought about hitting him then. In many ways he was close to the truth. But he needed action, not gratification.

He took a deep breath. 'I don't want her harmed by anyone, Mr Bloom. It is *Mr*, isn't it? You're a surgeon. A registrar. We wouldn't want anyone's career to suffer because of negligence.'

Bloom reddened and picked up an internal phone.

CHAPTER TWENTY-ONE

Humph nosed the cab into the northern gale. For five miles the road ran beside the main river. The ice was breaking up and the wind was making waves, piling the frozen shards against the banks. The water was a foot, maybe eighteen inches, from the top of the banks. Even now, as the floods rose inland, the Fens could be saved if the water could escape quickly to the sea. But the north wind was holding up the tide and bottling up the water in the rivers. The cloudscape was being ripped apart by the gale, leaving gaping holes of winter blue between the shreds of lead-grey nimbus. Seagulls were torn across the sky, screeching southwards.

The night came from the north too. As they drove, dusk killed the colours in the landscape and replaced them with sepia. There was little traffic and they were soon on the outskirts of King's Lynn. Around them stretched the sink estates of the 1950s and 1960s. Grey rain fell on thousands of identical roofs. Dryden heard 'Little Boxes' playing in his head.

The centre of the old port city, medieval and stately, had been evacuated in anticipation of the gale which was now bellowing in off the Wash. They parked on the wide quayside which had been ruined by some largely unsuccessful attempts to introduce trendy waterside flat developments into the old warehousing district. Out in the wide estuary several coasters had taken refuge to ride out the storm. The horizon at sea was clear and jagged, with white horses crisp and high more than ten miles to the north.

The press conference was in a converted spice warehouse, a glorious eccentric pile in golden brick with Victorian mock-Indian turrets. The presser, predictably, was in an airless, windowless, overheated room on the ground floor. The nationals had made the trip north, or at least their local stringers had, from Norwich, Cambridge and Peterborough, and the local TV stations had set up a camera, which was bad news for the print journalists who would now get second-class treatment as a result.

It was 3.15 and the impressive array of officials the press had been promised had yet to appear. Dryden felt a tap on the shoulder, and turned to find Detective Sergeant Andy Stubbs.

'Short straw?' asked Dryden.

Stubbs fiddled with the knot of his tie. 'County heard the TV was coming and we're one of the threatened areas. They wanted a copper on the press conference panel. Just what I need . . .'

'Tribunal?'

Stubbs couldn't help but wince. 'Unpleasant.'

'Story in *The Express* didn't help?'

'Oh, it helped. God knows what they would have done otherwise. But it didn't help enough.'

Dryden looked sympathetic. Sometimes he hated himself.

'I don't want this in the paper, Dryden.'

'Would I?' This was one of his favourite replies to any plea to keep things out of print. The answer was: 'Yes. He would.' What did people think he did for a living?

'They're considering demotion. I'm not suspended from duty in the interim. Final decision tomorrow.'

Dryden decided Stubbs was looking for sympathy and playing for time. And there was still no sign of the file on the Harrimere Drain accident.

Dryden checked his watch. 'I presume you want to know where the Lark victim died?'

A muscle twitched above Stubbs's eye. 'I've told . . .'

But the TV crew called for silence. A long line of the usual suspects trailed in from a room to one side of the dais. The silver-haired chairman of the water authority confidently took the central seat, flanked by officials from the emergency services, army, and county councils. Dryden couldn't resist a parting shot as Stubbs scurried unhappily forward. 'And I know why he died.'

Sir John Vermujden, chairman of the water authority, was silky smooth and about as trustworthy as the company's share price. As maps were handed out, showing those areas already under water and those areas likely to come under threat, Vermujden read from a prepared statement. The maps were colour-coded at various heights, or rather depths. These ranged from twenty feet above sea level to six feet below. If the riverbanks and, or, sea defences failed all the area under sea level would flood. The chances of that happening were now about evens.

302

Sir John flashed an orthodontic smile at the cameras. 'But we are doing everything in our power to make sure this does not happen.'

The rest of the panel shifted in their plastic bucket seats. In Dryden's experience they always started these things with the good news in the hope that the journalists would lose interest by the time they got to the bad. If Vermujden's fifty-fifty chance was the good news then the Fens were heading for disaster.

Next up was a scientist from the Met Office. Desperate attempts had been made to make him presentable for the cameras. His hair had been lacquered flat to his light-bulb-shaped head but now, as he moved in front of a large *Playschool* weather map, the adhesive gave way just above one ear and a spike of hair popped out like the indicator on a Morris Minor.

The cameras closed in. The scientist betrayed a slight twitch.

'The temperature is rising fast, the first danger signal. If twenty per cent of the snow still held on the land within the vast catchment area of the Ouse, Welland, and the Nene melts by dusk the riverbanks will not hold. There will be some respite overnight, and at dusk tomorrow, when the temperature drops below freezing again. But it will be shortlived.'

There was a buzz of excitement in the room and the cameras edged closer.

'The second danger signal,' said the weatherman, 'is rain. In the last twenty-four hours 1.7 inches has fallen. It does not sound very much.' Here he paused for a winning smile. 'But sometimes the Fens gets just ten inches in an entire year. The problem is that the catchment areas are so large, rain is falling much harder in the Midlands where the rivers rise. The combined effect will add several feet – *several feet* – to the water levels in the rivers.

'Danger signal number three: the tide. Tomorrow evening, at about 10 p.m., it will be at its highest point this year. This restricts the ability of the rivers to discharge the water into the sea. This would be bad enough but . . .' Here the weatherman tore off the map showing rainfall to reveal underneath a new map, crowded with the black arrowheads denoting windspeed.

'Danger signal number four. The current gale is forecast to reach storm force 8 by dusk. It could hold that speed for twenty-four hours. The wind direction – north-north-east – is precisely that which we would wish to avoid at this stage. It is blowing directly behind the tide, pushing the seawater towards the land and effectively damming the rainwater into the rivers. It is also driving more rainclouds towards us from the Arctic. Normally this would be good news – as it would bring a drop in temperature and freeze the water. But, as we have seen, the cyclone over the North Sea is dragging its air from the south of Ireland, where it has been warmed by the Gulf Stream, and turning it in a vast circle north of Scotland and out towards the pole before bringing it south. So, we have warm air from the north.'

The weatherman sat down abruptly with a self-satisfied smile.

Dryden got the first question in before the TV reporter had a chance. 'Sir John said there was an even chance the banks would hold . . . what do you think?'

The weatherman had a degree in meteorology and a doctorate in natural hazards – but no idea about public relations, which is why Dryden had asked the question.

He considered it. 'Oh. Er. Frankly, I don't think there's any chance at all, the question is where the banks will fail.'

Several of the print journalists started making mobile

telephone calls. The cameras closed in on Sir John, who was now running a beautifully manicured hand through his silver hair. The smile was beginning to slide to one side.

The TV reporter recovered quickly. 'The last floods in 1977 covered sixty thousand acres of agricultural land – how could this compare?'

Sir John cut the weatherman dead. 'I think that's a question for John Thoday – chairman of the joint county councils' civil planning unit. John . . .'

John looked like he'd just been offered a plateful of shite pie. The sheen of sweat on his forehead indicated that he was well out of his depth, a dangerous inadequacy in the circumstances.

'We already have some ten thousand acres under fresh water flooding in southern Cambridgeshire,' he said. 'That's due to the dykes and drains being unable to take the meltwater – the riverbanks are holding but we must prepare for the worst.'

At which point he tried a smile of reassurance. A big mistake which would get a prime spot on that night's local TV news.

'We can expect, I think, a hundred thousand acres to flood over the next forty-eight hours. Possibly half a million. None of you are old enough to remember but in 1947, three million acres went under. It was a national disaster.'

The BBC's East of England correspondent got to his feet. 'Is that possible this time?'

Thoday avoided the question: 'The banks of the main rivers are under great pressure here, south of the Isle of Ely. But that's not really the problem we face. It's sea water that is the greatest threat. The bottling up of the rivers just south of Lynn could breach the sea walls, then salt water could flow back across the already flooded fields; that would be an environmental disaster and could ruin the fertility of the fields for years. That's why we are taking the measures we are today . . .' Thoday sat, having effectively passed the pie back to Sir John.

The chairman tried to say thank you but it stuck in his throat. 'Today I've asked the Department of the Environment to enact emergency legislation by statutory order to allow the armed forces to assist us in reinforcing the sea defences on the upper Ouse and in ferrying livestock and people from the inland areas threatened with flooding. Just prior to this press conference I received notification that a state of emergency has been declared for the region. These are draconian measures but I, and the other representatives of the emergency services, feel they are entirely justified.'

One of the Fleet Street tabloid boys was first in with the boot. 'Could the privatised water authority not have spent more money on flood defences rather than paying its executives so-called "fat-cat" salaries?'

There was a brief flap as various press relations officers indulged in a frenzy of semaphore messages to their respective bosses.

'Perhaps I can help with that question,' said a silky voice from the back of the room. There was a collective groan from the print journalists who began to talk amongst themselves, while the camera team eagerly rearranged itself to light a man in a steel-grey suit and fake tan. This was the water authority chief PR, Christopher Slater-Thompson, known without a trace of affection as 'Mr Flannel'.

Dryden slipped out onto the quayside to a concrete and glass shelter with its back to the wind. Seagulls blew past, screeching, and heading inland.

The mobile signal was poor so Dryden kept it brief. He got Bill. 'It's the real thing. State of emergency declared. Time to go over the top. We should have the full story by deadline for *The Crow* tomorrow afternoon with plenty left for *The Express* next week as the water goes down. I'll work my way back through some of the danger spots. Woggle better start worrying about how he's going to get the paper out.' As he spoke the coasters bobbed in the tide like paper boats. He reckoned it would take Stubbs less than five minutes to find him. The detective did it in two.

'The file,' said Dryden. 'Then the information.'

Stubbs straightened his back. 'Look. I've told you withholding evidence is an offence. Not a great time for you to spend a day in the cells either, is it?'

'Friday's edition of *The Crow* remember. I'll make it clear the police have made no progress. Oh – and there's the forensic evidence at Stretham Engine. Evidence your men overlooked.'

Stubbs buckled. 'I got the call this morning. The file is ready to pick up – although I have to give a written reason for taking it away. It's categorised.'

'Why's it categorised? How?'

'It could contain sensitive information, or it could denote that the enquiry is still active, or that information in it was used, or may be used, as evidence in another enquiry. It doesn't have to be sinister.'

'Get it. Quick. I'll phone later – leave your mobile on.'

'And the written reason. What exactly would you suggest? I have a friend on the local newspaper with a personal interest? Don't think that . . .'

Dryden stood, bent down from the waist, and put his face

close enough to Stubbs to smell the faintest trace of sweat. It was like eyeballing a dummy at Madame Tussaud's.

'I've had a remarkable return of memory about the night of the accident. I've come to you with fresh evidence about the identity of the driver of the other car involved, the one driven by the man who saved my life but left Laura behind. The man who dumped me in the sub-zero temperature in a wheelchair outside the hospital and then drove off. You've decided to reopen the case and want to see the original file. Try that. Try it fast.'

Stubbs tried a sneer: 'Anything else?'

'Yup. The Tower. I'm worried about Laura. You don't need to know the details. She's been threatened, possibly by the murderer. The aim is to encourage me to concentrate on other stories. Over the next twenty-four hours it is going to become increasingly obvious that this is advice that I have declined to take.'

Stubbs pulled out his mobile and hit a preset number. 'I'll get a car to drop by. Put a man outside after dark.'

Humph pulled up in the cab. Dryden had some last-minute information for Stubbs. It wasn't much but it would whet his appetite.

'Stretham Engine. The rope ends are still in place, see the curator. I'd get it closed quickly, most of the forensic evidence should still be in place. He died in the pulley loft. The killer shot Camm there I think, then dropped the body down by rope, hence the neck injuries.'

Dryden slapped the dashboard and Humph produced a creditable skid as they pulled off. They got round the corner before they realised they had nowhere to go. It was too dark to work their way through the danger points on the way back to Ely. Planning a return trip in the morning was out as the roads could well be closed by then. Dawn would give them their first chance to head south.

They bought fish and chips and Humph headed north to Hunstanton, a bleak seaside resort on the coast of the Wash ten miles to the north.

'Honeymoon,' said Humph, by way of explanation. He seemed to enjoy revisiting bitter memories.

The sea was attacking what was left of the pier, a Victorian cast-iron structure largely destroyed by a wayward trawler a decade earlier. The cab reverberated with a deep thump as each new set of waves dropped on the promenade. They worked their way through some more of Humph's collection of miniature spirit bottles while happily watching the wind build towards storm force. Humph finally let his seat down and was instantly asleep. Dryden waited for dawn.

The schoolhouse at Isleham had been closed since the war but it seemed, even to the eleven-year-old Dryden, the right place for an inquest. The sombre single Victorian room was bare but for the pews, the teacher's pulpitum commandeered as a witness stand, and a large mahogany desk brought in to preserve the majesty of the coroner. Dryden sat in the front pew, next to his mother, and sensed around them a cordon of sympathy which left them entirely alone.

A man who had called at Burnt Fen after the accident to talk to his mother sat at the far end of the front pew making notes. When he wasn't scrawling with his pencil he fiddled rhythmically with a packet of cigarettes, and winked secretly at Dryden when everyone stood for the coroner. He seemed to be enjoying himself.

In the nightmare of the night before Dryden had seen his father's body stretched out on a settle before the coroner. The blood, black and streaked, and the body white from the days in the water but punctured with yellow bruises. The eyes had woken him up. They were fish-like and a strand of weed had circled the throat like a gangrenous cut. In the dream water dripped from the settle to the floor.

But there was no body in the schoolhouse at Isleham. There was never a body.

He knew the inquest was important but the witnesses spoke a strange language that he could only struggle to understand. So much was unsaid to spare them the truth. Papers were submitted but unread. Euphemisms replaced the facts. But he knew the story in the end. The man in the front pew had written it up in The Crow.

The floods of the winter of 1977 had burst the banks at Southery, north of Ely, and only a few miles from Burnt Fen. The army, already called out to help keep back the sea at Lynn, filled the breach with sandbags. Black and white pictures of the operation were up on the schoolroom wall, showing marching lines of men under a low sky, with the solitary trees bent down in the storm.

But the River Ouse had broken through at a second spot, ten miles south, near the lock-gate town of Earith on the night of 17th December – a Saturday. With the army needed to maintain the wall of sandbags at Southery they called for volunteers. Farmers mostly, with entrenching tools. The pictures, pinned up alongside those of the army, showed a scene as from the Somme. The men covered in the black sticky silt, lit by bursts of arc light, and behind them the lethal gunmetal gleam of the water. Some grinned out of the dark beside a mobile canteen, wisps of ghostly cigarette smoke catching the lights.

The army had brought amphibious vehicles – beaver tanks – upriver to the breach and chained the convoy together as a floating dam. The current had done the rest, drawing them towards the breach where millions of tonnes of water were spewing out into the Fens. Once the floating dam was sucked into place submarine netting was dropped overboard to form the first membrane of a new riverbank. Sandbags followed, and then hardcore, dragged along the bank from freight trains at the railway bridge at Earith. By ten that night the dam was in place. 'Operation Neptune' was a success. When a pistol shot marked the end of work the volunteers posed for pictures, but Dryden could never find his father's face.

The words of the final witness, a Captain Wright, Dryden knew by heart – memorised from the cutting in The Crow. *Six volunteers were needed to stay behind and mount the first watch.*

'First forward,' he said of Dryden's father, and the schoolroom had filled with the murmur of approval. Captain Wright had taken two men to the south end of the breach, two had been put to the north, and Dryden's father and a labourer from Chatteris had been ferried over the river by amphibious vehicle to watch the far bank.

'We all heard the noise at the same time,' said Captain Wright, and the schoolroom's hush was complete; the only sound a squeaking cycle wheel from the lane outside. Captain Wright had stopped then, inhibited, Dryden sensed, by his mother's careful attention. The coroner nodded by way of encouragement.

'It was terrible really . . . a vibration, in the earth. We checked the beaver tanks and they were fine. Our bank seemed solid too. That took a minute, I think – perhaps two. Then I heard a shout from the far bank.

'"She's going!" His mother had jumped at that – surprised by the strength of the witness's voice.

'They were both waving. Not panicking – just signalling I think. And then they sort of went away from us – that's as best as I can describe it. They had a generator and an arc lamp over there so they were in this pool of light. And then they weren't. They just moved away into the dark.

'The bank had gone. A huge slice – almost a hundred yards long. Blown out by the pressure of water. Blocking the breach had narrowed the river – increasing the force on the far side. There was

313

just white water then, crashing out. It was a huge noise. They heard it at the church hall at Earith where the volunteers were billeted – that's four miles.'

Captain Wright stopped again, taken aback by his enthusiasm for the story.

'We lit the distress rockets then. Sent out the outboards. But they'd gone.'

The phrase Dryden liked was 'went away from us'. He knew, even then, that his father had not meant to go away. But he felt lonelier anyway.

The labourer's body they found a week later at Upwell when it nudged the lock-keeper's gate one night. But Dryden's father they never found. He liked to think of him out on the Fen somewhere but suspected he'd been washed out to sea when the waters finally turned north in late March. He didn't mind that. His father was free there.

'Death by misadventure' was the verdict. Dryden didn't understand at the time. Didn't understand that it implied his father had taken a risk. Didn't understand that it robbed them of the insurance money.

In his verdict the coroner added a rider. A recommendation that both men be recognised for their bravery. They never were. Dryden thought that right now. After all, they hadn't been brave, they'd been unlucky. But the cutting from The Crow *said they were brave. So he liked the reporter even more for that.*

THURSDAY, 8TH NOVEMBER

CHAPTER TWENTY-TWO

He got out of the car at just after 7.30 that morning. The dawn was a white cold gash to the east. The sea was a molten lead grey where the light caught the waves still marching south. The shreds of a deckchair flapped from the railings on the front and wind screamed through the iron pillars of the old pier.

He got back in and turned on the radio. The state of emergency in the Fens was top of the bulletin. The forecast was the same. The wind would hold at storm force for another twelve hours piling up the tide, which was due to peak at just after dusk. The temperature had dipped below freezing overnight but was rising again. Some snow and ice would survive until the air froze again at nightfall but until then billions of tonnes of water would melt into the rivers. Disaster was as unavoidable as the setting of the sun.

Humph tracked down two bacon sarnies at the greasy spoon next to the town's cab rank. Most of the drivers had been out all night ferrying people around in the gale. All had stories of fallen trees, flooded roads, and stranded families. They filled Humph's flasks with tea and drove south under clouds stained with cordite. The gale, tailing them, buffeted the car. In the telegraph wires straw hung and the chaff blew past them on the wind. The first set of traffic lights they met were without power. At the second a military Red Cap directed the traffic.

The main A10 ran like a backbone through the Black Fen, the peatlands which surrounded the Isle of Ely. A breach in the main river would bring disaster swiftly by nightfall, but first each of the individual fen basins would have to fight its own, miniature battle of the banks as local dykes and drains filled with meltwater. An ice-blocked culvert, a weak earthwork, a fen where the peat had shrunk to take the field level below sea level, there were a hundred different reasons for the same result: inundation. Already the waters were creeping up into the fields.

Dryden studied his Ordnance Survey map, matching it to the one the water authority had produced of the danger areas. He found what he was looking for, a mobile home site on a fen six feet below sea level. To the east of them, Feltwell Anchor was already a grey sea. The water had brimmed up out of the main dyke an hour earlier and now flattened an already two-dimensional landscape. The wind whipped up a swell and the wavelets broke against the drove road sending spume flying into the field beyond.

They pulled off the road to the east and followed a drove. The cab rocked in the sidewind.

'Jesus,' said Dryden, looking east.

They'd found the Feltwell Anchor caravan site, the location

for nearly a hundred mobile homes. But it wasn't where it should have been. It had set sail, a flotilla of caravans, drifting south towards the road. The mobile homes dipped and nudged each other in the wind. Most of the families had got out but Dryden could see small groups clinging to the roofs. A dog howled from one caravan which, snagged by a fence post, had been left behind by the drifting fleet.

Ahead of them, coming west, a line of emergency vehicles was threading its way along the edge of the fen. Seagulls, blown inland, followed them in a cloud, mistaking them for tractors ploughing the land.

The unmistakable chainsaw whine of an outboard motor cut through the wind. Humph parked in a passing place on the single-track drove and handed Dryden a pair of binoculars he kept in the glove compartment, then he struggled out on the driver's side, stood for a second in the buffeting wind, and retrieved a camera and tripod from the boot.

Humphrey H. Holt, thought Dryden. *Man of Action.*

Six inshore rescue dinghies were out on the fen, edging their way forward in the flood, checking half-drowned farm buildings. One farm stood alone about half a mile from the drove road, the apex of its roof dotted with half a dozen people waving towards the boats. A barn, twisting in the gale, collapsed like a piece of origami, a cloud of chickens briefly rising from the debris.

They heard the crash on the wind, and something else.

'Dryden!'

Running towards them from where the emergency vehicles had parked up was Gary. He was fully kitted out for the operation: ankle-length leather coat, wrap-around fighter-pilot dark glasses, and black fake leather slip-ons. By the time he got to them the weight of the coat had almost done for him. Each slip-on had acquired about a hundredweight of cloying peat.

Unbelievably he was smoking. 'Hi,' he wheezed, 'this is a good one. They got most of them off before the water came over but there's still about forty out there . . .' The cigarette was torn out of Gary's mouth by the wind. He fumbled for a replacement.

A dog came ashore by the cab and shook itself before trotting off towards the nearest fire engine. 'Bill sent me out because of them . . .' Gary pointed further east, across a dry fen, to a line of terraced houses set bizarrely in a north–south line atop a raised bank. 'Lode Cottages. Apparently they don't want to move. The army's bringing in food and stuff. Bill wants me to do the story.'

Dryden felt the familiar wave of professional despair. 'And this?' He pointed out at the floating caravan site. 'Isn't this a story?'

'I guess,' Gary shouted. All three of them stood leaning into the gale.

'Stay with it. The most important thing is pictures. Got a camera?'

Gary opened his leather coat flasher-style. Underneath were three cameras.

'Take hundreds. We'll do the cottages. Catch us up.'

Lode Cottages were flotsam from the agricultural revolution. A lode was a fossil riverbed. When the rivers moved, snaking their way across the Fens over the centuries, they left behind their clay beds. Over time, as the Fens were drained and the peat shrank, the lodes were left as high clay banks, ideal for beaded villages. Lode Cottages were built for agricultural labourers in the early nineteenth century. They stood fifteen feet above the peat. In 1947 this had proved to be ten feet too low.

The dozen houses had been built as tied cottages for the farm across the fen. They were red-brick Victorian, an out-of-place remnant of an industrial suburb, strung beside the drove road facing west. From the high ground Dryden looked towards the cathedral, a distance of some fifteen miles. The Ship of the Fens was just that, a black solid superstructure on a watery horizon. A patchwork of drowned fens and peat-brown fields lay at their feet.

Water, rising. His father's body was never buried but his mother took him to the funeral of the labourer who had died with him. It had been Dryden's first Fen burial. Like all of them it had been wet, distinguished by the sound of a pine coffin being dropped into the black peat water. An unspeakable fear. Not only drowned in water, but buried in it.

The familiar panic came with a preliminary rush of adrenalin to the muscles, the pulse audible in his ears, and then the slight constriction of the stomach and the first intimation of a heave, like the barely perceptible roll of a boat as it leaves harbour.

But he had a mantra: *Keep talking. Keep breathing. Keep thinking.*

He retrieved the binoculars from his rucksack. To the north he could trace the course of the Old West River from close by the cathedral to his old home at Burnt Fen. The farmhouse still stood high and dry, sitting on its own miniature island.

It was time for 'T' to send another message.

Two ten-ton army trucks arrived with a crashing of gears. They were loaded with sandbags and soldiers – TA volunteers. A dog barked from an upstairs window in Lode Cottages. Out on Feltwell Anchor the mobile homes were still living up to their name. The flotilla had drifted towards a grass bank and the inflatable outboard rescue boats were circling them like sheepdogs. He could just make out Gary's flapping leather coat

321

amongst the gaggle of emergency rescue vehicles on the bank.

The wind, suddenly, dropped. If Dryden had known anything about meteorology he would have known this was a very bad sign.

He found an old man pulling up winter vegetables in his back garden. A pile of beet was at his back and he'd just moved on to the sprouts.

'Remember the last time?' asked Dryden.

The old man straightened up. 'Hardly likely to forget it, lost the wife.'

First prize, thought Dryden. *Idiot question of the year.*

The man was sweating in the wind. They both looked out over the fen.

'Pneumonia: that's the real problem. All this gets in the papers but we ain't gonna drown up here, are we? It's a winter in a damp cold house that's the killer. Everyone forgets when the water drops.'

'Here long?'

'All my life, sixty-eight years. Born here. Not this one, one on the end. We moved when we married.'

'How high did it get last time?'

'Made the bottom of our stairs. I sent her away, sister's. I sat on 'em for a week waiting. Freezing. At night there's a commotion. I come down and ground floor's aswimmin' with rats. Ratking, they calls it, just like a ball of string. Live string.'

Great, thought Dryden. *I have to find the village doomsayer.*

'I left in the end. Got back a week later. Lost everything. Roof went. I ain't going again. We're's all stayin'. Even the young uns. Ask 'em.'

Out in the fen to the north the water was beginning to edge

322

along the furrows. An army amphibious vehicle climbed up from the fields. A white-haired officer with three crowns on his collar flipped open the top hatch and spread out an Ordnance Survey map.

Dryden approached with due deference. 'Hi. Sorry to interrupt. Dryden, Philip Dryden, local paper.'

'Talbot. Captain. Peter, TA. Good ter meet ya.' The accent was upper-class sing-song slang. They shook hands in a very military kind of way.

'How many men have you got out, sir?' Army drill, always call 'em sir. Talbot began to fold up the map.

'All the county TA – about three thousand. Cambridgeshires.'

Dryden flipped open a notebook. 'These people don't seem to want to move.'

'We can live with that. We'll sandbag 'em. Bring in food. Can't have you chaps filming us dragging them off the land, can we?'

The wind was back, stronger and less predictable. Despite the sodden peat it was drying the topsoil and lifting it in red-brown dust clouds.

Talbot slapped the roof of the duck. 'We'll need more of these tonight, and the bridge-building kit. That's a bit beyond my boys, I'm afraid. Last time they brought amphibious tanks in to fill the breaches in the banks, parked them up and in-filled with sandbags.'

'I know.'

'Publicity stunt of course. They had to try something. Banks were bound to go eventually. Still, they might try it, who knows? Corker for you lot though, eh? Good story and all that.'

Dryden looked underwhelmed. 'Water's not my favourite element. I just live on it.'

'Swim?'

'No. Never.'

Suddenly the wind blew itself out and it was completely and blissfully silent. The soldiers stopped sandbagging and lit cigarettes. The old man stopped digging in his vegetable garden.

Dryden was looking west when the lightning forked down into the flood, seeking out the chimney stack of a half-drowned farmhouse. He closed his eyes too late – the lightning leaving a varicose-veined electric image on the retina which hung before him like a mirage as the flash was followed immediately by the rumble.

Talbot looked positively ecstatic at this development. 'Blimey. Spectacular, eh?'

A military motorcycle messenger arrived with an ace reporter as pillion. Gary, his spots in full disaster formation, tried to run to the duck but his black slip-ons, now ankle-deep in mud, slowed him down.

'This is Captain Talbot – Gary Pymore, one of my colleagues at *The Crow*.'

Gary saluted. Talbot winced.

Talbot gave Gary a briefing on the present situation from his map. Dryden used his mobile to check his answerphone. The two pieces of information he needed were waiting for him. One from the Land Registry at Stepney confirmed the Reverend John Tavanter's story of his £750,000 windfall. The other, from the Probate Registry for East Cambridgeshire, confirmed Dryden's suspicions.

Now he knew.

But he needed proof. He tore a page from his notebook and, leaning on the duck's bonnet, he wrote a message in neat capitals.

MEET ME AT THE OLD FARM, BURNT FEN. MIDNIGHT. T

He'd known for some time that it would come to this. With no forensic evidence and no witness it was the only way of catching Tommy Shepherd's killer. He had to meet him. The message was bait that the murderer could not resist. Dryden's problem was making sure he didn't become his third victim.

He folded the paper and wrote a full name and address. Then he gave it to the military messenger who, with Talbot's encouragement, agreed to deliver it on his return journey to Ely.

Gary looked longingly at the motorbike as it sped south.

Dryden took two of his cameras. 'The deadline for *The Crow* is three this afternoon. File what you've got by two – that'll give them a chance to get things in order. Then stay here tonight. Spend some time with these people. Human interest stuff. The village that wouldn't die, you know the line. Memories of the last time, what it's like spending a night surrounded by the floodwaters, boiling up for tea, etcetera.'

'You off?' Gary cast furtive glances at the floodwaters.

'Yup. I'll file the main story now for the front. Keep in touch.' Dryden shook Talbot's hand. 'Look after him, Captain.'

Dryden and Humph made the last five miles as dusk fell, via the level crossing at Shippea Hill. The smell of roast lamb drifted across the water to meet them. The overhead cables on the mainline to Norwich had toppled into the flood electrocuting an entire flock of sheep.

As they approached Ely the cathedral floodlights flickered and died. In the market square a dozen gypsy caravans were drawn up in a rough circle. Billy Shepherd, aka Joe Smith, was stretching a tarpaulin to create a windbreak. In town the wind was more bluster than power. But the streets were lined with broken tiles and moss balls fell from the old roofs. The flag on the cathedral was in tatters.

Billy Shepherd almost managed a smile. 'Council moved us, said the site would be under by midnight. But it's re-freezing fast. That'll give us some time until sunup tomorrow. We left the animals on the bank, I'm going back.'

Dryden saw his chance to enlist an ally. He hadn't planned it like this. That's why it was so good. 'I saw you out at Little Ouse.'

The gypsy wordlessly strapped the tarpaulin down with expert rope work.

Dryden skipped the silence. 'Tavanter can't know. Tommy didn't know. But if you want to meet him, Tommy's killer, you can.'

Billy stood in the lee of the caravan and expertly rolled a cigarette with one hand. The cat-green eyes were very bright.

'Burnt Fen Farm. Out by Shippea Hill. Eleven p.m. On the dot. Dump the car on the main road, walk the rest. The causeway is still dry. I'll need some help. No one else.'

Billy had no questions, which was answer enough. Dryden walked back towards *The Crow* with a light head.

CHAPTER TWENTY-THREE

He's coming.

In the moonlight Dryden watches him pause by the white van, calculating. A pale mac flaps in the storm. Around him the water rises and wavelets begin to slap at the wheel arches.

Out on the fen the moon lights an inland sea. A cow's bellow is ripped from the wind. The telephone wires sing and a mile distant comes the crash of breaking glass as the arched window of the Baptist Chapel at Feltwell Anchor implodes under the weight of the water. Unheard, the flotilla of mobile homes grinds itself to matchwood against Black Bank.

He's coming now, moving forward in a torchlight circle towards Burnt Fen Farm.

Dryden punches Andy Stubbs's number into the mobile and

listens to the recorded greeting. He's left two messages already, to meet at the Old Farm. Bring the file. And bring a gun.

'Where is he?' he asks the house, and climbs quickly to the schoolroom.

At one end, behind a partition, is the sink. At the other a large mirror reflects the moonlight streaming in through the dormer window. Icicles are beginning to decorate the beams as the frost takes a grip on the melting water from the roof. A small wooden Victorian children's chair remains in the room, and the sit-up teacher's desk and seat. His mother taught him here, until water destroyed their lives.

A blackboard fills the wall opposite the window. On it Dryden writes: 'Martha Jane Elliott. Pauper.' He feels again the crunch of the snow in the graveyard at Little Ouse. The broken shards of the headstones are at his feet.

'Kids,' the Reverend Tavanter had said.

'Kids,' says Dryden, out loud, to the schoolroom.

From the window he sees the figure crossing the yard. Confidently swinging the torch. But the build is too light, the head too small, the step too nimble. He's wrong. How can he be wrong?

Dryden flashes his torch twice into the shadows of the barn. There stands Billy Shepherd. The shotgun held expertly with the one arm. The lower body clad in waders. His father's waders, salvaged from their hook on the wall. Around him the water swirls. An inch now, but rising. Billy picks a blast of wind to cover the sound as he uncocks the gun at Dryden's signal.

He lets the figure pass, himself unseen.

Dryden crouches by the banisters on the first floor landing, an old haunt from his childhood, and a memory as vivid as the fear he feels. Below, water flows freely through the house, tumbling down the stone stairs to the cellar.

The minutes pass: one, two, and three . . . The back door, which has been banging rhythmically in the north wind, stops, missing a beat, then begins again.

He's in the house.

Another minute trickles by. Dryden sees a black polished leather slip-on shoe stop at the edge of the moonlight circle below, and the silence is full of listening. The newcomer takes a bold step and looks up. Andy Stubbs, framed by the bone-white collar of his shirt, could be ten years older.

He takes the stairs in pairs. Breathless, stressed, but oddly in control. A brief but specific fear freezes Dryden's heart.

Stubbs slides a hand inside his overcoat and draws out a brown manila file. The cover is stencil printed:

DRYDEN. LAURA – RTA. CLOSED.

Dryden grips it in relief. 'At last. You've read it?'

Stubbs hasn't taken his eyes off him. 'Yes. But I knew. Or guessed. That's why I played for time. I didn't want the tribunal to know. They might have decided to punish us both.'

Dryden took a step closer. 'You knew who it was?'

'Now I have proof.' He tapped the file with a gloved hand. 'Your evidence.'

Dryden almost spat it out. 'My evidence was worthless. If I'd known the driver's identity we wouldn't be here. My statement says nothing, nothing but the smell of dogs on old leather and a large blue paper parcel with a silver . . .'

'Moon,' finished Stubbs. 'A silver, single moon, on a blue paper parcel that I wrapped.'

'For who?' Dryden asks, guessing the truth.

Outside a flash of lightning forks to the flood and for a second they see it all through the schoolroom window. The ragged white horses, the tree by the farm gate bent to the water, and the sky in black shreds screaming south.

'There's no mistake. I checked. Last Friday of November two years ago. It's in the station diary. "Retirement of Deputy Chief Constable Bryan Stubbs". Lunchtime do, nothing sordid. Top brass from Cambridge. Home Office rep. Speeches, buffet, a few drinks. I was on duty but I called in for the speech. We kept up appearances, then. I organised the whip-round, wrapped the present – the water clock. The cronies were drinking half pints and orange juices. Didn't fool anyone.'

He turned his back on the storm. 'My father has been an alcoholic for nearly twenty years. My mother left him a decade ago. He used to be violent, now even that emotion is beyond him. He'll have gone on drinking somewhere; they had bars, people who turned a blind eye. Golf clubs, the nineteenth, ha bloody ha. And then he'd have driven home. Or tried to. That's when he slewed in front of you beside Harrimere Drain.

'The coincidence. Your accident, his binge, didn't go unnoticed. There were rumours. Talk in the station. Alibis quietly made. It has its own stench – a cover-up. I looked the other way with everyone else.'

Stubbs met Dryden's eyes. 'He's never been a physical coward so he deserves some credit for saving you, but he wasn't thinking clearly, and it showed. Presumption, a great vice in a policeman – as he told me so many times. He presumed you were the only person in the car because you were the only person in the front. He drove you to the Princess of Wales

330

but he couldn't take you in, not in his state. I'm surprised he got the car that far. And the alcohol would have kept his temperature up, he probably didn't even think about the cold. Alcohol made him reckless, unthinking, blundering. But not evil. He was that to start with.'

The lightning strikes again. They look out into the darkness and see the bolt cut down the sky and ignite a telegraph pole. It crashes into the water in a plume of steam. Overhead the thunderclap rocks the farmhouse.

'When you called looking for help after Tommy's body was found he couldn't stop himself, he saw it as a way of paying off his debts. And of course he sought vindication for his deceit. He always said Tommy Shepherd was guilty. The fact that he'd fabricated the evidence didn't mean he was innocent. He wanted you to prove it.'

Dryden presses his forehead to the glass in the schoolroom window. 'The water clock. Clepsydra.' He saw again the gurgling glass mechanism and the ornate fretted face of the clock in Stubbs's conservatory.

'And the tribunal?'

Stubbs sighs deeply. 'Busted me down to DC. Wish they'd thrown me out.'

The next sound is not nature's. The shotgun blast is sharper than the thunder, nearer. When they get to the window they see Billy sprawled in the slush, a dark black, spreading river running from an ugly jagged hole through the thigh of the waders. The shotgun, still uncocked, lies beside him.

The banging back door misses another beat.

'Who?' asks Stubbs, but there is no time. There are only seconds now until they must meet Tommy's killer.

Dryden leads the way into the front bedroom. Stubbs casts his torch beam across the iron bedstead, the wardrobes, the two armchairs coated with melting frost.

In one corner stands a screen Dryden's mother used to block the draught. A large silvered mirror, blackened at the edges, hangs over the bed. On the window ledge a crow's carcass twitches in the wind.

'I need a minute with him,' Dryden said. 'Just listen. He thinks I'm alone. Go behind the screen.'

Stubbs hesitates.

'I asked you to bring a gun.'

The policeman takes a pistol from his jacket pocket. 'It was his. Shooting club,' he says, slipping behind the screen.

Dryden plays decoy and settles in the armchair by the window. He counts sixty seconds in which his life does not flash before his eyes. Then he sees a torch's swaying beam touch the wallpaper in the hallway. Then it dazzles his eyes, and he braces himself for the shot, but knows it will not come. A second's silence deepens and the doubt blossoms. But then he hears it, the wheezing breath. The torch moves quickly on, checking the screen, the wardrobes, the bedstead, and the mirror.

Dryden's eyes reassemble the greys and blacks to form a picture. Josh Nene stands in the doorway, a shotgun held in the crook of his elbow. His boots glisten with water over the ever-present blue overalls.

'Dryden.' A cloud of steaming breath rises and catches a moonbeam. The ice is returning with the night. 'My congratulations.'

Nene takes a step closer. The barrel of the shotgun shakes and his fingers clench and unclench themselves around the stock.

'Who was the man outside?'

'Billy Shepherd. I don't blame you for not recognising him. It's been a long time.'

Nene's eyes widen, the whites catching the flicker of the lightning outside.

Dryden keeps talking. 'Surprised? That was one of the keys of course. He was alive because you thought he was in America. No need to kill him when Tommy's body was found. But if he'd been here you'd have tracked him down. He didn't know your name, but you couldn't have risked him finding you if he knew Tommy was dead.'

He cocks the gun. 'We have very little time, Dryden, but I am intrigued. May I ask how we find ourselves here?'

Dryden hears a footstep slide behind the screen, Nene misses it.

'We find ourselves here because of Martha Jane Elliott – 1891 to 1976. Or rather because of her gravestone.'

'My wife's aunt.'

'Your wife's aunt and benefactor. The woman who left a small fortune to your wife, which enabled you to buy the building yard and a business in which, until then, you had been merely a lowly employee.'

'A badly paid, exploited and abused employee.' Nene takes another step forward into the light. Despite the cold Dryden can see a sheen of sweat on his forehead.

'The churchyard at St John's at Little Ouse tells a different story. Martha died a pauper. She had no money to leave. I checked with the Registrar of Wills to make sure. That was a mistake, vandalising the headstones.'

Nene's eyes flicker, calculating. 'One mistake. I left the stone. There was no hurry. But things got out of hand. I had to act quickly.'

'You were there that night I visited John Tavanter?'

Nene studies the room and makes no answer.

Dryden keeps talking. 'Did Reg have to die? You'd ruined his life of course, but was he the killing type? But then he wanted to die anyway, he'd tried enough times. Perhaps he would have come after you, or gone to the police. That's more likely. A confession would have been fatal for you. You'd have lost everything. And you'd risked so much to keep it.

'And he'd never guessed. No one had. Pretending your wife inherited the money was a masterstroke. And you waited ten years. That's impressive. A decade of patience. Perhaps you were Gladstone Roberts's silent partner in Cathedral Motors? Good return, no doubt. And silence guaranteed.'

Nene laughs but his calculations are running too fast now, out of control.

'What did you tell your wife?'

Nene humours him with an explanation. 'That Aunt Martha had left her a fortune. I got a friendly solicitor to produce a will. That way she didn't have to lie.'

'But you paid a price. More than thirty years waiting for Tommy's body to be found. Bad heart?'

'I don't have a heart, Dryden.'

Nene backtracks to the landing and glances down to the hallway below. Nothing. He checks the view from the dormer window, then the gun, and reloads the empty barrel.

Dryden lives by words. Now he needs them to stay alive.

'I looked back over the council minutes. Every year you added your little bit of wisdom, just enough to postpone any work on the south-west transept roof. Removing the body was tricky and dangerous, but one day you could have done it. So why rush?

'One mystery. How did you find out Tommy's secret signal?'

Nene smiled, reliving the past. 'Broke his fingers. He was never very brave.'

'And the postcards?'

'We do work in the States. Heritage stuff. It was Boston that year. I sent the cards over with the shipment of stone and asked for them to be sent back.'

They smiled together.

Dryden pushed on. 'But this year it backfired, emergency work was needed and you had twenty-four hours to do something about it. So you sent a note to Reg.'

Nene shivers. 'Reg bit all right. Pathetic really.'

'What did you tell him?'

'Said Tommy had been back in touch, wanted to repay some of the money. Restored Reg's faith in human nature it did. I think he wanted to believe it. Believe something, anything. It got him there. That's all that mattered.'

Lightning torches across the sky outside the dormer window and the crash follows almost instantly.

'Did you push Tommy? I imagine you'd envisaged a private killing. Time to get the body out, or perhaps find a place in the walls? You were in every day on restoration work. But instead you had to push him . . .'

Nene sneers. 'Wrong again. He was always unreliable. He jumped.'

'What'd you have – a knife? Did he have a choice?'

Nene shrugs, checks his watch. Dryden's life is ticking away.

'After Tommy fell you must have looked round the base of the tower and found he'd fallen into the high gutter. But it wasn't that much of a problem in the short term. If the body was found it would look like suicide and you'd tell the others you hadn't met him and they could have their money back. But then he wasn't found, and you thought he might never be, or at least when he was Reg might have left town, moved on. And Billy was set on the States. So you kept the money, banked it, and waited.

'There were the winnings as well – how'd you get them off him before he jumped?'

'He wanted to count it out. With the cash from Crossways. See how rich he was.'

Dryden draws his legs up under him. 'Crossways. Amy Ward did recognise you of course, or thought she did. You'd done the building work at the garage the year before. Fitted the strongroom.

'What was the plan after you killed Reg? You got George Warren to steal the car. My guess was, you were the driver on the night. You were heading for the new marina at Feltwell Anchor. I presume the caretaker owes you some favours. He told you I was moving the boat there.

'And those pits dug for the bridge piles are ready-made graves. But they're flooded – which is why you weighted the body. You missed the turning and ended up in the Lark. You were lucky to get out with a bad cold.'

But Nene doesn't laugh. Dryden's time is up.

'And Laura. That was Gladstone Roberts of course. Applying some pressure. But you checked it out first. The lie of the land. That's when we spotted you and followed you to Stretham Engine. Why there?'

'I had a gun there.'

Dryden feels his blood freeze. Nene might have killed him then, if he'd been alone.

336

Nene is bored now. Dryden has nothing new to tell him. *Now*, he thinks. *For God's sake do it now, Stubbs.*

Nene raises the gun and aims expertly from the hip.

There are three simultaneous loud bangs, the sound of the screen being thrown back, and two shots. A brutal red light captures Stubbs halfway across the room – like an overexposed photograph. The blast catches him in the shoulder and flings him back with terrifying force against the wall. In the second that the red light bathes the room he seems to hang there, pinioned like a butterfly.

The scene seems to freeze then with the soundtrack a buzzing painful echo. Only Nene is moving. Walking towards him with the shotgun raised. Something is coming out of his mouth. Black and thick it rolls over his chin and spatters his overalls. A spurt jumps from his neck and he lifts a hand to staunch the flow. His eyes are startled and white, but fixed and unblinking.

Dryden rushes him, throwing him back against the mirror, and then dives for the open door. But Nene catches his arm with an almost mechanical force. Dryden wheels to face him and the blood spurts again, blinding him. He smashes a fist into Nene's face and the grip instantly releases as he tumbles to the ground. Then the thread breaks – the thin line of sanity that had brought him to Burnt Fen snaps. He senses the water outside, encircling, and the panic rises with the flood.

Half blind, Dryden scrambles down the stairs. The water is knee-deep in the hallway below. Frantically he wades to the front door and throws it open as the lightning comes again. The world outside is a riot of water. Ice, cracked and floating past, gathers against the farmhouse walls. He backtracks down the hall and hears upstairs Nene's stumbling footfalls.

The panic buzzes in his spine and lifts the hairs on his head. He runs across the yard as the thunder crashes again and, passing Billy's body, rounds the barn. Here, in his childhood, he fished in the pond which stretched to the road. In the darkness he does not know he is on it until his feet slip on the surface. The still deep water, in the long shadow of the barn, has kept its carapace of ice.

He skates for a few seconds and then falls, breaking through, and the water goes over his head. The shock almost stops his heart and he sinks, blindly struggling now, out of the light.

And back. Slowly back, as he falls into the darkness and the pain begins to fade. The panic has obliterated the present. He leapfrogs the years to his childhood, past Laura, past Fleet Street, past school. A newsreel of his life in reverse.

And then it's Boxing Day again. So he closes his body into a ball so that he can reach the skates. The Christmas skates. It's his nightmare and he's living it again. He finds the laces and releases them and the weights fall away.

For a moment he hangs in perfect balance. Then slowly he rises. Rises to the clear ice surface above. The pain has gone and he gulps the anaesthetic water until his face touches the ice and his hair begins, instantly, to freeze to the surface. His hands press up with a feeble force.

The sense of loss is overwhelming, as it always is. The warm farmhouse at Christmas. The fire. The present still to be opened. And his parents. All of this, just the other side of the ice.

He hears the footsteps before he sees them. The thuds rhythmic and ever stronger. For a second he finds a new fear. That they'll pass him by. But then they're over his head. The familiar patterned soles of his father's waders.

The blow is stunning when it falls. Cracking the ice and covering the world with millions of silver fissures. And the sound! From the cotton-wool silence of the frozen water to the storm above. The sudden crackling of the lightning, the rolls of thunder and the liquid rush of the flood.

A hand, massively strong, reaches down and drags him back into the world. He hugs him then. And calls his father's name. And Philip Dryden cries for joy.

Billy Shepherd pulled Dryden from the ice. The shotgun had removed a chunk of thigh muscle but nothing worse. He had been conscious when Dryden had run across the farmyard. His call had been lost in the sound of the storm. Once he got him out of the water he used the mobile to phone the police. By the time they arrived he'd lost three pints of blood. He made a full recovery and returned to New York with his daughter and grandchildren. Dryden paid for the tickets.

Josh Nene died from a pistol shot which severed his windpipe and jugular.

Detective Constable Andy Stubbs was severely injured by Nene's single shotgun blast. He was hospitalised for six months. He appealed against his demotion without success. His father visited him the night after the events at Burnt Fen Farm. Bryan Stubbs stayed for an hour. Then he returned to his country house, fed the dogs, and took an overdose of sleeping pills. He left a note that said he wasn't sorry for anything except the events at Harrimere Drain. He repeated his belief that Tommy Shepherd had been at the Crossways.

George Parker Warren was charged with car theft and convicted. In the dock, scandalised by the quality of prison food while on remand, he decided to cut his sentence and cooperate with the police. He said he had stolen the car for Gladstone Roberts. Roberts in turn admitted giving Warren £200 for the car, having been paid £800 by Josh Nene to get a vehicle at short notice. He'd pocketed the difference. Warren got six months.

Roberts had a less comfortable time. The police requested details of the partnership that had set up Cathedral Motors. His silent partner had indeed been Josh Nene. Roberts had bought him out in 1976. He escaped a charge, there being no evidence that he knew the origins of Nene's capital. But his fingerprints were found on PK 122. He said Nene had told him to stop Dryden's investigation or face the consequences if the builder was arrested and revealed the source of his capital. He also admitted twice getting into the Tower and moving Laura to leave the cuttings from the maps under her pillow. He was jailed for two years.

John Tavanter, Liz Barnett, and husband Roy, read about the end of the case in The Crow.

Gary Pymore spent forty-eight hours stranded on a roof at Lode Cottages in the middle of the worst natural disaster to hit the Fens for a century. He filed regular news stories and features by army radio which were syndicated in the Daily Telegraph. He won an award as Provincial Reporter of the Year as a result and Henry gave him his own desktop PC by way of reward.

Kathy recovered her sight but was plagued by headaches and dizzy spells. She was offered £16,000 by the town council's lawyers to settle out of court. She took it. She packed what she owned into the red MG and left Ely for Fleet Street. Dryden got her the job. They never met again but he smiled when he saw the by-line.

Laura is still in the Tower. If Gladstone Roberts's evidence could be believed he had broken into her room twice. This suggested that the first time she had shown signs of coming out of her coma – on the night of Friday, 2nd November – she had indeed made a critical breakthrough in her recovery. If Gladstone Roberts was telling the truth . . .

Dryden is at her bedside. Waiting.

Humph is listening to his latest language tape in a lay-by. Polish.

ACKNOWLEDGEMENTS

The reissue of *The Water Clock*, *The Fire Baby* and *The Moon Tunnel* is due to the vision and energy of my publisher Susie Dunlop at Allison & Busby, ably assisted by my editor, Kelly Smith, and sales and marketing assistant, Kirsten Munday. To see books relaunched in this way, some twenty years after their publication, is a rare joy for a writer.

I would like to thank Beverley Cousins, my original editor, for her skill, determination, and patience in championing *The Water Clock*, Faith Evans, my agent, for living up to her name, and Martin Bryant for meticulous copy-editing. Dorothy L. Sayers deserves some belated glory for the inspiration provided by *The Nine Tailors*. I am indebted to Renee Gillies, Donald Gillies, Bridie Pritchard, Eric Boyle and Jenny Burgoyne for helping with the text. I read many accounts of the 1947 floods in Fenland but must thank all those at The Cambridgeshire Collection for their work in the archives.

The landscape of the Fens is, of course, real but details of geography and history have been altered for the sake of the plot. All characters are, however, entirely fictitious.

DON'T MISS THE NEXT DRYDEN MYSTERY

THE FIRE
BABY

Summer, 1976. A plane crashes on a farm in the Fens and out of
the flames walks Maggie Beck, clutching a baby in her arms ...

Twenty-seven years later, Philip Dryden is witness to Maggie's
deathbed confession. But some secrets are best kept secret, and
what started out for Dryden as a curious story about the only
survivor of an almost-forgotten plane crash soon escalates into a
full-blown murder investigation.

THE MOON TUNNEL

From beneath a wartime POW camp near Ely, a man crawls through an escape tunnel. But he won't emerge until fifty years of peace have passed.

When he does, unearthed by archaeologists seeking a saxon tomb, Philip Dryden knows he has a mystery to solve. First the man appears to have been shot in the head – and second, he was breaking into the camp not out. Dryden digs deeper – and soon unearths a corpse of much more recent origin ...

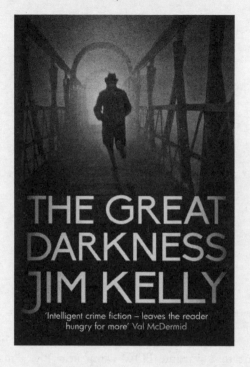

Cambridge, 1939. The opening weeks of the Second World War, and the first blackout – The Great Darkness – envelops the city. Detective Inspector Eden Brooke, a wounded hero of the Great War, takes his nightly dip in the cool waters of the Cam. Sirens wail and yet in this Phoney War the enemy never comes.

But daylight reveals a corpse on the riverside, the body torn apart by some unspeakable force. Brooke investigates, calling on the expertise of his fellow 'nighthawks', all condemned, like him, to a life lived away from the light. Within hours there is another victim slaughtered under cover of The Great Darkness. War has many casualties, but what links these crimes of the night?

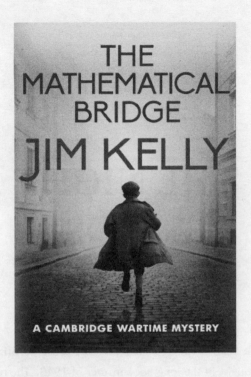

THE MATHEMATICAL BRIDGE

JIM KELLY

A CAMBRIDGE WARTIME MYSTERY

Cambridge, 1940. Snow is falling thick and fast on a cold winter's night. As a college porter makes his nightly rounds, he is startled to hear a boy's desperate screams for help coming from the icy river below. But by dawn the river has claimed its victim.

When the following night an Irish Republican slogan is left at the scene of a factory explosion, Detective Inspector Eden Brooke questions whether there could be a connection between the two events. As more riddles come to light, he begins to close in on a killer, but there is one last twist: it seems that the boy had his own startling secret.

THE NIGHT RAIDS

A lone German bomber crosses the east coast of Britain on a moonless night in the long hot summer of 1940. The pilot picks up the silver thread of a river and, following it to his target, drops his bomb over Cambridge's rail yards. The shell falls short of its mark, and lands in a neighbourhood of terraced streets on the edge of the city's medieval centre. DI Eden Brooke is first on the scene and discovers the body of an elderly woman, Nora Wylde, beside her shattered bed in a terraced house on Elm Street, two fingers on her left hand severed, in what looks like a brutal attempt by looters to steal her rings. When the next day Nora's teenage granddaughter, Peggy, a munitions worker, is reported missing, Brooke realises there is more to the situation than meets the eye.

Jim Kelly was born in 1957 and is the son of a Scotland Yard detective. He went to university in Sheffield, later training as a journalist and worked on the *Bedfordshire Times*, *Yorkshire Evening Press* and the *Financial Times*. His first book, *The Water Clock*, was shortlisted for the John Creasey Award and he has since won a CWA Dagger in the Library and the New Angle Prize for Literature. He lives in Ely, Cambridgeshire.

jim-kelly.co.uk
@thewaterclock